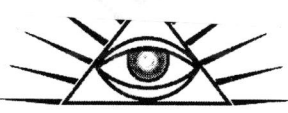

The Eyes of Athena
Spencer Hawke

Copyright © 2014 Spencer Hawke
All Rights Reserved.

www.lonemesapublishing.com
Spencer Hawke, www.spencerhawke.com
Eyes of Athena

ACKNOWLEDGEMENT

As an avid reader I have often glossed over the acknowledgement page penned by many successful authors as an introduction to a new novel. My mistake... The common denominator of these successful authors is that they have an unseen hero or heroine in the background without whom the novel might never have been read.

Many of you followers of Superman or Wonder Woman believe that this comic figure is the only superhero stronger than steel. You are sadly mistaken. There is one other figure flying over the vistas of Lone Mesa Publishing in Texas. She is not only a woman of steel, but I swear (and she doesn't allow me to) she flies faster than a speeding bullet to my aid.

My unsung heroine in the background is Teri Piearcy. She edits my manuscripts with the grace of a ballet dancer and the savoir-faire of a magician.

It is with the most sincere thanks and appreciation that we offer this book for your reading pleasure.

~ Spencer

CHAPTER ONE

Athena Campus, Bethesda, Maryland
March 27, 1999

It was a quiet evening at the Athena Ops Center. Major Tom Burke was enjoying a cup of coffee in his office, his long legs stretched out with his feet on the desk in front of him. The rich aroma of the Columbian blend was tantalizing, and he closed his eyes, pushing his head back to luxuriate in the quiet, basking in a rare minute of solitude and peace in what was normally a hectic world.

Out of the blue, his office door catapulted open, slamming noisily into the wall behind. It was impossible to jump up, drop his feet to the floor and spin around without spilling his coffee. Burke looked around angrily, feeling the heat of his coffee spreading down his leg, to see a junior analyst standing in the doorway, panting as if he had been running.

"Sir!" the young man shouted, "I just saw a Reuters report in the break room; a U.S. Stealth F-117 Bomber has been shot down over Bosnia."

Burke ignored the coffee running from the pool atop his desk full of drenched reports to the floor. He immediately did two things. First, following protocol, he placed a call to his direct superior; the Athena Board Member from Massachusetts who was on call that night. That completed, he switched on the television to see if the 10 p.m. NBC Nightly News had any more information. He was just in time to hear a newsflash.

> "This is Tom Brokaw reporting from New York. NBC News can now confirm that a U.S. Air Force B-117 Stealth Bomber was shot down over Bosnia today. The unthinkable has happened. An 'undetectable' Stealth Bomber has somehow been

discovered during operations in enemy territory over Bosnia and Serbia. The exact location is being withheld by the military for reasons of national security.

"*It is believed that the pilot ejected safely behind enemy lines. We can only assume now that the question is, will the enemy find him first or can American rescue teams get there in time? As the pre-dawn darkness clears in Eastern Europe, the race is on.*"

Burke switched off the set. All he could think was, *Why does this have to happen on my first day in charge of the OPs center?*

He was an old hand around Athena, having been part of the organization for more than a decade. He was an agent before becoming a handler and was now moving into leadership of the whole OPs center at Bethesda. He was seasoned, and not much got to him, but having a major international incident go down within the first four hours of your first day in charge was just a little unnerving.

To make matters worse, his direct superior had not returned his call. Burke was analyzing all the possibilities, planning what he would do if the Member from Massachusetts did not get back with him.

His thoughts were interrupted by the main telephone ringing. Thinking it may be the Member from Massachusetts returning his call, he grabbed the phone quickly and practically shouted into the receiver, "Sir, thank you for calling me back; we might have an 'issue' here."

Burke was startled to hear a voice very different from the one he was expecting. "This is George Tenet calling."

Through his surprise, Burke managed a response. "This is a secure line, Mister. You must have a wrong number. I'd appreciate you not calling this number again."

The caller was also surprised at hearing someone in the intelligence community not recognizing his name. He raised his voice an octave, "I think if anyone in this country can call a secure line it would be me, sonny boy."

Burke, still in a state of confusion, was determined to follow protocol to the letter. "What did you say your name was, Sir?"

THE EYES OF ATHENA

"George Tenet... the Director of the Central Intelligence Agency."

Realization suddenly slammed into Burke like a flaming meteorite. He was so surprised that he leaped from his seat in an involuntary urge to salute the well-respected leader of the premier spy agency in America.

Stating the obvious, he stammered, "I wasn't expecting you to call, Sir. I didn't think you were aware of our existence."

"Burke, we don't have time for small talk. Your boss is in the situation room at the White House with the President. You've heard the news, haven't you?"

"Yes, Sir."

"We have to move quick, son. We already have an elite team on its way to Yugoslavia to rescue the pilot. But these Navy SEAL paratroopers are going to stand out like chocolate chips in vanilla ice cream without some assistance on the ground. I need someone there to meet them or they'll be minced meat," Tenet added.

"I need someone there who knows the country, speaks the language, and knows the people. Once they hit the ground, they will need someone to help them fulfill their mission and get back to a safety zone for extraction."

"That makes sense, Sir." Burke said no more, expecting Tenet to continue with the reason for his call.

"I don't think you do get it, sonny boy. I want you to solve my problem."

Burke was still not following Tenet's line of thought. "Your problem Sir?"

Tenet was sighing, exasperated. "Yes, Burke. Get me someone on the ground."

"Yes, Sir. I'll have to make arrangements ... I'm not sure how close our nearest agent would be..."

Tenet sighed again. "Think outside the box, boy. Mossad has been running OPs in that area for months now. The President, your Boss and I want you to call your friend Ben Rosenberg in Tel Aviv and get him to put his best man with Bosnia and Serbia experience on a plane to the crash site in the next 30 minutes."

He paused to let Burke grasp his orders. "It is vital that the pilot not fall into enemy hands. We're clear on that, right, Burke? He has information on the functioning aspects of that technology that we don't need anyone else getting hold of, correct?"

"Of course, Sir."

"Well, Burke, that team will need to do more than rescue the pilot, if possible. From what we can tell, the self-destruct mechanism in the Stealth malfunctioned.

"That means all that super-secret technology is just laying out there in a field there behind enemy lines just ripe for the taking. We need our boys try to destroy that plane if necessary.

"And it won't be a walk in the park, either," Tenet added. "In case your special little geeks there haven't alerted you yet, satellite imagery is showing us what we believe to be a large concentration of Yugoslav troops mobilizing in an area less than an hour from the crash site. We've got to believe they're after our pilot and our plane.

"Yes, Sir." Burke sounded as if he were still working through the issue in his head.

"So find someone fast, Burke, and find someone good. I mean, really good. He needs to not only keep up with my Navy SEALS, he needs to add to everything they're bringing to the table. When he's airborne, we will synchronize his arrival with our special team. Got it?"

Burke was dialing the phone almost as quickly as he hung up the receiver. It was going to be a long first day...

Yugoslavia

Ari Cohen hit the ground hard, rolling forward in a standard maneuver designed to reduce impact from a fast landing. He came to a halt and crouched down on one knee while he pulled in his straps. He breathed in deeply, enjoying the familiar scent of evergreen from the nearby forest. He checked out his perimeter, the smell bringing back childhood memories of boar hunting trips he used to make with his uncle.

In those days, all he had to worry about was disturbing an angry wild pig, disrupted as he was foraging through fields and forests in search of his favorite food – the morel mushroom.

Ari reminisced as he waited for his senses to adjust to his new environment away from the noise of the military transport plane that released him less than three minutes ago.

THE EYES OF ATHENA

His uncle used to love hunting pigs, watching them roast over a large spit in the family room of the local inn. His uncle's ulterior motive was that the pigs used to eat the morels he wanted to buy, so culling the local population made economic sense. Uncle Bruno made a good profit taking the mushrooms back to Italy to sell in his grocery store.

But those carefree days were long gone. Today Ari had to concern himself with a country gone mad fighting a civil war that pit sons against fathers and brothers against brothers, all started by power-hungry oligarchs trying to spread their wealth and influence. The chief agitator was Russia, now trying to spread her influence through Bosnia-Herzegovina.

Ari was within 5 miles of the Stealth crash site. He knew he would not be the only one searching for the downed pilot. He had been warned by his boss and recruiter, Ben Rosenberg, in Tel Aviv before he left.

"The Stealth bomber is a very advanced technology but the homing beacon used by the U.S. Air Force is so old that the Russians, the Yugoslavs and the Iranians will also be able to track it. In fact, it's so antiquated, even the Romans could home in on it," Ben had said with sarcasm. "Be careful; they might even be broadcasting a false signal to lead you into a trap."

Ari checked his watch; twenty minutes to the main drop. He pulled out his GPS device; he was within 1 1/2 miles of the drop zone.

He whispered a silent prayer, adding just under his breath, "I hope it's secure." He knew if the enemy could track a stealth bomber, it stood to reason that they would be able to track the transport plane the SEAL paratroopers were going to use.

Shortly after midnight, Ari was in position, his Uzi cocked and on semi-automatic, his knives – his preferred weapon – ready for instant retrieval. He checked his watch again; two minutes to drop. He thought he heard the distant throb of airplane engines. He was ready. He checked the locater beacon; the pilot was three miles away.

A scowl formed on his dark features. "Wait a minute. That can't be right," he whispered into the darkness. There was another, fainter signal coming from close by.

"That doesn't make sense." Ari pulled out his night-vision binoculars, searching the edge of the landing zone; all clear. Suddenly, he picked up movement, an animal? He zoomed in closer, trying to keep his hand steady despite the flies swarming irritatingly around his exposed neck. He ignored them. He was right, somebody was there, dressed in black, an ammunition belt swung nonchalantly around his torso like a Mexican bandito.

It was his posture that worried Ari. He had his head cocked slightly to one side; he was listening for something. That could mean only one thing; the enemy knew the paratroopers were coming.

"How?" he gasped through gritted teeth. A question for later; now was the time to act and act fast.

Ari had been told to maintain absolute radio silence. Ignoring those orders, he switched on his microphone. "Abort! Abort!" he spoke as loudly into the mic as he dared without being heard by the intruder across the way.

No response; Ari knew he was too late. They were going to jump into an ambush. He pulled his silenced FN into position and centered the scope to the edge of the forest with the cross-hairs closing in on the soldier. Ari could see him swatting at flies around his face.

Ari fired and watched through the telescopic sight. It was as if in slow motion; his target stopped suddenly, the hand that had been chasing away flies, ceased in mid-swing – almost as if he had seen the muzzle flash.

The target's head turned toward Ari like he could see him. His eyes seemingly grew larger, like he could focus on the leaden projectile barreling toward him. Then the target's head suddenly dropped forward, then backward, as his body jerked back into a tree. Ari could almost hear the collision, the thunk of dead meat hitting wood. Momentarily, the corpse was suspended against the trunk, then the legs spasmed and he slid to the ground.

Ari reached into his pocket to wipe the sweat off his hand and felt a piece of paper. Puzzled, he pulled it out and in the rising moonlight he could see it was his ticket to watch the Vienna Philharmonic playing with the Santa Cecilia Orchestra in Rome, Italy, where he had planned to be that night.

THE EYES OF ATHENA

Perhaps the man I killed, in another time, would have enjoyed the same rendition of Mendelssohn's Symphony Number 4, he thought. Ari had left his radio comm on, hoping he could raise an alarm. The pulsating engines of the plane above jerked him out of his compassionate thoughts; men were running out of the forest, firing at will.

The first paratrooper of the 10-man unit appeared out of the dark sky; they didn't stand a chance. Seven soldiers ran toward him firing mechanically. The majestic gentle swaying movement of his parachute was interrupted by machine gun fire and the jerking human moving spasmodically in the last throws of life – a puppet controlled by a puppeteer gone mad. The destroyed parachute crumpled to the ground on top of the dead paratrooper.

Ari – focusing on his target through his scope – could just make out the emblem of the Iranian Republican Guards on his sleeve. He continued to fire, but they seemed to pour out of the forest in an endless stream.

In quick succession, eight more paratroopers drifted down through the darkness, sitting ducks for the Republican Guards who ran fearlessly to each successive SEAL. Ari reloaded his FN, firing as many shots as he could, killing with a ruthless efficiency. As the last paratrooper glided into view, Ari shot the final standing enemy soldier.

He was overcome with sadness, running out to the only survivor in order to provide covering fire. Ari zigzagged, just in case he was being watched, to make himself as difficult a target as possible. As he reached the trooper, he jumped on top of him to protect him.

The stunned trooper initially resisted, but Ari shouted to him, "Stay still!" All was quiet, eerily so.

Ari and the paratrooper were very close to the edge of the forest where he had landed. Hearing no more pursuit, Ari got up, followed by the paratrooper. Instantly, Ari regretted his impulsiveness; from the forest, he heard a noise – the sound of a broken tree branch. He looked around quickly, saw the officer of the slaughtered enemy approaching, walking with a mechanical certainty, with his pistol at arm's length aimed toward both men.

Ari was paralyzed by surprise; the guy had him dead to rights. He looked at his opponent; the man was scruffy –

hadn't shaved for day – smoking a cigarette cockily. The Iranian officer was fuming, his face contorted in anger.

In an educated English accent, he shouted out angrily, "You imperialist pig! You spoiled my surprise! You have killed my men!"

Ari would never forget that face. The Iranian pulled the trigger, but it fell on an empty chamber. As if in slow motion, the Iranian stood still, not understanding, then looked down toward the gun and turned it so that he could examine the chamber, clearly not believing what his mind was telling him. Ari, against every bit of training he had sweat through, had stood still in shock, but at least he recovered first. His body, not understanding why he was not shot, finally moved; he reached for his pistol and turned back toward the Iranian, only to see the back of the man rushing into the obscurity of the forest.

Ari was still in shock, adrenalin surging through his veins and overwhelmed by the sudden appearance of the enemy officer. A little more wary this time, he turned to check out his perimeter. He remained uneasy as he continued his visual inspection until he had checked out the entire area. Ari saw nothing; he sensed that they were alone, that the battle was over.

He turned to look at the lone SEAL survivor, visually inspecting him as if uncertain. "Why did God choose this one?" he couldn't help but think. "Why let this one live, when so many had died?"

Finally, he broke the mental spell his shock had him under, and held out his hand to the man before him. "I'm Ari Cohen." He whispered.

Still stunned, the paratrooper offered his hand eagerly. "I'm David, David Gray."

"Let's move it," Ari responded. "I want to get that lunatic." He turned around to grab his gear and radio. It was still switched on, and as he lifted it up he heard a report. "The pilot is safe; we have the pilot."

Gray looked over at Ari. "What just happened?"

Ari squinted his eyes, frowning thoughtfully. "They knew you were coming; they were waiting for you." He still had that creepy feeling that all was not over yet. "Let's get outta here."

He turned to move back away from the forest edge. As Gray made to follow, he stumbled but recovered, still on his feet.

Ari looked him over. "You've been shot; let me look at that."

Gray got down to the ground, wincing in pain as he extended his leg, where a bloodied area was spreading on his thigh.

"Give me your med pack." Ari proceeded to clean up Gray's wound. When finished, he told the trooper, "That wound is too serious, we are going to have to evac you."

"No way. I'm going after that monster, that heathen who killed my team," he growled out angrily.

"Not with that leg." Ari looked up to see the determination on Gray's face. "Don't worry. I'll take care of him."

Ari shouted loudly into the radio. "I need a med flight; we have one injured. I'll wait until he's picked up then I am requesting permission to pursue the enemy responsible for this!"

Ari was prepared to wait while the radio operator checked with Ari's superior; he was surprised by an immediate response.

"Request denied, soldier. We're coming to pick you both up."

Ari was speechless, this response he did expect. Gray had been watching the exchange. "I guess you're coming home with me," he said with resignation.

Ari was adamant, although no longer on the mic, he turned to Gray, "No can do. We were set up; they were waiting for you to jump, and I need to find out who sold us out."

Ari was explaining his stubbornness to Gray. "I can't go with you, if I don't get that mad man, his face will haunt me for as long as I live."

Decision made, Ari looked around, needing something to do. "I need to go check on your team, see if there are any other survivors while we wait."

Gray stayed where Ari had left him, realizing that Ari needed some time. He watched as Ari would kneel, check a comrade and man-handle him over his shoulder to take the fallen hero to an evacuation spot close to Gray. Neither spoke as they waited for the sound of helicopter rotors.

CHAPTER TWO

One moment Ari and Gray were hidden in silence at the far edge of the clearing and the next, the throbbing beat of the Med Evac choppers sounded in the darkness. The powerful rotors pummeled them from overhead. Ari looked up, squinting against the wind, to see two choppers, coming in for a lightning-fast rescue mission. As soon as they landed, a medic jumped out waving at Ari and Gray to hurry them aboard.

As Ari climbed in helping Gray, the pilot leaned back from his seat and looked at him. "Are you Cohen?"

"Who wants to know?" Ari was in no mood for pleasantries.

"I got orders, Sir, to bring you in." The pilot looked almost apologetically at Ari. "I'm sorry, Sir."

As they talked, the medics carried the bodies of the nine dead SEALs to the chopper. Once the last one was loaded, Ari and the pilot looked over at the bodies, then back at each other – a look of two brave warriors assessing one another respectfully.

"Do you want to let them get away with this?" Ari asked, nodding his head in the direction of the bodies.

"What do you have in mind?"

"How about you comply with your orders? I'll come aboard; your evac route could take you in the direction of the Stealth crash, flying according to protocol at low altitude. Then I could happen to jump out halfway to the Stealth, which is just where the murderer who planned all of this is going. If we get moving, I can get in front of him."

"What rank are you, Sir?"

"Captain."

"Hop aboard, Captain. I do believe we got ourselves a plan. Wish I could go with you."

~

Ari felt the chopper go into a steep bank, cutting its speed to just above a crawl as it hovered over the tree tops, momentarily. The pilot didn't dare turn around, his concentration riveted on the enemy positions around the downed Stealth. When the pilot had the chopper as close to the ground as he dared, he shouted out to Ari, "Go!"

Ari calculated that he would land at a little over the optimum speed of 15 miles per hour, given the height from which he was jumping. Ari saw the branches – just visible in the faint moonlight – rushing toward him. It was as if he were falling through a narrow center of a green Christmas tree, the evergreen boughs appearing one second and slapping him in the face the next. Although painful, they acted as a speed brake as he cascaded through the blinding vegetation. He heard the plop of his pack hitting the ground before him, so he braced, knowing that his hard landing was next. He hit the ground rolling forward before coming to a final stop, just thankful that he hadn't hit the trunk of a tree.

He turned to look at the departing chopper; it was already nearly out of sight and silent. Just the distant sound of sporadic rifle fire came to him now. Slowly that diminished, too. Ari was alone, his only company, the claustrophobic silence of a mountain night in a dense forest.

He clutched his only friend, an electronic GPS locator the chopper pilot had given him, saying, "You've got nine hours before they ship me out. Find a safe evac location, hit the switch, and I'll come get you."

Holding his get-out-of-jail-free device, Ari was tempted to push the on switch as the reality of his situation hit him like a tidal wave. He worked to get a grip and tune his ears to the forest. Slowly, his senses began to work. Down the mountain, he could just hear the sound of straining diesel engines surrounded by excited Russian voices.

Must be the crash zone, he thought to himself. From further off to the west came the sound of yapping dogs thrilled to be on the chase. It sounded like the dogs were happy to be running, not yet the crazed, wild yelps of a pack on the scent of its quarry.

"I must be bloody mad," he said under his breath. "This is a cesspool of land mines. One false move and I'm a dead man."

THE EYES OF ATHENA

He reached into his inside jacket pocket, put away his life line and zipped it tight then pulled out his night-vision goggles to perform a circular sweep around him.

He checked his watch, by now Gray would be back at the temporary base and his new friend the chopper pilot would be refueling, waiting anxiously for the rescue beacon from Ari. He had to get this right, to make a plan that was survivable. The Russians were partially dismantling what was left of the Stealth less than two kilometers away downhill. That way was blocked.

To the west, a search party of Russian soldiers with hounds was patrolling the crash site perimeter unaware that the pilot had lucked into a ride in a farmer's cart to a small village down the way. From there, he had been ferried by kind-hearted locals far enough out to be picked up by a chopper once he felt safe enough to turn on his beacon.

The enemy Ari sought was uphill, hopefully coming from the east.

He checked his watch again, eight minutes since he landed. The Iranian should be getting close. If his calculations were correct, he had less than five minutes until crunch time. That Iranian officer would never expect Ari to come from in front of him.

It was time. He pulled out his Zeus thermal imaging scope, switched it on and ran its beam in a circle around him. He was facing uphill, which meant the man he was after would be coming downhill, probably moving fast. Nothing yet.

He switched gears. Behind him, he focused on the crash site just visible with his NVGs. The area was surrounded with heavy equipment. Russian military guards were posted every ten meters around the perimeter, each one supported by a Gorgovsky armored personnel carrier. Each vehicle was equipped with a mobile searchlight, switched on, roaming skyward, prepared for another U.S. invasion of paratroopers that Ari knew wasn't coming.

In the center, he spotted the man in charge, judging by the ribbons on his chest – a general wearing the red elite GRU Spetznaz crest. Portable cranes were helping military transport people load the wreckage onto trucks. Ari realized he couldn't get close enough to even place a tracer on the transports to keep track of the plane.

No matter, he thought. *Right now there is only one trophy I am determined to take home with me.*

Without warning, he heard the sound he had been seeking, coming from uphill. Somebody was coming down toward him at quite a clip. He turned around and focused his NVGs toward the motion. About a hundred meters in front of him to the west, he saw the flash of an image. Almost immediately, he heard someone else approaching his position, but this one was to the east. There were two of them coming; he had to make a choice.

His decision wasn't made consciously. His subconscious vote went for self-preservation, his mind knowing if he had gone west, he could have also walked into the patrol of Russians and their hounds. Ari moved to the east.

He was cautious, knowing he had to make a silent approach. If forced to use his silenced weapon, he might kill the enemy without getting the answers he wanted – how did they know the paratroopers were coming and how did they know the location of the drop zone?

It was a trap; of that he was sure. Ari reached inside his jacket to retrieve his homing beacon. With a determined set to his face, he pressed the button, summoning his new friend. That gave him five minutes to get the information he wanted, kill the man responsible for all those deaths, find a clearing for the rescue chopper and get the heck out of dodge.

His plan was already made before he knew it. He started off slow, searching the forest floor for a limb as close to a baseball ball bat as he could find. He couldn't risk the noise made by breaking off a limb to fit his requirements. As he rushed to intercept his target, one eye kept watch for his target while the other looked for a weapon.

Closing in on the sound, he spotted a limb out of the corner of his eye and diverted to pick it up, but as he turned around with his weapon, something hit him and hit him hard, and he went down.

He realized his quarry had spotted him. "Careless idiot!" He cursed himself.

He scampered away quickly, tried to get up, but received another sharp, hard poke to his ribs. He went down again, grimacing in pain. On his way to the ground, he grabbed the attacker's weapon – a stick like a baseball bat, just like the one Ari had sought. He held on, forcing his attacker to bend forward. Now Ari had an advantage and he used it, kicking both feet off a tree in a circular fashion toward the attacker; whose legs went out from under him.

As he fell, the attacker released his weapon. Ari, now free of his attacker's grip on the stick, pivoted up and landed with force on top of the man. The attacker's head smacked into a branch on the forest floor, and he was dazed momentarily. Ari relaxed too soon, and his attacker recovered and twisted around so that his back was down on the ground, then he launched three quick, powerful jabs to Ari's gut, and Ari fell back away from his assailant.

Ari was winded now and wary. They both got up slowly, circling each other. The attacker was blinking fast, the streaming blood from a cut over his eye interfering with his vision. It was too much, and he lifted his sleeve to wipe the blood away. Big mistake; Ari jumped, coiled his left leg, and released it like a jackhammer on the jaw of his assailant.

The man stumbled back, dazed, confused, and not knowing what just happened. Taking no chances this time, Ari drew his knife and launched at his opponent, striking him in the shoulder and sinking the knife deep into the flesh. Quickly, Ari covered the attacker's mouth, smothering the sound as he tried to scream, "Der...!"

Ari's hand cut off the rest of the Russian curse word, and he almost recoiled in shock; he kept his hand over his prisoner's mouth, whispering, "Russian?"

His prisoner nodded, and Ari put his finger in front of his mouth to indicate silence. The Russian nodded enthusiastically. Ari removed his hand.

"Where's the Iranian?" The prisoner nodded to the west. "Who is he?"

The Russian, in broken English, responded, "Iranian Republican Guard; Mahmoud."

As he watched his Russian prisoner, Ari noticed that he suddenly moved his eyes, he seemed to look past Ari, his eyes widening in fear. Too late, Ari's sixth sense picked up something or someone behind him. He turned to see Mahmoud, face contorted in rage, leveling a pistol at Ari's head.

"This time, my gun is loaded, American pig." As Mahmoud mouthed his hate, Ari heard the pulsating throb of a chopper approaching.

Mahmoud, too consumed by his own rhetoric, didn't hear it. Ari jumped sideways from his kneeling position just as Mahmoud fired two quick shots.

Ari looked down at his chest to verify that there were no holes. Mahmoud looked in shock at Ari then at the Russian solider. The man lay in front of Ari, eyes wide in shock, two blood-soaked holes draining the life out of his chest. Before Ari could recover from his surprise, Mahmoud turned and ran off through the forest.

Ari turned to the Russian, close to death, and gently stroked his face, trying to comfort him. "How did Mahmoud know about our rendezvous with the paratroopers?"

"They came from base in Aviano, Italy. Mahmoud has spy there."

Ari still didn't understand. "But why?"

The Russian struggled with his last words. "Iran has money... wanted plane. Russia does not pay generals well."

The man exhaled one final time as his eyes took on that unfocused, distant look. Ari slid his hand over the Russian's eyelids almost lovingly, as if mourning a friend. He tried to ease his passing, saying a silent, private prayer. Ari laid aside his remorse aside when he felt the sudden change in air pressure and his ear drums began rebelling against the noise of his rescue chopper overhead.

CHAPTER THREE

Athena Campus, Bethesda, Maryland
April 5, 1999

Ari felt uncomfortable sitting in Tom Burke's office. He still wasn't quite sure why Rosenberg had sent him back to Bethesda to debrief the Americans. In all his years with the Mossad, he had rarely ever worked an OP with the U.S. much less been "loaned" to them.

"Good to see you in one piece, Cohen." Burke was tall but stout. It seemed to Ari like his Texas accent elongated every other syllable as he spoke. Ari shook the hand Burke offered before he slid behind his government-issue metal desk.

"I hear things didn't go quite as we had hoped." Burke was looking down at the file on his desk. Ari knew everything he had told the original debrief team at the airbase was right there in black and white. No need for this additional conversation.

He seethed. "Nine men dead for nothing and the man responsible is still out there. Yeah. I'd say the operation was not a total success."

Burke eyed the man across the desk. He was unused to hearing that kind of sarcasm issued at him from the men in his command, but he reminded himself, Ari Cohen was not in his command ... yet.

Ari didn't flinch. The hard glare he gave back was unmoving.

"You want a chance to go after that monster, don't you, Cohen?"

"Oh, I plan on it, Sir. One way or another."

Burke sat for a moment studying Ari. His face – still bruised from the hand-to-hand combat in the field – could not quite hide the righteous anger bubbling underneath. Burke admired the fact that this man felt such loyalty to men he had never met who weren't even soldiers for his own nation. They had been his responsibility and that meant something to Ari.

Burke made up his mind. He had already green-lighted the addition with the Member from Massachusetts. Now he would make it formal.

"Ari," he said, switching to a more personal first-name-basis as he rose from his chair and headed toward the doorway. "Come with me. I've got something to show you and quite a tale to tell."

Confused, Ari followed Burke down a long hallway past offices and workstations for a large operations center. He found himself wondering what unit of government Burke represented.

The hallways became a maze of turns, ending finally at a nondescript door. Burke pulled a simple key from his pocket to open it and they stepped through. Later, Ari would wonder at how the greatest secret of his life was kept behind such a loosely locked doorway.

"Watch your step," Burke warned as he reached to switch on an overhead light. The door opened to a set of stairs leading down into an undeveloped tunnel. After some time, the tunnel led to a set of old, wooden stairs and another unassuming wooden door. Another key came out of Burke's pocket, and Ari was led into what seemed to be the library of an old mansion.

An older gentleman sat in a brown leather chairs, reading a newspaper. He seemed not the least bit surprised when two men appeared from out of a doorway hidden in the bookshelves.

"Hello, Tom." He looked up from his paper with a warm smile and favored Ari with his glance. "You must be Mr. Cohen, and you must be confused."

The big man chuckled at himself, rising to shake Ari's hand. "John," he said by way of introduction. "Have a seat. We have a lot to talk about."

Burke quietly took up a position in the back of the room while Ari sat in the chair next to John. "Tell me, Mr. Cohen, have you ever heard of the Eyes of Athena?"

Ari shook his head to indicate he had not. He glanced at Burke and then back at John.

"Excellent. Good, good," John said. "We try to keep a low profile." Again he chuckled.

"The Eyes of Athena is a secret organization founded by the fathers of this nation that has been around for more than two centuries." John paused to gauge Ari's reaction. Seeing only curiosity, he rose from his seat, and pacing the room, he went on.

"We are the brainchild of Thomas Jefferson himself, who saw a need for a group to run outside the control of the government, politicians, even the President, to safeguard the true values, beliefs, safety and needs of the United States.

"Jefferson and the men he worked with had learned firsthand about the abuse of power that can come in the role of any 'ruler' while they were under the thumb of good old King George in England. So, shortly after the nation was born – almost before the ink was dry on the Declaration of Independence and the guns were put away from our hard-won fight for freedom – these men came together to form the Eyes of Athena."

Ari hung on every word, wondering what this could possibly have to do with a member of the Mossad and why in heaven's name a U.S. agency would lay itself naked before a foreign agent.

"Thirteen representatives – one for each of the colonies – formed the organization at first and fought secretly for the safety of a newborn nation. Today, things have progressed way beyond muskets and carrier pigeons." There was John's chuckle again. The man did seem to find himself funny.

"You just came from one of the most sophisticated operations centers in the world – far ahead of anything at the CIA, FBI, NSA or anything overseas. The leadership of Athena is still governed entirely by representatives of those original thirteen colonies – now states – keeping the number of those who know about us small, but not hindering our circle of influence.

"The secret is passed from representative to representative, and each President of the United States is made privy to some limited knowledge of our existence in case he ... or she ... ever needs to call on us.

"I am the Eye from Massachusetts," John said with a flourish of his hand and a dramatic little bow, a big smile on his face. He then stood before the bookshelves and rested his arm against them, looking intently at Ari as he waited for some response.

"That is all very fascinating," Ari said, opening his hands before him in a gesture of questioning. "But ..."

"But why would I tell you all of this?"

Ari simply nodded.

"Well..." There was a twinkle in John's eye. "How would you like to be the first Mossad member of the oldest secret society in America?"

Ari stared. "Why?"

"We have agents from all over, Mr. Cohen. We only recruit the best, and you, I'm told, are one of the best. After what I heard of your performance in this latest caper, I suspect you are also as highly motivated in this current endeavor as we are."

Ari's stare turned hard.

John nodded. "That, I would say, makes us perfect partners. As for Mossad, Rosenberg works with us often. He has agreed to loan you to us long-term with an appropriate cover story for the folks back home."

He returned to his seat next to Ari and sipped casually from a small glass of water. "Your first mission will be to find the Iranian, discover his plan and eliminate the threat. Interested?'

"Where do I sign?"

CHAPTER FOUR

Bethesda, Maryland
May 12, 1999

"So this is home." Burke flicked the light switch as he entered the small hallway. "Kitchen to the right here. It's stocked with the basics – pots, pans and plates, all that stuff. You'll need to stock your own pantry and fridge though.

"Living room," he said as he moved forward, "and the bedroom is through there. Again, all the linens, towels, and what have you are there for you. I think they even stock it with soap and shampoo if I remember from my rookie days."

Burke sat on the plain beige sofa and awaited Ari's judgment.

The new apartment was on base at the OPs center, where Ari would bunk for the duration of his first year with Athena. Between missions, he would train and learn more about the procedures of the organization. He had, of course, lived in much worse conditions.

"Looks great," he said with little enthusiasm. His grueling hours of debrief and travel – not to mention the failed operation – were wearing on him. All he wanted now was a hot shower and time between some clean sheets.

Burke took that as a sign to make his exit. "I'll see you back in my office at 0800." He handed Ari his apartment key and let himself out.

Ari only had the small travel case, and he unpacked it in the bedroom before stepping into the shower. "I swear. I have pain in places I didn't know existed," he said to the shower walls. The steaming hot water cascaded down his back, and he stood there a long time thinking about the mission, the men that had been lost, and that face he could never forget.

Halfway around the world, the man in Ari's thoughts was harboring thoughts of Ari, as well. Dawn was breaking, but Hamid Mahmoud had been awake for some time. Despite the success of his mission in Yugoslavia, he had not moved forward with his plan. He was worried about the agile dark-haired man who had nearly bested him. A man like that doesn't back down. A man like that could ruin everything.

He bellowed through the thin walls of his office at the assistant he had dragged into work in the middle of the night. "What news, Karim?"

Karim Kahn had been working their contact at the Italian base, a man with deeper connections within the U.S. government than anyone knew. He hurried in to tell his impatient boss what he had discovered thus far.

"He wasn't American." Karim entered the room talking. "He was brought in through some vague channels that our source cannot track, but he was definitely Mossad."

"Mossad? That makes no sense," Mahmoud said. "Since when do those dogs work with the American pigs?"

He moved around his desk and walked to within inches of Karim. Nose to nose Karim could smell the wretched stench of cigarettes and coffee on his boss's breath as Mahmoud whispered dangerously, each word crisply emphasized, "Find me a name."

~

Ari was standing outside Burke's office at 0759 about to knock when Burke bellowed, "Enter!"

Before the new Athena agent could even take a seat, his boss jumped into his Intel. "We've got eyes on your Mahmoud character. He flew straight back to Tehran from Yugoslavia and went right back to work at the Ministry of Information and Security."

"When do I leave?"

"Not so fast, cowboy. We need to watch this character, get an idea of what he intends to do with that technology, get a handle on who the players are, because that guy isn't getting anything done on a grand scale all by himself. We already know he's playing house with the Russians."

THE EYES OF ATHENA

Burke moved to sit on the edge of his desk and took a hard look at his new recruit. "I know you're anxious to get hold of this guy, and I don't blame you, but we've got a lot more riding on this than settling that grudge. You follow me?"

Ari nodded. "Then what is the plan?"

"We wait and watch, see where this guy is going with his new found information, and then we take him and everyone involved out of the picture. In the meantime, you work your connections and see what you can find out about him."

Ari nodded again and headed toward the door. "One thing, Tom," he said, turning back. "When the time comes, the Iranian is mine."

This time it was Burke's turn to nod.

CHAPTER FIVE

Bethesda, Maryland
July 6, 1999

The annual meeting of the Eyes of Athena Board was still held on the first Tuesday following the Fourth of July. The only difference was that it was not held at Monticello, Thomas Jefferson's Estate in Virginia, but rather at the Athena Intelligence complex near Bethesda, Maryland.

Twelve members were sitting around the meeting room waiting to see if the member from New York had appointed a successor before he died. As was tradition, the Secretary called the roll.

"Order! Order!" The member names were called out, one by one. "Massachusetts."

"Aye."

"Virginia."

"Aye."

And so it went.

All present except the Eye from New York State. Athena still maintained its original board of thirteen founding colonies – now states – and their representatives. They were Delaware, Pennsylvania, New Jersey, Georgia, Connecticut, Massachusetts, South Carolina, New Hampshire, Virginia, New York, North Carolina and Rhode Island. Each member was known as an "Eye," pertaining to the society's symbol – a pyramid with an eye in the center surrounded by 13 shafts of light.

The Secretary called the meeting to order. "The first order of business should be the replacement of our Eye from New York. It would appear that the succession plan in place failed. Do we have any suggestions?"

The athletic member from Massachusetts stood up. "May I speak, gentlemen?"

"Aye," resounded throughout the room.

THE EYES OF ATHENA

"I have been giving our board a lot of thought lately, and I suggest that we all do the same. Throughout our history, we have confronted many challenges in our nation, and now Athena must face one more – and that challenge is the current makeup of our board, the concentration of our professions and, quite frankly, too many old men."

There was a general nodding of heads, no disagreement among those assembled.

"Our world is changing, and we must change with it! It is time for us to get some younger blood on our board.

"Additionally, we have not had anyone join us that might be a potential Presidential candidate," he noted. "Our candidate should have worldwide, real-time diplomatic experience. A member of the fairer sex might also be prudent. This person must be a unifier of our people... and of our board. In short gentlemen, we need a real leader."

In an almost humorist tone, he questioned, "Do we have any members that aim to run for the presidency?"

He knew the answer to his rhetorical question, as most members were too old or set in their ways to seek the seat. Seeing the smiles and the shaking of heads, he continued. "In short, gentlemen, we need to take some bold steps to prepare Athena for a new century, a new generation."

He paused for effect, surveying the room, saw heads nodding in agreement and could hear some slight sounds of affirmation, but there was no consensus yet. *Not surprising,* he thought, *they don't know who I am going to suggest.*

The member from Virginia asked, "Who do you have in mind?"

When the Eye from Massachusetts answered, the room fell silent.

North Carolina managed to stammer in his shock, "But isn't she a resident of Arkansas and therefore not eligible to join our board?"

Massachusetts took his time; he finally had their attention. "I have not approached the candidate yet, so I am going to need a little time, but I believe this is a doable proposition."

The eleven other board members sat forward animatedly, not one was slouched back in his comfortable chair. They all looked from one to the other, gauging each member's interest in this brazen idea. The Secretary stood up as Massachusetts sat down.

"Do we have a second to the Member's suggestion?"

"Seconded!" was the unanimous response. The Board voted and agreed.

Once all was hammered out, the Eye from Massachusetts was granted an extension of thirty days to try to realize his plan. It was agreed that the opportunity was worth leaving the seat vacant for the six months or more that would be required to make things happen.

CHAPTER SIX

Washington, D.C.
July 16, 1999

The President was in an Oval Office meeting with members of his staff, the daily "State of the State" discussion on the agenda. He found it difficult to keep his mind on the meeting, his thoughts instead turning to the affair he had attended last weekend.

Ronald "Rocky" McQueen had always had a great admiration for the Kennedy clan, and consequently he had accepted the invitation to go to the wedding in Martha's Vineyard of one of the Kennedy clan members, Rory. He couldn't help but think about the disappearance of John F. Kennedy and his wife, Carolyn, who never showed up.

One of his secret ambitions, after the end of his second term, was to learn to fly – get his pilot's license, do it properly, get instrument rated. *Now,* he thought as he looked down at a press release Reuters was about to publish, *there wasn't a chance in on earth that my wife or the Secret Service would ever let me fly my own plane.*

He thought that even if he defied his wife's wishes, there was no chance she would ever fly with him, nor would she let him fly with their daughter. He was thinking that the President of the United States of America was meant to be the most powerful person in the world, but he supposed that meant only if you excluded the First Lady.

McQueen turned his attention to the press release he was holding,

"Reuters -- On July 16, 1999, John Kennedy, his wife, Carolyn, and sister-in-law, Lauren Bessette, were reported missing when the Piper Saratoga he was piloting failed to arrive at its planned destination in Martha's Vineyard. John

Kennedy, as the pilot, had checked in with the FAA tower at the Martha's Vineyard Airport in Vineyard Haven, Massachusetts.

"The trio was en route to attend the wedding of Kennedy's cousin, Rory Kennedy. A search commenced more than 15 hours later to locate them, finally ending in the late afternoon hours of July 21, when the three bodies were recovered from the ocean floor by Navy divers.

"The bodies were taken by motorcade to the county medical examiner's office. The National Transportation Safety Board has opined that the plane had crashed into the Atlantic Ocean off Martha's Vineyard, the probable cause being pilot error. NTSB noted the likely cause as being Kennedy's failure to maintain control of the airplane during a descent over water at night as a result of spatial disorientation."

McQueen's thoughts were interrupted when an aide walked in and stood beside him, awaiting his attention. He turned to his aide and nodded and was then given a card emblazoned with an eye inside a pyramid surrounded by 13 shafts of light.

The President tensed and looked inquiringly at the aide, who approached and whispered in his ear, "He is waiting for you in the White House gym. He has been cleared by the Secret Service."

McQueen nodded affirmatively to his aide. He finished his meeting with his team, establishing a list of priorities for the next press conference. At the top of the list was his desire that Congress send to his desk for signature – without further delay – the reasonable gun measures already passed by the Senate.

In the White House gym, the Eye from Massachusetts was pacing, thinking about his mission. He heard some activity approaching, so he turned his attention to the door just as the President entered, looked around in mild confusion and approached the stranger.

"I was beginning to wonder if I would ever hear from you guys."

THE EYES OF ATHENA

"So I gather you have seen and read the Book?" Massachusetts was pleased to see that Athena's charter and existence was still being passed from President to President in a private ceremony at the beginning of each new President's term.

"Yes I have. I must admit I am glad to finally meet you; I had wondered if you really existed, and I'm privileged to make your acquaintance." McQueen oozed good old fashioned southern charm.

Massachusetts was encouraged by his reception. "Mr. President, these are perilous times. It is imperative that Athena be ever vigilant. You are familiar with our bylaws from the Book? He hesitated a moment to be sure the President signaled in the affirmative. "So you know that we always need to have thirteen board members, one from each original colony-now-state?"

"Yes, Sir, I am aware."

"We have recently had a board member vacate his position without a named successor, so we have an opening for a member from New York State."

The President simply nodded, having no idea where this conversation was going.

"Where do you and your wife intend to live when you leave the White House?"

McQueen was a little thrown by the unexpected question, but answered, frowning in his puzzlement.

"Why, we ... uh ... why, we had planned on returning to Little Rock."

Massachusetts pressed, "Have you ever considered a move to upstate New York?"

McQueen was slow to catch on, and stood before Massachusetts completely mystified, his face showing it. "No, we haven't."

"There are some beautiful communities in upstate New York, like Chappaqua." His voice was leading now; he had not anticipated it would be this difficult to make the suggestion.

Finally, he gave up. "We'd be happy to arrange financing for a suitable residence if you were planning to move your residency to New York."

The President looked inquiringly at his visitor, as if questioning him, still not understanding.

Massachusetts began to wonder how the man ever got elected. "Your final term will expire in January of 2001, and we have decided to leave the New York position open for a short term in order to find the right person ..."

McQueen finally understood and contemplated what he thought he was being offered. "I'd be happy to serve as the representative from New York," he replied.

Massachusetts sighed under his breath. After all of that, he had not been clear. He was embarrassed now. "Mr. President, you flatter us, but..." he hesitated only a little, "it is your wife we want."

CHAPTER SEVEN

Bethesda, Maryland
July 27, 1999

The Athena Board meeting resumed promptly at 10:00 AM at the Bethesda headquarters of Athena. On this occasion, it was handled as a conference call on Athena's own secure network.

The Secretary called the meeting to order. "Massachusetts, do you have a report for us?"

"Yes, Sir, we are a go." Massachusetts repeated, "We are go for New York."

"Do we have a second?" The Secretary's question was greeted with unanimous cheers.

The Secretary asked the conference call moderator, "Do you have New York on standby?"

Receiving a response in the affirmative, he stated, "Please admit the proposed member from New York to our conference call."

There followed a moment of silence. Then he continued, "Madam First Lady, can you hear us?"

A strong, determined, but decidedly feminine voice floated back across the line. "Yes, gentlemen."

"Madam, it is our custom to refer to each other by our representative state, if you don't have any objections, New York?"

"None, Sir. I'll be proud to serve her."

"Good. You will be glad to know, New York, that 220 years ago, Athena members were obliged to have a mark tattooed on their inner wrist to identify themselves one to another. This practice has now been modernized; each member and operative has a microchip embedded in their arm for security purposes. May I assume that this meets with your approval?"

"Yes, Sir, you may."

"In that case," the Secretary replied, "Madam, we are honored to have you join us. Henceforth," he added with dry humor, "we will try not to refer to ourselves as a brotherhood, but as a society!"

Not to be outdone she responded, "Mr. Secretary, did you say society or sorority?"

Hearty chuckles could be heard all around. The Secretary continued, "As Massachusetts is your sponsor, he will take over and introduce you to our ins and outs. Thank you for your service and God Bless America."

CHAPTER EIGHT

Washington, D.C.
July 27, 1999

Sitting in the room with the Eye from Massachusetts, Jade McQueen didn't seem the slightest bit nervous considering she was the first woman to ever be made privy to one of the nation's greatest secrets.

"Well, John, what now?" she said to her long-time friend.

"You have a lot to learn, Jade." He rose from the rich leather sofa on which they had been sitting and poured himself a glass of water. "You have just become part of a long and rich history, and a very powerful ... ahem ... society." He turned to look at her with a smile.

"After more than 200 years, the influence, prestige and resources of Athena are without equal. Our first financial resources and budgets officer was none other than Benjamin Franklin. He had instituted some strict financial disciplines, which included a prohibition on any type of borrowing or pledging of Athena's assets for any purpose."

Turning back to McQueen, he offered her a glass of water as well, which she took.

"Smart ... if they stuck to it."

"Yes. Franklin reasoned that if you had bankers involved in your business, the confidentiality and secrecy of the organization would be impaired. The founding members also agreed to bequeath 10 percent of their estate to the Eyes of Athena upon their deaths. Consequently, the wealth and resources of Athena grew significantly from the beginning.

"Over the years, Athena has further protected its massive wealth with some very wise investments and shrewd placement of its assets in safe tax havens around the world."

"Smart and sly," McQueen said over the top of her glass.

"The rationale behind this decision was made clear in one of those founding board meetings – an objection to taxation without representation was a major factor leading to the Declaration of Independence. Besides, if the financial affairs of Athena were subject to government scrutiny, the secrecy of Athena would be threatened."

John stopped his stroll around the room and seated himself in a comfortable chair opposite McQueen.

"So, we have strong resources. What exactly do we do with them?" she asked.

"Anything we want," he replied without humor.

"Sounds dangerous, John."

"If such a society was in the hands of any other group of men ... er, and women," he said with a nod of his head and a tip of his glass in her direction, "it would be. The members are chosen for their strong moral standards and complete commitment to the foundational beliefs of this nation. For that reason, Athena has served for more than two centuries to protect the American people and their freedom from all threats – inside and out."

"Well then, John, I'm on board."

CHAPTER NINE

September 29, 1999

"His name is Ari Cohen, but no one at Mossad has seen him since the crash. Word is he's in deep cover," Karim stood proudly at Mahmoud's desk awaiting a kind word of appreciation. He should have known better than to expect so much as a nod from his boss; Mahmoud simply did not do kindness.

"Where is he now?"

"Our American contact could only track him to a military flight into Bethesda from Italy. No one has seen him since."

Mahmoud sighed. He rubbed the space between his eyes, a sign that told Karim he was trying to control himself. He spoke in measured tones. "Then we must find him. Get me Heinrich."

Cafe Orleans, Buenos Aires, Argentina
October 13, 1999

Heinrich Gosslau was a walking contradiction. He was a cold-blooded killer who loved the crisp feel of autumn and all that was Buenos Aires.

As he strolled down the street, he indulged in the early morning aroma of a rousing populace used to indulging their fetish for pastries, caffeine and tobacco. As he traveled the Avenue Cordoba, he approached one of his favorite haunts, the Cafe Orleans.

Luscious scents of Arabica beans, delicate pastries and expensive perfumes mixed together to radiate an irresistible smell that surely must have been one of the original deadly sins. He entered the cafe and inhaled deeply, heading for his favorite table while surveying the local talent. It was filled with a clientele of females like no other city in the world, he thought. They were all immaculately dressed, almost as if they were waiting to be asked to Tango.

He meandered to his seat and maneuvered around to put his back to the wall. He often imagined himself to be Argentina's answer to James Bond, but in fact, the reason he sat with his back to the wall was to ogle the ladies before him. He had never found a partner to put up with his selfish nature and mean eccentricities.

His job at the Secret Police did not keep him very busy, being given only an occasional assignment – usually one that no one else wanted – to neutralize a political opponent the top brass and political elite had ordered eliminated. Due to his peculiar talents, he had an inflated view of his own self-worth and abilities.

He had just ordered his favorite cafe latte when a colleague from the Secret Police entered the cafe and stood still for a moment scanning the customers, obviously looking for someone. After scanning the crowd, his eyes finally reached Heinrich. He squinted a little, as if to make sure he had the right man before approaching the table. Heinrich recognized Emilio immediately.

He watched as the smaller, Latino man deliberately sidled up to his table and asked in a most mocking and innocent tone, "Ah, Heinrich, mind if I join you?"

No one used his last name. Heinrich assumed it was a sign of camaraderie, but in fact it was disrespect. Heinrich's father was a well-known scientist deserving of great accolades, while his son's position in the Secret Police – or even at the Russian Military Academy that trained him – was never earned.

Heinrich was instantly on alert. This was the last thing he wanted – somebody's company when he was indulging his favorite past time, stalking Buenos Aires' prettiest women.

"Of course, Emilio, it's so nice to see you," he tried to say in his most sincere voice. "Is this a chance encounter?" If his forced smile widened any further, his face would break.

Emilio considered Heinrich to be the lowest form of life that existed but he played along because he had been so instructed.

"Heinrich, you old scoundrel, how did you know?"

Heinrich ignored Emilio's question, knowing he had no real friends at the office, but rather acquaintances of convenience. He imagined it was because his co-workers were afraid of him and respectful because of his special status as a Secret Police hit man; he did not know or suspect that they despised him with a passion as a man with no conscience and found him a person to pity, not admire.

Heinrich decided he had no reason to play games with this man. He dropped the smile and got straight to the point. "What do you want, Emilio?"

"I have been sent by an old friend who wishes to purchase your... services." Wiping his mouth with an ivory silk handkerchief, Emilio made the word sound as dirty as it should.

Heinrich perked up at that. He enjoyed his work and no one had needed him in quite some time, but he was cautious. "And do I know this friend?"

"You have worked for him before... Our friend Mahmoud? He is in need of the removal of a pesky Mossad agent."

Emilio slid a piece of paper across the table discreetly. "Call this number if you are willing to accept this... opportunity."

And with that he left.

Heinrich took the paper, paid for his barely touched drink, and headed out onto the busy sidewalk. He hurried down Avenue Cordoba. Due to the frigid temperatures of autumn in Buenos Aires, he hurried down the sunny side of the street. As he anticipated his coming assignment he began to sweat. His attention was soon brought back to reality as he turned into the electronic doors of his office building at the Argentinean Secret Police – a place the public avoided like the plague. The rule of General Juan Peron was still forefront in many Argentineans' minds even though he had died more than 35 years ago.

Heinrich quickly began removing his coat and scarf as he walked into the lobby, swiped his ID card through the secure access machine, and gained entrance to the building's elevators. He took the elevator to his office on the 6th floor, feeling a rising excitement over the chance to get back to work. He hurried over to his desk, picked up the secure phone and dialed the number off the piece of paper Emilio had provided.

It seemed forever before the call connected. Heinrich began to rub the scar he had received as the result of a fencing duel at the Moscow Military Academy. He thought back to that week, the very idea of that tragedy making him rub his scar until it was beet red.

The academy was one of the most prestigious schools in all of Russia. As a result, the competition to get into the academy was intense, as was the competition to get the best grades formidable. The intense competition to get into the academy had resulted in most of the accepted candidates being members of the political elite, the Politburo, the KGB or GRU.

Heinrich often wondered how his father had arranged for the academy to accept him. He knew of his father's work for the Russians before they moved to Buenos Aires, knew his father had continued the work his grandfather began for Nazi Germany. But where did the great Hermann Gosslau cultivate such a strong connection to the elite society of Moscow? Heinrich had never been able to figure out what his father – who was an expert in pulse powered jet propulsion engines – had found to occupy his great talent in Argentina of all places.

Still rubbing the scar, he remembered how he had initiated the duel. Challenging the son of one of the highest members of the Politburo to a sword fight had not been a good career choice, even though Heinrich lost the duel that resulted in the ruination of his face and his being sent back to Argentina.

The telephone finally clicking through brought him back to the present. A stranger with a heavy accent did not waste any time.

"Arrangements have been made for tomorrow morning. Get on the plane to Chicago O'Hare and check into the Hilton O'Hare. We will have a room reserved for you, await instructions." The phone went dead.

Unfazed, Heinrich grabbed his passport from the safe in his office and headed for his apartment to pack.

CHAPTER TEN

International Hilton O'Hare
October 14, 1999

After Heinrich cleared customs, he walked down to the baggage claim area to retrieve his suitcase. The gangway was crowded, and he used that as his excuse to rub up against the women exiting the plane with him, oblivious to their looks of disgust.

As the crowd began to spread out and his attention refocused to the world around him, he saw an advertisement for the Chicago O'Hare Hilton flashing on the side of the walkway. "Discover the best of the Windy City from the comfort of the Hilton Chicago O'Hare Airport. Connected to the airport via the walkway, the hotel is located a short train ride from downtown Chicago with its abundant shopping, dining and entertainment."

How convenient, he thought, *I don't even have to get a taxi; a walkway takes me right to the hotel.* It was even easier than he imagined and within no time he was checking in at the Hilton. He loved American hotels. The front reception area was as long as a swimming pool and the hotel wanted their guests checked in as quickly and comfortably as possible. He thought that at a hotel of this size in Argentina, he might have to wait for an hour to get checked in.

After a late lunch and an afternoon siesta, Heinrich rose to answer a knock on his hotel door. A bell boy was waiting, envelope in hand. "Delivery for Mr. Gosslau."

Heinrich turned around to retrieve his money clip, peeled off a ten and gave it to the boy.

"Thank you," the boy replied enthusiastically, handing him the envelope.

Heinrich closed the door and went over to his coffee table to open the dispatch. Inside were instructions, identification paperwork, money and credit cards.

CHAPTER ELEVEN

Georgetown, Washington, D.C.
October 14, 1999

David Gray had been on medical leave for months. His career as a Navy SEAL ended in that dark field in Yugoslavia with one bad bullet placement. Although he had recovered reasonable use of his leg, it would never be strong enough to endure the rigors of life as an active SEAL.

And so he had been growing anxious, pondering his alternatives when the Secret Service came calling. The change of pace seemed like just what he needed.

Gray had only arrived in Georgetown a few days ago. His sister – the little homemaker of the family – had already found him a place to live and had it furnished and decorated before his plane touched down.

Coming in from a long jog through his quiet neighborhood, Gray wiped the sweat from his face, grabbed his cell phone and checked for any messages. He refused to take the thing with him when he jogged – his own little oasis from the hustle and bustle of the world – at least until he started life as a Secret Service agent 24/7.

"This is your platoon buddy, Mike. I'm sorry to bug you, but I really need your help," Gray froze at the sound of pain in his friend's voice. Mike had saved his bacon more than once when they served together. They were more like brothers, and there was nothing he wouldn't do for the man.

"I'm in Fairbanks, sitting in my car in the parking lot at the Bear Lodge. I don't know what to do an' I'm broke."

The message ended. Gray's fingers flew over the buttons of his phone calling 411. "Please give me the listing for the Bear Lodge in Fairbanks."

The female operator, in a high-pitched, totally disinterested voice, said, "You mean Fairbanks, Alaska, Sir?"

Were there any other Fairbanks in the U.S.? Gray had no idea, he sighed deeply. "Of course I mean Fairbanks, Alaska."

"Putting you through, Sir."

After a few switching clicks, the call was answered almost immediately by a man in a deep confident voice. "Bear Lodge Motel. May I help you?"

"I need to make a reservation, please."

"How many people and how many nights, Sir?"

Gray decided to give him the whole story. "Look, I have a service buddy sitting in the parking lot. He's down on his luck, and he needs my help, and that means I need your help."

"Sir, I'm a vet, too, Iraq. It'd be an honor to help. I'll do my best to take care of him. What's his name?"

Gray breathed a sigh of relief, thankful to find a vet who felt a bond with other vets and a military code of honor. "Mike Rogers. He has PTSD. Here's my credit card info."

Once the clerk had everything down, Gray asked, "Can you give him a room and access to room service on my tab? I'll be there tomorrow or as quickly as I can."

As soon as he hung up with the manager, Gray was dialing another number. Since they met on that fateful night, he and Ari had become fast friends, and he needed to talk to a good friend right then.

Never without his cell phone, Ari answered on the first ring. "David! How are you?"

"Ari, I've been better."

"Tell me, brother. What can I do?"

"Have you ever been to Fairbanks?"

"Alaska?"

Gray almost laughed at that. "Is there any other?"

CHAPTER TWELVE

Fairbanks, Alaska
October 15, 1999

Fairbanks International Airport in October can be a cruel introduction to Alaska. Gusty winds blow most of the time at well below zero.

Heinrich's flight from Chicago was going to arrive on time, but the gusty crosswind meant it was going to be a bumpy landing. By the time Heinrich had checked out of his hotel in Chicago, his contact had already found out that the target was scheduled to arrive in Fairbanks and meet one David Gray, former Navy SEAL, at the Bear Lodge Motel. Once they had found Cohen, they had made it their business to track his every move.

Heinrich's contact did not say why the man was there, only that Heinrich was ordered to 'take him out.' He had been told that someone would meet him in baggage claim.

His plane had the predicted bumpy landing, after which Heinrich made his way down to claim his suitcase. As he was leaving, walking outside in the blustery snow, a man approached. It was hard to see who he was with his hat pulled down over his face. He also wore sunglasses, which was not unusual considering the bright snow all around.

"Mr. Heinrich?" the man asked as he approached much too close for Heinrich's comfort.

"Yes."

"I was told to meet you here, Sir. Follow me, if you please."

The contact did not say another word until he had led Heinrich into a parking area, where he stopped. "Here are the keys. She's stolen; false plates, so no worries where you leave her. Got a good rifle and scope in the trunk."

The man turned and walked away. Heinrich opened the car door and slid behind the wheel. On the passenger-side

THE EYES OF ATHENA

seat was a map of Fairbanks. Heinrich thought to himself that he was going to enjoy working for these people; they seemed well organized with assets everywhere.

He familiarized himself with the map while the car was warming up, then drove out of airport parking toward Fairbanks. It was only mid-afternoon and was already getting dark. *A real strange climate,* he thought.

As he drove down the highway toward town, he saw an illuminated billboard flashing:

SIGHT YOUR GUN HERE
A&A GUN RANGE
NEXT EXIT

Heinrich was surprised. *Only in America,* he thought, *would a business advertise a gun range on a billboard.* Still he needed to sight-in the rifle and get the scope fine-tuned so he took the next exit and pulled into the range.

After parking his car in the deserted parking area, he paid the attendant his fee, retrieved his ticket stub and walked over to the range. He unzipped his rifle case and pulled out an FN-FAL with a 1-4X scope.

He loaded the 20-round FN-FAL magazine with 7.62 mm rounds, inserted the magazine and put it on semi-automatic. He adjusted his stance and turned his attention to the scope. When he had adjusted it to his satisfaction, he started firing. Fire, adjust. Fire, adjust. Eventually, he was satisfied – 1/2" groups at 100 yards.

The range attendant watched Heinrich's grouping through some binoculars from a perch behind and above the firing range. "That's some pretty good shooting, fella."

Heinrich didn't reply; he just left the range and drove into Fairbanks. He parked behind an abandoned office building about 800 yards from the Bear Lodge Motel. His instructions included the room number Gray had been given. It faced into the parking lot along the highway.

Heinrich climbed up to the roof of the abandoned building, the bitter cold wind blowing snow up all around him, and spent the day checking out Gray's room with the scope on his rifle, knowing the FN-FAL rifle was ready.

He saw Gray in the room moving around. Through the long, cold hours he waited, eyes on his quarry. Later in the day, Gray opened the door for maid service, dragging Heinrich out of his boredom, there were no other visitors.

"Where is little Ari, David?" Heinrich said in a sing-song voice. "My patience is running thin."

After a full, cold day lying as still as possible, he moved stiffly, as if his joints were frozen. He decided to descend the outside metal access from the roof and drive back to his own motel. He would come back for the Mossad after a hot shower, a good meal and a night's rest.

CHAPTER THIRTEEN

Fairbanks International Airport
October 16, 1999

Gray was a vet's vet – immensely loyal, he always had an almost paternal concern for his comrades in arms.

Luckily, it was a sentiment that his friend Ari understood completely.

Ari had listened intently as Gray told him everything there was to know about Mike Rogers. He had been quiet a moment and then he had said simply, "This is a man we must help."

Over the years, Ari had been witness to man's worst brutality and the damage it could do to other men. He had experience with helping people like Mike and had readily agreed to meet Gray at the motel the following day.

Gray arrived on time in Fairbanks. Carrying his overnight bag, he had no need to wait in the baggage terminal for a suitcase. At the main terminal, he went down the escalator to the baggage claim area and over to the car rental desk. As a Gold card member, he didn't have to wait in line. He looked for his name on the reservation billboard, picked up the rental packet with keys under his name and went straight to the parking area.

Ari wasn't due to land for another hour, so Gray located his rental, stowed his gear and drove out. After verifying his identity with the rental car check-out clerk, he was on his way. He went directly to the Bear Lodge Motel. It was dark already, windy, cold and wet. He drove into the motel parking lot, scanning the doors for room number 114.

He knocked on the door and waited. The motel was typical for those built back in the 1960s. The reception and lobby was closest to the road with one long line of very plain, identically drab rooms spread out to the side and behind, forming an L shape.

Inside, his old friend pulled the curtain back to see who was knocking, and on recognizing Gray, threw open the door, beaming, and grabbed his pal in a bear hug.

Mike was overcome with excitement. "Thanks for coming, David," he said repeatedly, as they sat down. He seemed to feel it necessary to explain himself, or at least try, almost stammering in the attempt. "I guess sometimes... sometimes things don't work out the way we want them to. I had such big plans when I came back from overseas. I wanted to use the G.I. bill to go back to school, you know and..."

Gray felt his friend's pain and didn't want him to have to relive all those lost dreams. "Don't worry about it, Mike," he interrupted. "You don't owe me any explanations."

But it seemed to him then as if Mike just needed to hear himself speak, rationalize it to himself, so he decided to let his friend go on – the words coming quickly now mixed with tears, as if he were trying to cleanse his soul.

"My wife left me. I lost my job." Mike hung his head. "She said I drink too much."

Gray felt so deeply for his brother. "Mike, it's the story of many of us. We were there for our country when she needed us. But when we returned home after serving, the country wasn't there to help us."

Trying to change the subject to a happier note, he slapped Mike on the leg and said, "Go take a shower, then we can go grab a steak. How does that sound?"

He decided not to tell him about Ari just yet.

Mike was still a little sullen but trying to recover. "I don't have a change of clothes."

Gray gave Mike a razor out of his kit. "Clean up. I'm going to go buy some clothes for you. Have a shower and shave. I'll be back within the hour."

Gray headed out, intending to find some kind of big box store on his way to or from picking up Ari.

From atop the building across the highway, Heinrich watched Gray come and go wondering what drama was unfolding in room 114. He knew from his instructions that his target was a Mossad agent – dark hair, dark skin – and even in his winter coat and ski cap, Heinrich could see that Gray didn't fit the bill.

"Must be the SEAL," he said to himself. "So, who's inside the room?"

It was dark now and freezing cold. Heinrich was losing his taste for this job rapidly. Watching Gray pull out of the parking lot, he could only hope that Cohen would turn up soon.

~

Ari was waiting just inside the terminal doors when Gray pulled up. He hustled out, threw his kit in the back seat and climbed into the warm car. He was bundled up like an Eskimo and still looked half frozen just from that short walk.

"Welcome to the Tundra." Gray laughed.

Ari shot him a look that could kill. "Remember, bird man, my desert people were not meant for your frozen wastelands."

Ari only called him "bird man" when he was agitated. It was his pet name for the man he met falling from the sky.

Almost an hour and one hunt-and-kill shopping trip later, Gray turned back onto the highway, headed for the motel parking lot.

Just as Gray climbed out of the driver' seat and Ari turned to exit on his side, a shot shattered the back window and split the air between them. Instantly, they were on alert, rolling out of the car and heading for positions of safety behind it.

The hotel manager came running out of his office three doors closer to the street and shouted, "Did you hear that shot?"

"Get down!" Gray warned.

The manager slid across the snow covered gravel to stop next to Ari. He and Gray had their heads together, whispering and scanning the rooftops behind the car looking for a likely spot for their shooter.

"Can you see anything?"

Ari peered into the blinding whiteness of the snow-covered terrain. Nothing seemed to move. Nothing seemed out of place.

The door to 114 opened, and Mike stood in the freezing cold, wearing only a towel and carrying the hunting rifle he had taken into the room when he checked in.

"What in the sam hill is going on?"

"Get inside, Mike!" Gray started toward him, but Ari grabbed his arm as a shot rang out.

Gray broke free, ran full out the few feet to the motel door and dove through. Ari followed, and both hit the floor. Shots rang out behind them, ricocheting off the sidewalk and the brick walls, whizzing past Ari's ear.

Mike lay motionless, his towel draped body in a pool of blood, muscles still twitching in a last vain protest against an untimely death.

In a flash, Gray was up again. He turned to Ari, "Call the police, and see if there is anything you can do for Mike. I'm going after him!"

Again, Ari grabbed his arm. "Mike's gone. I'm coming with you."

Gray took a deep breath and exhaled slowly. "Then let's do this."

Rather than exit through the door they had entered, the two headed for the rear. As with many older hotels, the Bear Lodge had two doors to each room, and they went out the back. Once they had made their way back around to the corner of the building and could see the parking area, they stopped to take stock of the situation.

"I'd say by the position of those bullet holes, the shooter's got to be in that office building across the street," Ari said.

He looked at the office windows, noting they did not open. "Had to be from the roof," Ari said, scanning it for several seconds before running in a crouch behind the motel office and across the highway toward the building itself from the far right, alert for the slightest movement.

Gray followed close at his heels.

A light snow was falling, hindering Ari's sight. Suddenly, he stopped in his tracks. Something out of place had tickled his subconscious. His ears pricked up at the sound of metal clanging on metal; the shooter must be descending the fire escape at the back of the building, banging his gun against the metal protective barrier.

They both ran full out now, figuring there was very little danger of being shot. As they approached the front of the building, they heard a car door slam followed by the sound of an ignition.

THE EYES OF ATHENA

Gray kicked in a burst of speed that ripped at the still-healing muscles of his leg. He skidded around the back corner of the building in time to see a car illuminated in the parking lot lights. It was ten feet in front of him and heading for the exit where he stood. As he slid to a stop, he looked into the driver's side front seat and saw his assassin looking back.

It was a face he would never forget. He raised his gun to fire just as Heinrich hit the gas. Ari grabbed Gray by the back of his shirt and pulled him from in front of the speeding car, knowing he would never get a shot off in time.

From the snow-covered pavement, with the swelling anger consuming his soul, Gray screamed into the blackened sky, "I will find you and I will kill you!"

In the car, Heinrich, too, had seen his pursuer and as he sped away, he swore to himself. For the first time in his life, he felt real fear.

CHAPTER FOURTEEN

Bear Lodge Motel

Ari and Gray raced back toward the rental car in the motel parking lot, but the sound of a wailing police siren drawing ever closer stopped them from following the assassin.

If they charged after Heinrich, the police would surely give chase and start asking questions they couldn't or didn't want to answer. Ari didn't like the situation. This was not the kind of low profile his new employer preferred.

He managed to reign in his friend and together they plodded back dejectedly toward the motel as two police cruisers pulled up, sirens still screaming, tires screeching for a grip in the slush.

At this point, Ari had no idea what they were going to tell them. In fact, he wasn't really sure what had just happened. As Gray headed straight for Mike's body, Ari hung back to place a call. On the other end, Burke was instantly wide awake and working.

Athena OPs Center
October 20, 1999

Ari didn't waste any time; as soon as he got back into town, he went to Bethesda and straight into Tom Burke's office.

"Welcome back. You want to tell me what happened, Ari?"

"At this point, Tom, I'd be willing to bet you know as much as I do. Lone sniper set up on the roof across from the motel.

"Yep. But you can fill me in on just what you were doing in Alaska."

"Providing a favor for a friend."

"Gray, right?" Burke was looking at a file on his desk. "He was the lone survivor of that paratrooper unit."

"Yes. He asked for my help with a buddy suffering from PTSD holed up in a motel in Fairbanks, so I flew in."

"You have any idea who the target was, Ari?"

"Nothing solid but I'd be willing to bet it's most likely me over Gray."

"That's not a bet I'd go against." Burke looked up from the file. From the description you gave of the shooter and the MO you described, it would appear to be our old friend Heinrich Gosslau. He works ostensibly for the Secret Police in Argentina, but we know him to be a man for hire at the right price.

"And since you're still breathing here in my office, I'd say your luck was holding that day. Heinrich is not usually one to miss his target."

"I am not an easy target to hit." Ari stated it as fact.

"So I see. I have scheduled a meeting with the team. Let's see what they've come up with."

The two left his office and walked across the hall to the Situation Room.

"OK, folks, we are going to refer to this assignment as Project H."

Burke nodded at the senior analyst in the corner. "Sam, why don't you fill us in on Heinrich Gosslau?"

"Of course, Sir. Here's what we know. Gosslau, born in the town of Flores, in Buenos Aires province, in 1968; attended bi-lingual schools where he had a reputation as a bully and a slow student. Father Hermann Gosslau was the son of Nazi scientist Fritz Gosslau, who designed the V1 and V2 bombs in Germany used during World War II. Father is also an accomplished scientist living in Argentina with strong ties to the Russian government.

"In 1988, Heinrich started popping up on our close-watch list due to some 'unusual talents' he learned in Moscow that he employed on behalf of the Argentinian Secret Police. Apparently he had acquired the skills of an assassin."

"Thanks, Sam," Burke said. "From what we can glean, Heinrich Gosslau is a bit of a low life. His comrades at the Secret Police have little respect for him, and it seems they keep him around to do the dirty work, but it's his little side jobs that took him to Fairbanks.

"Our sources in Argentina strictly deny any involvement in that debacle and are interested in finding their little wayward ward, as well. Seems he disappeared after Fairbanks and the Secret Police deny being able to locate him."

"You believe that, Tom?"

"Let's just say we do not take Intel from those sources at face value."

CHAPTER FIFTEEN

**Inside the MOIS Military Complex, Tehran
October 15, 1999**

"Nothing happens in Iran's Ministry of Information and Security, unless it is within the strict guidelines as set forth by the Supreme Leader. Period."

Mahmoud sat at the desk in his office at the Ministry of Information and Security in Tehran.
"Now that that insolent Mossad dog is being handled, the time has come to move forward," he told Karim.

His office was deep in the interior of the building – a maze of offices in a giant security complex where analysts worked day and night delving into the lives of any Iranian they chose. According to Iran's constitution, all organizations were required to share information with the MOIS.

On the wall of Mahmoud's office, two framed pictures hung – one a portrait of the Ayatollah and the other a photo of the Liberty Bell.

Mahmoud sat looking at the photos as he contemplated the rogue Mossad agent. He constantly flexed the muscle of his upper cheek in a nervous twitch, which exaggerated the dark stubble on his face and general unkempt look about him. A chain smoker, he dragged heavily on a Turkish cigarette.

He smiled at the picture of the Liberty Bell and kept his eyes centered there a few more seconds, then his smile turned to an evil sneer as he said to himself, "Soon..."

To Karim, he said, "Call to make an appointment with the chief. I need to see him as soon as possible."

As Mahmoud's overly attentive assistant turned to leave, his curiosity got the better of him and he asked, "Why do you have the photo of the Liberty Bell on your wall?"

Mahmoud looked over at the photo again and replied, "I won't rest until I have turned that very symbol of American liberty to dust."

Karim shuddered at the look on the man's face.

After Karim left his office, Mahmoud reopened the newspaper article he had tucked away months ago and started to re-read it.

> *"Reuters -- March 28th, 1999. An American F-117 Stealth fighter went down in Yugoslavia on Saturday, the first allied loss in the four-day Balkan conflict, even as NATO officials announced a broad new phase of the air assault on Serbian targets.*
>
> *"Besides the loss of the plane in Serbia, the United States faces a loss of the secret technology that allows the F-117 to evade detection. That technology includes the composite materials used for the outer surface of the plane, which absorb radar instead of reflecting it back to be picked up at defensive missile sites.*
>
> *"Military sources say any secrets lost to the Serbs could find their way to the Russians, who have been supporting Serbia."*

Mahmoud carefully folded the article, reached for his wallet and stored it safely. He could not contain his excitement. Finally he was ready to go to the man in charge at the MOIS.

~

Despite his appointment, Teymour Nassiri kept Mahmoud waiting by his secretary's desk for twenty minutes. Mahmoud's face twitched as he glared straight ahead, incensed that he was treated with such disrespect. His dark scowl frightened the woman next to him, who tried to focus on her typing.

"I'm sure it won't be but just a moment longer," she said nervously.

THE EYES OF ATHENA

Mahmoud did not look up. His excitement over this meeting had drained away moment by moment. *If this self-important, over-bloated egotist knew what I am bringing him...* he thought bitterly, his teeth grinding. He reached into his pocket to pull out a cigarette just as the door to Nassiri's office opened. Without a word, he beckoned Mahmoud forward with an indifferent wave of his hand.

Mahmoud walked into the office and took a seat in one of the metal chairs. He knew very little about this new chief who had just been promoted to the post – a political move that had more to do with his family's connections than with his work at the MOIS. The man was much younger than Mahmoud, well dressed and handsome. Mahmoud suspected this was just his first stop on a fast-paced career path.

Without looking up from the files on his desk, Nassiri said, "What is it you wanted to see me about that you think is so urgent?"

Mahmoud pulled out his wallet and retrieved the well-worn article on the Stealth crash. He went to hand it to his superior, but the man simply looked at him with little interest.

"I assume you know of the American Stealth bomber crash, Sir?"

Nassiri returned his attention to the files on his desk. "Of course."

Mahmoud struggled to maintain his composure. He decided skipping to the end of the story might best serve his purposes here.

"I have the plane."

That elicited the response he wanted. He had his supervisor's full attention. "You have the plane?" Disbelief dripped from every word, but at least he was looking at Mahmoud.

Mahmoud began at the beginning then, and two days later, Nassiri had arranged for his subordinate to have a meeting with the Grand Mullah himself, Ayatollah Ali Khomeini.

~

Some consider Ayatollah Khomeini the father of the modern day Holy War – or Jihad – against the West. The Ayatollah had an intense hatred of "infidels" and particularly the U.S.

He hated America, not only because he viewed the nation as infidels, but also for the years of support for his arch enemy the Shah of Iran and his family. The original Ayatollah Khomeini died in 1989, but his successor, Ayatollah Ali Khomeini inherited the same hatred of the West and its infidels.

Granted his meeting with the Ayatollah, Mahmoud wasted no time. He pulled out his wallet and the New York Times clipping concerning the downing of the F-117 Stealth Bomber over Serbia. The Ayatollah nodded his head, confirming that he remembered the news.

Mahmoud said, "A Russian general in my ... sphere of influence has the downed plane, but the Russians do not know, and even if they did, they do not have the scientists or the expertise to dismantle, analyze and re-build a better model."

The Ayatollah looked at him, studying him closely, as if evaluating whether this was a man he could trust. Then he seemed to make his decision and asked Mahmoud, "Why don't they have the expertise?"

"Since the Great Satan himself, Ronald Reagan, instigated the destruction of the Berlin Wall in November of 1989, all the best scientific talent fled the country. In fact, many of those same scientists came to Iran to work for the new regime, developing our nuclear and military capabilities."

Mahmoud felt expansive suddenly, filled with the greatness of his own genius.

"I have secured the technology with my Russian contact and have developed the right expertise in addition to our own scientists to unlock the secrets of the Stealth technology. We will be able to not only improve on their technology and build a stealth plane, but also develop other stealth bomb delivery systems, as well."

The Ayatollah looked sternly at him. "If you have done such great things on your own, why are you here with me now?"

Mahmoud instantly felt terror, suddenly aware that his overzealousness could get him killed.

"Forgive my foolish eagerness," he begged. "I have only made the most basic of plans for the glory of your regime. If you will permit us to continue and will finance the development of the new technology, we may be able to put an atomic warhead on a stealth missile and aim it at Tel-Aviv or even Washington, D.C., and they would never know it was coming."

Not many people ever saw the Grand Ayatollah smile, but Mahmoud saw it that day, and such evil malevolence radiated from the Ayatollah that it scared even him.

The Ayatollah simply said, "Don't fail me Mahmoud; we will create a new department in MOIS that is answerable only to me. We shall call it, 'The Arrows of Islam.'"

CHAPTER SIXTEEN

After his meeting with the Ayatollah, Mahmoud was exhilarated. There was no turning back now. He had committed himself to the Ayatollah; it was either perform or die.

He entered his office bellowing at Karim. "Get me Andropov!"

Mahmoud began to put his plan in motion. First, he needed to speak with Dimitri Andropov, his counterpart in Russian Military Intelligence called the GRU. Andropov was awaiting his call.

"Is our toy safe?" Mahmoud asked with no introduction.

"And good day to you, as well, old friend." Andropov chuckled at the eagerness of his Iranian counterpart. "Yes. All is well here. Are we finally ready to set things in motion?"

"The time has come, General. We need to meet."

The two set up a time for the following week. As Mahmoud hung up, his mind raced. Where to take the plane? It would have to be a neutral country, accessible from both Russia and Iran and it would have to be a location where supplies, machinery, etc., could be shipped without raising suspicion. Still, Tehran would have to ramp up other diversions so that the U.S. would put its intelligence and political resources elsewhere.

At that moment, Karim knocked and entered his office, waiting to be acknowledged. "Have you found a location for our project yet?"

"Yes I have," Karim replied. "Baku, Azerbaijan. I think you will find it suitable."

"Why?" Mahmoud asked.

"It meets all of your requirements, but principally it is the scientific, cultural and industrial center of Azerbaijan, so attracting and keeping a highly skilled technical team there should be easy.

"The only disadvantage is the smell," Karim added in a jocular fashion.

"What do you mean?"

"Oil. Oil is in the air one breathes, in one's nostrils, in one's eyes, in the water of the morning bath, in one's starched linen, in fact everywhere. This is the impression which one carries away from Baku," Karim replied with a shrug.

Mahmoud thought that was a perfect idea for the location – Baku, Azerbaijan, on the Caspian Sea. Baku was only about 2,000 miles from the Russian southern border and close to the Iranian northern border, and more importantly, close to the hidden location of the plane. Definitely doable.

The next step was to send Karim to Baku to search out appropriate sites and political allies. He would then need to find a scientific advisor who could help him understand the technology and how he could adapt it for his purposes.

Moscow
October 21st, 1999

Mahmoud checked into the Metropol on Teatralny Proezd. He would have much preferred to use one of the American hotels, but the Metropol had a lower profile, at least he hoped so. As usual, Moscow was wet and cloudy, and the weather did nothing to improve his disposition.

He had just been told the Mossad agent had escaped. That fool Heinrich had failed. But having already gone to the Ayatollah, Mahmoud had to move forward. Karim had searched in vain for Cohen. The man was suddenly a ghost.

In his room, Mahmoud stood at the window looking across at the Kremlin and felt a shiver run down his spine. He could see Red Square lying beneath the Kremlin's east wall and at the south end, the famous Cathedral of St. Basil the Blessed, a monument to Orthodox art. It was strange that such a beautiful scene could have been the home of so much death and intrigue over the years and that it still generated so much fear among Russians.

This town gave him the creeps. He didn't want to go out, so he looked for the room service menu.

"Room service, please."

"Room service is closed tonight, Sir."

Angrily, he slammed the phone down. Shaking his head in disgust, saying to himself, "I almost wish I was in New York; I could get anything I wanted at any time of the day or night."

He checked around the room for something to read, settling on the "Moscow Tourist Guide." The guide opened naturally to a story about Whitney Houston at the Kremlin. He read, slightly incredulous that a star of her quality would appear in Moscow.

> *"MOSCOW (AP) -- The renovation of the Grand Kremlin Palace, a famed concert and meeting hall that is one of Russia's most valued landmarks, cost $335 million, an official said Wednesday.*
>
> *"The three-year, recently completed project included restoration of ornaments in the palace's elaborately decorated meeting halls and installation of new equipment in the halls and offices.*
>
> *"Kremlin manager Pavel Borodin, who gave the price tag, told the Interfax news agency that the renovations were done mostly by Russian workers, although companies from Italy, Austria and other nations were also involved.*
>
> *"To celebrate the completion of the project, Russia will be sponsoring a concert by famed American singer, Whitney Houston."*

Mahmoud couldn't believe his bad luck, he had just missed the two Moscow performances of Houston on her World tour, "My Love is Your Love." He was secretly vexed that Moscow of all places could get Houston to perform when Tehran could not. Instead of reading to relax, he was getting agitated again, so he decided to take a bath and go to bed early.

The next morning, he woke early, impatient for 10:15 AM to arrive. At 10:00, he grabbed his coat and started toward the elevator; he was going to be on time for this meeting. At 10:15, he was standing outside the hotel entrance, thick overcoat pulled up over his ears. A bone-chilling wind was whistling through Moscow from the north, winter holding the city firmly in its snowy grip. Fortunately, Andropov was right on time.

He walked up to Mahmoud and took him by the arm. "Let's take a walk."

It was extremely cold waiting for Andropov outside the hotel's main entrance and even worse walking up the exposed street as they moved west toward Alexander Gardens. Mahmoud was uneasy, sensing that something was wrong behind him. He turned around and saw a Zil following them, crawling along the curb.

Andropov noticed and calmed his guest. "Don't worry, my old friend, they are my security detail." After about 10 minutes, Andropov asked Mahmoud, "So, what shall we talk about?'

Mahmoud did not play such games. "I did my part, keeping those paratroopers out of your crash site. It is now time to begin work on deconstruction of the plane and creation of the new technology. What will it take to get the plane out of Russia and into Azerbaijan?"

Andropov continued walking, nodding his head slightly, then stopped. He motioned Mahmoud to look over his pointing arm at the Grand Kremlin Palace and whispered in his ear, seeming to the onlookers as if he were giving the foreigner a history of the palace.

In that moment, Andropov told him what it would take, and Mahmoud simply said, "Done."

Mahmoud offered his hand to Andropov as if to say thanks, and in his hand was a note with an address of the warehouse in Baku. Mahmoud, matching Andropov's quiet voice, said, "This is where we want it delivered."

Andropov nodded his head in confirmation, climbed into the Zil and left. Mahmoud turned to walk back toward the hotel. Now that he was alone, he was able to look at the Alexander Gardens. He walked past the memorial to the soldiers and civilians killed during the Nazi invasion in World War II, noting the prominent flame, glowing for all time.

CHAPTER SEVENTEEN

Bethesda, Maryland
October 23, 1999

Ari closed his apartment door and leaned back against it. He needed time to unwind.

"What have I stumbled into?" he said to himself as he sunk into an oversized armchair in the living room. An innocent man was dead and he was pretty sure he had been the intended target. Gray was practically homicidal with rage over the shooting and Ari couldn't blame him.

Ari sat back in the chair and closed his eyes, trying to figure things out. At first, the only vision he could see behind his closed eyes was that of his beloved Stradivarius, his only true refuge in times of extreme stress.

"I promise," he said aloud, "as soon as I get a handle on this, I will come to you."

His Stradivarius was locked in a safe room at the Lowy Concert Hall in Tel Aviv. Ari didn't think a non-musician could ever comprehend the love a master held for his favorite instrument. He smiled as he mused to himself that playing his violin was as sweet to him as making love to the woman of his dreams.

And with that thought, his focus was completely lost. He had broken his cardinal rule – never let love enter his mind. Now, instead of thinking about that heathen Mahmoud, he mellowed with memories of his Stradivarius allowing the other love of his life to come to the forefront.

"Jasmine..." It was a whisper thin as spider's silk but laden with pent-up emotion.

Immediately, his words turned to prayer. "God, what price must I pay for the gifts you have given me? Couldn't you just let me be a concert violinist?"

Would that he had never met Jasmine Cooper.

THE EYES OF ATHENA

How long had it been now? Ari had been so young then. After months of training and office assignment, he had begged for a chance to go out into the field. In fact, he had pestered Rosenberg unmercifully.

"Ben should have known then what a pain I would be for him," Ari said aloud with a chuckle. It amazed him that the man had kept him in his direct supervision all this time, grooming him and, in fact, treating him like his own son.

The cajoling finally worked, and Ari found himself a courier in Pakistan carrying information to and from another Mossad agent that was so deep undercover even Ari didn't know who he was.

All Ari did know was that this agent was so deeply inserted into the Pakistani military intelligence that he could not risk communicating with anyone directly himself. Instead, the agent managed to get his messages out through a young girl, and Ari took them from there. He had been "installed" as a clerk in a specialty store that provided silks for bridal wear, and as such, he was constantly on the move delivering samples all over the capital city of Karachi.

It was the perfect cover for Ari's courier services but was also his undoing. On one of his trips to an affluent area called Saddar, he was waiting for a consignment of silk when he noticed five teenage boys trying to rig a suicide vest on a five-year-old girl. She was crying and confused as the boys tried to prod her to walk into a local café and pull a string to detonate the bomb.

Ari, still leaning back in the comfortable chair with his eyes closed, could see her soft brown eyes, rounded in terror and filled with tears. He sighed, thinking of it. Even now, he could not regret his decision. He had chased the boys away, carefully removed the vest, destroyed the detonator and thrown the contraption at the boys as they stood watching from a distance, seemingly undeterred.

Despite having been told to keep a low profile, he could not turn a blind eye. He had taken the little girl on the back of his moped to a police station.

What a fool I was, he thought. *I should've run for it then.*

Instead he had gone back to his sleeping quarters as if nothing had happened. With the dawn came the arrival of the military police.

They swooped in to find me curled up in my bed like a fool, he thought ruefully.

He screwed his eyes up tight, a clear vision in his mind. Rosenberg had pulled in every favor he was owed for the rookie to whom he owed nothing.

Ari rose from the chair and walked into the kitchen for a drink of water. He felt the need to move as the memories became more vivid. He could never repay Rosenberg for saving his life, and Ari knew that God had surely blessed him richly for his act of kindness in that alleyway behind the silk shop.

Still, his life had changed that day.

Ari could see her now, leading a team of Rangers to rescue him. He had been tied up in a primitive cell behind a wooden door. He was lambasting his own stupidity at sticking around after he helped the child, feeling terribly sorry for himself, when a small explosion obliterated his cell door.

In charged a Ranger who towered over him as he lay on the floor. Face hidden behind camo paint, body cloaked in black fatigues and a bullet-proof vest, Ari thought at the time the man was menacing in the sheer efficiency of his every move.

"Nearly scared me to death." Ari was smiling at the recollection now.

The man stood over Ari, inspiring his own fear and uncertainty, and in a voice surprisingly dripping with nectar and an octave higher than he expected asked, "Ari Cohen? Are you Ari Cohen?"

Ari still smiled at the thought; it was as if an angel had been sent to save him. His eyes opened wide in surprise at the female tone, and all he managed to say then was a stuttered, "Yes, I'm Ari Cohen."

"We've come to take you home." No sweeter words had ever been spoken.

He would later learn she was a CIA agent directing a Ranger extraction team. The Mossad had no team close that they could risk without blowing their cover within the Pakistani militia.

The Rangers led Ari out of the isolated cell block and into the remote countryside. Soon, they were maneuvering to make their rendezvous on a beach outside of Karachi. A

Ranger had been left to guard their inflatables for the short ride to meet a U.S. submarine on station a few miles out in the Arabian Sea.

That Ranger wasn't answering his call, and Ari suddenly caught the pungent, bitter aroma of cheap Pakistani cigarettes as they waited on the beach. He knew a Ranger on mission would never take the liberty of lighting up a smoke and was moving before his mind had even processed the thought. Despite his lack of experience, those months of training and an innate sense of survival took over, and he leaped over at Agent Cooper, knocking her to the ground, just as an enemy lying in ambush opened fire.

Ari was on top of Jasmine, returning the favor by saving her life. He quickly pulled her military knife from her boot harness and advanced on the enemy. It was all instinct now, and it didn't take long for Ari to kill off the three surprised terrorists and find the Ranger they had killed.

His rescue team had remained on the beach in protected positions. Cooper, after recovering from her unceremonious throw to the sand, had not been able to give her team permission to engage without a directive. They had made the trip out to the sub in silence, one fallen Ranger in the bottom of the submersible.

The team and Ari spent three days in the sub before they docked and disembarked to go their separate ways. Despite the weight of the situation, Ari and Jasmine had spent most of that time together talking, playing chess, and simply sitting in each other's company. A connection was made between them that neither could have explained.

"She wormed her way into my soul," Ari said with a sigh.

She was still there, but he had left that dock knowing it would never work. On the day they met, she had nearly been killed for him and seeing her in harm's way had maddened him. He could never see her in danger again – even if she was a formidable agent in her own right.

Ari came from a nation where women were conscripted into military service, but it was not a part of his personal heritage or background. His own mother had been an English educator living in Israel when she met his Israeli father. He and his siblings had been raised with more Western ideals of chivalry, and his sisters had been sent away to boarding school and college before they were of age to be asked to serve. While he had worked many missions with female operatives over the years and had served with women in the Israeli military, he retained an ingrained need to protect the women in his own life.

As Ari sat in his armchair, a tear of remorse escaped his eye and he caught himself wondering what Jasmine was doing at that moment. He stood suddenly, angry at himself, but somehow renewed. He reached over to a cheap violin he had bought as his only touch of individuality in his American apartment.

As he pulled his bow back to play Jasmine's tune, he thought to himself, *One more indulgence before this world of darkness draws me back in...*

CHAPTER EIGHTEEN

Baku, Azerbaijan
December 12, 1999

Mahmoud's scouts had found a perfect location in Zabrat, just on the outskirts of Baku. It was an industrialized suburb of the city that had its own airport and decent hotels, altogether a great choice.

Mahmoud's Iranian Air jet landed at Baku International Airport and he walked through the terminal and flagged down a cab. As he did not want to attract attention, he had asked that no official delegation meet him at the airport. The first thing he noticed on leaving the terminal was the smell; it was as if he had landed in an oil refinery. It wasn't an offensive odor, just very noticeable.

"Take me to the Sheraton Baku Airport Hotel," he ordered the taxi driver in English.

The driver seemed to understand. As the taxi made its way to the hotel, he was thinking of the irony – he loved American hotels yet he wanted to destroy America.

After arriving at his hotel, he checked in at reception and went up to his room. He drew the curtains aside and looked north out over the Caspian Sea. *Quite a view*, he thought to himself. He opened his window and was nearly blown back by the strong wind, which was even more noticeably oily and salty.

He decided to rest a while before Karim arrived to update him on their progress. He had been lucky again. He needed a lieutenant to manage the Baku project and Karim had been able to find a young Iranian educated in Europe who wanted to serve his country. Mahmoud felt so safe here in Baku that he decided to take a swim.

Two hours later, he was back in his room to answer a knock on his door; Karim had arrived. *Now down to business,* he thought.

Karim entered the room, bowed to Mahmoud, and they sat down. "Karim, what is the status?"

"We have rented a warehouse to store all of the components that arrive until you make a decision as to the final location of our project."

"What do you recommend?"

Karim responded, "We do have an opportunity to buy a ball bearing plant that is for sale in Zabrat. It is a very large facility, and as it is a going concern. We would have a great cover for all the people we need to hire as well as the equipment we will need to bring in. In other words, Sir, a great camouflage."

"That is a workable idea; make the arrangements."

"Sir, we have received the plane. Initial clean up and photography from all angles is nearly finished. We have assembled the scientific team from Iran, and following your recommendation, we have identified and contacted a lead scientist that we think fits your profile.

"I'm sure you are familiar with the V1 and V2 bombs used on London toward the end of World War II?"

'Yes, of course."

"The chief designer for the Germans was a Berliner by the name of Fritz Gosslau. He died in 1965, but what few people know is that he had a son born in 1946, called Hermann. After his father died, Hermann moved to Argentina. Fortunately for us, Hermann is an even more accomplished scientist than his father. He is probably the best brain in the world when it comes to pulse-jet-powered weaponry."

"Gosslau? Why is that name familiar to me?"

"His son has been of use to us in the past for certain ... unsavory projects. Heinrich is a member of the Secret Service in Argentina."

"Ah, yes. And he failed me, no?" Mahmoud still seethed, knowing Cohen lived. They had lost track of him after Heinrich failed in his duty. Mahmoud wanted to make Heinrich pay for his carelessness, but had not had time to consider what evilness he might visit upon the wretch of a man. Now, if he needed the father ... Perhaps, using the bumbling fool in this project would allow him a chance at redemption. He would have to think on that...

THE EYES OF ATHENA

For how, Mahmoud tried to contain his excitement, smiling like an alley cat.

"He has ... agreed to work for us," Karim said with a strange inflection.

"I take it there was some coercion on the part of our friend Andropov?"

"That is my understanding, Sir."

Perhaps he would not need to play nice with Heinrich after all. This would take some careful thought.

"Fine. I am heading back to Tehran. I will be sending you a secure dispatch with the design parameters that I want our team to focus on."

Karim answered excitedly, "Yes, Sir."

Mahmoud was thinking hard now, pleased with the progress, "We must make all haste. Contact me when you have an update."

Baku, Azerbaijan
December 13, 1999

The next morning, Mahmoud was on his way back to Tehran and decided to use the time to write down his operational requests for Karim and the scientists.

He only had limited knowledge of the stealth bomber. He knew the engines were buried in the fuselage to minimize infrared signature. He also knew the skin was composed of small flat surfaces that reflected radar signals from every direction, but he didn't know of what material. And he knew almost all of the external surfaces were coated with radar-absorbent material.

He listed his demands:

A long-range missile capable of holding nuclear material, hidden by Stealth technology and able to reach the U.S. east coast.

A mid-range missile capable of carrying a nuclear payload with Stealth capability.

A self-propelled, underwater shuttle or torpedo-like device that would deliver weapons and dirty bombs to coastal destinations. Stealth capability would also be required.

A missile-like weapon that could be fired from Iranian submarines.

Mahmoud decided this was enough for a start and he would forward it to Karim as soon as he reached a secure facility. He was like a child with a new toy, so excited with the possibilities.

CHAPTER NINETEEN

**Georgetown, Washington, D.C.
July 4, 2004**

"You know, my friend, you should really consider hiring a decorator – or getting a girlfriend." Gray stood in Ari's sparsely appointed kitchen sipping on a cold beer and taking stock while Ari prepared a salad to go with the roast lamb he had prepared earlier.

Ari was rarely in his kitchen – or his home for that matter – since his work with Athena kept him on the move all over the globe. When he was home, he spent as much time as possible with Gray, who was also a busy man.

Ari turned to pull the lamb out of the oven, where he was keeping it warm. Gray looked once more at the meal and shook his head.

"As long as you've been here, brother, and you still don't get it. The Fourth of July is meant for hot dogs and hamburgers, fireworks and ice cold beers."

"You are free to seek whatever repast you prefer," Ari said with some annoyance. As he was rarely home, he rarely had the opportunity to cook, and when he did, he preferred to do it right.

"I will not be partaking of your mystery meat stuffed in a tube no matter how much horrid yellow mustard you pour over it."

Gray laughed then. He slapped Ari on the back. "You'll never be one of us, Ari, but God bless you if you aren't awesome just the way you are!"

Besides that, Gray noted, the lamb smelled amazing.

"But seriously," Gray continued as if his thought had never been interrupted by a whole culinary conversation. "You should look into that whole girlfriend thing. I hear they are pretty handy at picking out curtains and pillows and such."

He grinned widely at Ari, who didn't bother to give him as much as a nod. "And who has time for a girlfriend? Who has time for curtains or pillows? No one is here most of the time anyway. I swear I only get the newspaper so that my neighbor can read it while I'm away."

Gray laughed. "I'm not joking, David. He dropped his own subscription. When I am home, he comes by after work to see if I've read it yet so he can take it off my hands."

"You need to slow down, my friend. Surely the CIA has other operatives."

Ari only shrugged. Despite the nature of his business being espionage, he tried never to actually lie outright to his dearest friend. He had never told Gray where he worked; he had just never corrected his friend's assumptions. When he had said he was on long-term loan to the U.S. from the Mossad, Gray had jumped to the CIA conclusion, and Ari had thought it best to leave that be. Now, he just avoided the subject.

Ari began carrying the lamb and potatoes to the table as Gray grabbed the salad. Another indulgence of his was using his dining room – complete with linen table cloth and napkins and good china and silverware – whenever he ate. Ari had spent his first year in America living in the apartment at Athena OPs. As soon as he was able, he had moved to Georgetown. While he had not decorated much or purchased much in the way of artwork or knick knacks, he did bring over a few things like china, silverware and linens that he had stored in Tel Aviv – as well as his beloved Stradivarius.

Just as they sat down to eat, Ari's phone rang. With a heavy sigh, he answered, knowing the only friend who ever called him was sitting at his table. Without looking at the caller ID, he answered, "Hello, Tom."

"Sorry to cut your holiday short, Ari, but we've got a situation."

"I understand. I'll be there in 30." Ari disconnected his call and headed for the stairs to his den, which housed his gun safe and equipment locker. Over his shoulder he told Gray, "Don't stop on my account. You have a key. Just put the leftovers in the fridge for my neighbors and the dishes in the sink for the housekeeper."

THE EYES OF ATHENA

Gray hadn't so much as paused his eating. "Will do," he said through a mouthful of lamb. "Go get 'em, Tiger."

Athena Ops, Bethesda, Maryland

It took Ari more like 45 minutes to make the drive because of the holiday traffic. When he walked into Burke's office, Burke was just hanging up with the Eye on duty.

"Let's go into the Situation Room," he said without preamble, and Ari followed him across the hall.

On the screen were a handful of blurry black-and-white satellite photos. The men they showed looked determined, mean and armed for bear, as Burke would say.

"So, what's up, Tom?"

"Sorry to pull you away from your burgers and dogs, Ari. It's a real shame we can't get even today, of all days, off around here."

"Yeah, I had a really nice lamb waiting for me to take my first bite," Ari said with true regret.

"Lamb? Oh, son..." Burke just shook his head. He turned to the screen and pointed. "This cast of fine characters is the issue today. Seems they took out some of our better Russian contacts this morning – and half a restaurant with them – in broad daylight with submachine guns.

"No one has any idea who they are or where they are affiliated, and that's a problem. With so few good contacts in Russia these days, we're loathe to be losing any ... especially en masse like that."

"So I'm on a plane to Russia?" Ari asked, and at Burke's nod, added, "And do I have any good contacts left to meet me?"

"Of course, Ari, we'd never send you in blind. We've got a couple of excellent operatives in Moscow, but they need to keep a low profile and we have reason to believe poking your nose into this case is going to make you very visible."

"Excellent," Ari said with a sigh.

"Don't worry, son. They'll have your back. They just aren't going to go charging around asking questions and stirring up trouble."

Burke patted Ari on the back. "And we all know that's one of your strong suits."

Ari had to laugh at that. He did have a knack for stirring up trouble.

By 8 PM, he was on a flight to Moscow.

Sheremetyevo International Airport, Moscow, Russia
July 5, 2004

It was 2 PM Moscow time when Ari walked down the gangway and into the airport. He carried one bag with him and had no checked luggage. Burke had told him his contact would meet him at his terminal, so he kept an eye out for what he imagined his Russian counterpart would look like.

He had never been so wrong. The agent who approached him with her hand extended was at least half a foot taller and statuesque with marble-smooth skin, long, ebony hair and bright-red lips. She looked like she had stepped straight off a fashion runway, and when she spoke, her heavy Russian accent was enchanting.

"Welcome to Moscow, Mr. Cohen."

Ari took her offered hand, thinking to himself that he liked the concept of Athena agents in Russia. As he stood, holding her hand longer than he realized, an internal struggle danced behind his eyes. He was, after all, a man looking at a stunningly beautiful woman, but he was also an agent meeting an agent.

"Get it together, Cohen." He had no idea that whispered phrase actually passed his lips until he saw her smile. Obviously, she was used to this reaction from men, but he was embarrassed to be so typical. He dropped her hand as if it were on fire.

"My apologies, Miss ..."

"Azarov. Katarina Azarov." She smiled sweetly at him then, not the slightest bit annoyed by his behavior. "If you are ready ..."

"Yes, of course." He found his hand placed quite naturally at the small of her back and again removed it as if touching molten lava. He thought he heard her giggle.

This is ridiculous, he thought to himself, determined to get his behavior under control immediately.

She turned to him then and with the most unassuming smile said, "It's quite alright, Mr. Cohen. Please do not worry so about your political correctness and you will find you become much more comfortable around me."

She faced forward then, but he could see a sly smile at the corner of her mouth. "I assure you I do not make a habit of suing handsome men just for finding me attractive."

Ari had to laugh at that, and he did indeed relax. It was a short car ride to a small safe house just outside of Moscow's inner city.

As Katarina escorted him inside, she handed him a set of keys. "You will find the house is well appointed."

She turned on the lights as she entered. The small house was sparsely furnished, but comfortable. Katarina pointed down the hall. "Bedroom. In the closet are all of the various ... implements you may need while you are visiting." She smiled at that and headed toward the kitchen.

"We do not stock the kitchen for foreign guests because ... well, we never know what you Americans like to eat." She laughed at that, and Ari laughed with her.

"I understand completely," he said. "I've only been in America a short time, and their penchant for meat-stuffed casings and casseroles has me stymied."

She turned to him then. "Ah, a gourmet, then are we?"

"Well, I dabble."

"We shall see," she said, turning toward the garage. Inside was a simple two-door car, black and unassuming.

As Ari moved to stand next to her in the doorway she whispered in his ear, "Don't worry. She's much faster than she looks."

With that she headed for the front door. "You'll also find a laptop set up in the bedroom with secure satellite access to Athena OPs."

She turned and looked down at him with that serene smile in place. "I'll let you settle in and get a little rest. Try to acclimate to the time change, and we'll be back in the morning to fill you in."

Ari couldn't help but wonder if the others would be quite so delightful.

After she left, he walked the interior of his new temporary home and checked the equipment he'd been given.

"Ah, Tom, you do know me," he said as he looked over the handsome set of knives included with the Glock and ammo as well as a long-range sniper rifle. He checked his watch, 10 AM Moscow time. With the 8-hour time difference, Burke should be settling in with his coffee about now. Ari made for the laptop and set up the link.

It took a moment for the analyst to bring Burke into the frame, coffee cup in hand.

"Morning, Ari. Good flight?"

Did Ari see a sly smile on his face, or was he imagining it? Did Burke know the agent who met Ari at the airport?

"All's well, Tom. Just settling in."

"Good to hear. Everything there to your liking?"

"All well appointed as usual, Tom." Ari didn't trust him. He still thought he saw a smile peeking around the coffee cup as he took a sip.

"Get along with your contact ok?"

"Yes, fine. Thanks." Ari wasn't going to play into this. "Anything I need to know before I meet with the team tomorrow, Tom?" He tried his best to sound all business now.

Burke laughed out loud. "No, Ari. They have all the Intel you'll need. Just get some sleep and be ready to roll when they arrive."

Ari glared at his boss and friend through the laptop screen. "Will do, Tom."

"You take care, Ari." Burke said. "Keep in communication."

"Of course, Sir."

Ari made to switch off the laptop, as Burke finished his goodbyes, "And, Ari?"

Ari's finger hovered over the disconnect key. "Yes, Tom?"

"Don't do anything I wouldn't do."

The former Mossad agent may have hit the key just a little harder than was necessary.

Grumbling, he headed for the kitchen. While they had not fully stocked it, there were a few essentials there to tide him over until he could go out for provisions. He found some cheese and crackers to snack on, grabbed his MP3 player from his bag and sat in the living room.

As soothing classical violin music filled the air, he began to relax, wishing he had his own instrument to play. It had been so long since he had been struck by a woman the way he had been with Katarina. To be honest, since Jasmine, he had rarely noticed other women.

THE EYES OF ATHENA

But Katarina had certainly been striking. "Hard to miss, really," he said to the empty room. He wondered if that meant his passion for Jasmine was fading. Could he really love a woman he had only met once so many years ago? How was she still so much a part of his heart?

Sitting there in that unfamiliar room, Ari drifted off to sleep. It was rare for him to fall asleep without intention – without making arrangements, securing his location, assuring himself of his safety – but he was exhausted both emotionally and physically, and sleep simply stole him from his waking thoughts.

CHAPTER TWENTY

Ari came to with a start, disturbed to find himself sitting on the sofa in the living room with a handful of lukewarm cheese and crackers.

"Way to go, Cohen," he said, wiping the sleep from his eyes and heading toward the bedroom. His carry-on had three changes of clothing in it as well as his shaving kit. He grabbed it and made for the bathroom to take a shower and change.

Ari stood under the running water until it began to turn cold, hoping it would work out some of the tenseness in his muscles. He was anxious now, having given up control by falling asleep like that in a strange place – without any kind of weapon close at hand.

He stepped out of the shower and wrapped a towel around his waist. He wiped the steam from the mirror and stared at his weary face. He had no idea what time it was, but day light was coming in through the window in the bedroom, so he better get his tail in gear, he thought.

He had just started shaving when he heard the front door open and close and the sound of Russian be spoken in the living room. He finished quickly, threw on his clothes and headed in to meet the other agents, his hair still wet and his feet bare.

Katarina looked at him with an approving smile. "I see you took my advice about relaxing."

She had two men with her, both much less approving of Ari's casual appearance.

Ari reached to shake their hands, apologizing for running late as he did so. "I overslept. It is not like me."

"Do not fret, Mr. Cohen," Katarina had moved to sit in an oversized chair across from the sofa. She folded her long legs beneath her and beckoned for the men to join her. "We are all friends here."

THE EYES OF ATHENA

Ari was not too sure the men looked all that friendly, but he sat in a chair on the other side of the room as they took up positions on the sofa.

Katarina frowned exaggeratedly at her companions, who had yet to speak to Ari. "These two gentlemen are Abram and Nestor." Each nodded toward Ari as she said his name. "They do not speak much English and they are wary of our foreign guests. But they are good in a fight and will follow my orders without fail."

Ari smiled at the men who remained stoic. "Good to know."

He turned to Katarina. "So, I'm told you will brief me."

"You are an eager one aren't you, Mr. Cohen?" She cocked her head then and looked at him quizzically. "Have you even had a cup of coffee yet?"

Ari's stomach chose that moment to turn on him, growling loudly in protest to the solitary meal of a few crackers and some cheese during the past 24 hours.

Katarina laughed, and Ari couldn't help thinking to himself that the sound was almost musical.

"I see." She unfolded herself from the chair, and her companions were instantly on their feet. "Please put on some shoes, Mr. Cohen. We shall have to do something about your belly."

Ari headed for the bedroom. He threw on a pair of shoes and a light jacket then grabbed the Glock from his equipment stash and tucked it into a holster at his back. Needing that extra bit of comfort, he strapped on a knife at his ankle, as well. Feeling much less naked, he stepped out to join the trio of Russians as they made their way outside and into a compact four-door silver car.

Ari wound up in the back seat with Katarina. Nestor chose to drive. There was a small, quaint café just around the corner, but the ride seemed to take forever in the silence of the car. Ari stared out at the neighborhood with an unwarranted intensity. Why did this woman make him so uncomfortable? He did not understand himself at all. He was not a man used to being nervous in any situation.

Nestor and Abram took a table close to the window at the front of the café while Katarina led Ari toward a booth at the back. As she slid into the seat facing the front of the restaurant, he was forced to either sit next to her or slide in across from her with his back to everything. A choice that most people wouldn't give a second thought became a maddening decision for Ari, who finally had to slide in next to the Russian beauty.

She smiled as she moved to make room. "All the better, Mr. Cohen, for we have much to discuss, and it would be best said in quiet tones."

Katarina handed Ari a menu from her side of the table. "Are you used to Russian meals, Mr. Cohen?"

"No. Actually," Ari said. "I have been in your country often, but now that I think of it, I have rarely had a chance to eat."

She smiled. "Since you have said you are not a typical American, I cannot assume that you are used to a heavy breakfast of fried eggs and bacon."

"No. Usually toast and oatmeal," Ari said. He had set the menu aside, unable to make much of it.

She took it from him. "I will order you the kasha. It is a kind of porridge made of different grains. And of course coffee."

There was that brilliant smile again. When the waitress came, she ordered the same for both of them. The waitress took their order, but her eyes never left Ari's face.

"She was quite taken with you," Katarina said, putting her own menu away.

Ari hadn't really noticed. "Was she?"

"How funny you are, Mr. Cohen. You really don't know yourself at all."

And while Ari pondered that cryptic remark, she pulled a small notebook from her bag and began to tell him about the reason for his mission.

Ari refocused on the photos in the notebook – the same blurry satellite photos he had seen back in Bethesda. "Have you identified them?"

"We know who they are," Katarina said. "That is not the problem. The problem is what they want and who they work for."

Ari waited for her to explain.

"No one has taken responsibility for the killing spree. We traced these men back to a known Pakhan of the Bratva – this would be a Godfather in your American Mafia –

Ramiz Polad. The men in these photos are Boyevik – what our Bratva calls warriors and your Mafia calls soldiers.

"They are not actually Russian, but are Azerbaijani operating in Moscow, and we are unsure of the motives behind these killings."

"Who do we believe was targeted?"

"There were 12 people killed in all," Katarina turned to another sheet in her notebook listing names and details on the deaths of those in the restaurant.

"Because these men simply walked in and sprayed the place with automatic gunfire for as long as they dared, then fled before being caught, it is hard to tell who they intended to hit and who was collateral damage."

Ari took the list. Two were waitresses and one a bus boy, hardly likely targets. One table had been taken up by a meeting of Russian banking executives and a couple of realtors – five in all, two with ties to Athena. In the back, a young couple had been having lunch. An elderly lady had been sitting alone at the front of the restaurant and the last man had been running for the kitchen exit.

That caught Ari's attention. Every other victim had been caught unawares and unable to get away, since there were four assailants firing into the crowd at once directly through the large plate glass windows that made up the restaurant's storefront.

"Who is this man?" Ari said, pointing to the name.

"One of the realtors." Katarina took back the notebook and turned to additional details on some of the victims. "Mikhail Danshov had a small realty company that recently posted some large sales. He had been invited to the meeting with bankers as an up-and-coming realtor who might be beneficial in some of the deals their clients were looking to make in various Russian provinces."

"One has to wonder why his little company was suddenly doing so well," Ari said, finishing his coffee. "So, where are the shooters?"

"Officially, no one in Russia knows where they are or who they are," she said. "Unofficially, Athena has tracked them to a Bratva safe house 20 miles outside of Moscow."

"Have an address on Danshov's realty company?" Ari asked.

"Yes, it's in the notebook." She handed it to him. "Anything else we have discovered is all there. I'm sorry we cannot be of more help. Our position here requires that we be very ... subtle in our dealings."

Ari smiled as he slid from the booth to let her slide out as well. "Lucky for both of us, no one has ever expected me to be subtle."

CHAPTER TWENTY-ONE

Katarina and her compatriots dropped Ari back at the safe house with a few groceries and the all-important notebook. She also gave him her cell phone number in case he needed her and a promise that she would check in on him often.

Shopping in the small market had been a strange experience with the beautiful Katarina drawing everyone's attention and the strange Nestor and Abram following behind like overgrown petulant twin toddlers.

Ari put his groceries away and headed into the bedroom thinking he would check in with Burke. He checked his watch, noted it was only 10 AM here and thought better of a 2 AM call to his boss.

Instead, he grabbed the notebook, doubled checked that the GPS on his phone worked properly in the foreign nation, and turned toward the garage to get the car. He had in mind two errands for the mid-morning. First, he would drop in on Danshov's realty company and see what he could find out about the victim's most recent deals. Then he thought he would make his way out of town about 20 miles to take a gander at the Bratva safe house location Katarina had given him.

His first stop was only a 10-minute drive. He managed to figure out what he thought was a suitable parking situation, given he knew nothing of Russian signage, and made for Danshov's business. Lucky for him, Katarina had envisioned he might need more than an address and had provided the GPS photo of the location so that he would know the building when he saw it.

"Bright girl," Ari said, as he neared the storefront.

It was a small building. Inside, one sad young woman sat at a desk. She barely looked up as he entered. "I'm sorry, we're not really handling customers," she said, her voice beginning to break as she added, "due to a death."

"Yes, I know. I needed to ask you a couple of questions if I could."

The young woman looked up then. Her eyes were raw with the tears she had shed and Ari saw that she was packing up a box with the things from her desk.

"I'm not really supposed to speak to the police," she said. "I'm just here clearing out my things. His ..." Her voice caught again then and she took a deep breath. "His wife will be in later today if you'd care to come back."

Ari could read people, and her body language had just told him quite a story. The name plate he saw sticking out of her half-packed box said Natalya Pavlenko.

"I'm so sorry for your loss, Mrs. Pavlenko," he said, emphasizing the married honorific.

"It's Miss," she said, breaking down entirely.

"Miss Pavlenko. Of course. You must have been very close to Mr. Danshov."

She looked up at him now a completely broken little girl in a woman's body. "Yes." She squeaked out.

"I see that they are closing the business, then?" Ari looked around, noting only the young woman's desk was being cleared.

"No." She sounded angry now. "His wife will be taking things on."

She was tossing things into the box with fervor now.

"Oh. I see," Ari said. "I didn't think the company could go forward without your assistance. I know Mr. Danshov felt you were a vital employee."

"Really?" She looked up again with that little lost girl look.

And Ari knew. "Mrs. Danshov doesn't feel the same way, I take it?"

Natalya looked down into her lap.

"I see," Ari said. "She found out about your special relationship with Mr. Danshov, didn't she?"

Natalya's head snapped up then, shock on her tear-stained face. "No one knew! If I hadn't broken down like a stupid baby! But he was my life. And his stupid wife... She doesn't love him. She only wanted his money!"

Her words ran together quickly until she seemed to just run out of steam. "But that's all gone now."

"His money?" Ari asked. "I was told Mr. Danshov had made some very large deals of late – very lucrative arrangements."

"Yes." She began packing the box again as she talked, forgetting that she wasn't supposed to tell this stranger anything. "But it was all a front. Those deals were all on paper, and there were some very nasty men behind all of it. In the end, he was supposed to be well paid for his services, but then Mikhail started to act like it was all real – talking to bankers like he was a big shot.

"That's what got him killed." She whispered the last sentence, rose with her full box and headed toward the door. "None of it was real," she said walking out, not even caring to lock up behind her. Ari had to wonder if she was talking about just the real estate or something more.

~

Just down the street, an unpleasant man in a gray suit sat in his car watching Danshov's storefront. He had seen a man enter and watched the crying woman leave with a box in her arms before the man followed. The man in the gray suit snapped a picture on his phone and uploaded it for identification. Not so connected as Athena, the Bratva still had ways of finding the information they wanted to know.

Ari made his way back to his little car and headed into the countryside, following the directions to the safe house that Katarina had given him. She had also given him explicit instructions not to go looking for trouble out there without backup, but he wasn't following those.

He had seen the Suit in the car outside Danshov's place – caught the snapping of a photo out of the corner of his eye – and knew he was being trailed.

"Gonna be an interesting day," he said to himself, using his cell phone to dial in to the satellite feed on the laptop at his own safe house. By now, Burke would be awake and waiting on a report and Ari had twenty minutes of drive time to kill.

Ever the multi-tasker, he kept an eye on the more aggressive Russian traffic, the tail he didn't want to lose, and the GPS directions on his phone, while waiting for Burke's voice to come through the hands-free speaker.

"What have you got for me, Ari?"

"And hello to you, too, Tom." Ari could picture his boss at his desk, coffee cup in hand, paperwork spread out before him. His voice was stressed, meaning he had too much to do and not enough time to get it done.

"Sorry, Ari. A lot going on here. I've got people waiting on a report."

"No problem, Tom. Not much to go on as of yet, but you can assure the board that Athena contacts were collateral damage and not the targets."

"You're sure of that, Ari?"

"I just left the office of one of the realtors, Mikhail Danshov. Turns out he was playing hard ball with the Azerbaijani mob, basically. I'm headed out to check on our suspects, but from the briefing I received this morning and the discussion I just had, I'd say he was the target."

"These guys took out a restaurant full of people to get one guy?"

"I'd say they like to make a statement." Ari gave a glance back at his tail then, wondering if his current undertaking was such a good idea after all.

"Sounds like the kind of people you need to take seriously, Ari. Don't go lone ranger on me out there," Burke said, as if reading Ari's mind.

"Got it, boss."

As soon as Ari hung up, his dialed Katarina's number. As she answered, he spotted a small market and pulled in. His shadow stopped along the curb several cars back.

CHAPTER TWENTY-TWO

Ari wandered around the small market looking at the exotic offerings while he awaited Katarina's arrival with the petulant twins.

She had scolded him playfully for starting out without proper backup and made him promise to sit tight until they arrived. His tail had remained in his car, obviously not too concerned with losing Ari out the backside of the building.

It had been almost 20 minutes when he heard that melodic Russian accent call his name. He turned and found that she filled the doorway. He wondered at how a woman that tall still found the need to wear heels that high. It always amazed Ari how women walked in those torture devices, but she glided toward him in knee-high boots with five-inch heels as if she had been born wearing them.

"Ah, there you are, Mr. Cohen." She bent slightly to kiss both his cheeks, and he was embarrassed to find it made him blush.

"Where are the boys?"

"They are keeping an eye on your new friend," she said as they headed back toward the front door. "It would seem you have already found one of our four shooters. He must be quite interested to see why you are driving directly to his hideout."

Katarina had pulled a small handful of flowers from a stand next to the old woman's front counter. She paid for them and exited with them pulled up to her nose to enjoy their delicate scent.

"And why are you driving to his hideout, Mr. Cohen?" Ari was surprised to look up and find she had stopped and was staring at him quizzically. "Did you not get the information that you sought at Mr. Danshov's office?"

"It's true, Ms. Azarov, that the target was not directly related to Athena nor, it would seem, any American-held assets, but there's something there that's niggling at the back of my mind."

Ari shrugged. "I just wanted to see the men in person, maybe have a chat." He smiled the grin of a mischievous school boy then, and she laughed.

"No, Mr. Cohen. You are not subtle."

As they approached the car, Nestor and Abram nodded from the front seat. Katarina and Ari climbed into the back, leaving Ari's car at the market.

"Shall we, Nestor? Mr. Cohen would like to see the safe house."

Nestor looked at Ari for a long time in the rearview mirror before he pulled out into traffic.

~

Several car lengths back. Adem was on the phone with his superiors.

"You are sure he is going to the safe house?"

"It would appear so. I cannot think of any other reason he would be out here. And now that woman and the men..."

"What is Mossad doing in Moscow?" They had tracked Ari as far as his identity with Israeli Intelligence, but no further, as was Athena's intent. "Follow them to the others. They have been warned to be ready for anything."

~

As Ari's little group pulled within sight of the house, they stopped at the curb and Katarina looked at him questioningly. As he turned from her to the house and back, he caught Nestor's glare in the mirror again.

"Wait here."

Katarina's face changed to one of surprise as he got out of the car and began walking up the street and into the driveway of the house. Ari walked up to the front door and knocked.

Two car lengths back, Adem was dumbfounded. He had no idea whether he should pull around the people still in the car at the curb or wait. Considering there were three heavily armed men in the house and one Mossad agent, he opted to keep an eye on the car.

Ari waited what seemed like an eternity for the door to open. A very confused man stood in the barely cracked door, the barrel of his gun poking out at Ari.

"Hello." Ari gave him his brightest smile. "Do you speak English?"

The man didn't speak any language in answer to Ari's question, but he opened the door just a little wider.

"Can I come in? I have a question or two to ask you."

There was no training in the spy handbook for what to do when your enemy walks up and knocks on the door. The man hesitated a moment, closed the door and began arguing with the other two men inside.

Ari stood on the front porch, hands in the pockets of his coat, and whistled. Katarina's mouth fell open when he turned his back on the door to face them and gave them the thumbs-up sign.

The door opened again, and another man looked Ari up and down. "Gun. Give. Now."

"That would answer the English question," Ari said in a friendly tone, handing his gun to the man. The door opened just wide enough for Ari to be pulled inside.

Nestor turned to Katarina then. "Your American is a dead man."

CHAPTER TWENTY-THREE

Ari did not so much walk into the small, sparsely furnished house as he was whisked inside by the three large men in gray suits.

Always gray, he thought to himself with the kind of humor doomed men often employ in those last moments to keep the terror at bay, *they must own stock in the company.* But he had to admit, as uniforms went, the gray suit spelled class.

He was propelled into a small, beige chair, and the largest of the three men took up a position behind him, while the other two stood in front of him with their arms crossed.

"Speak!" This from the only one who had said anything thus far. Ari could tell from even those few words, however, that the accent was more Turkish than Russian.

"Surely," he said in a conversational tone. "I'm guessing you understand more English than you speak?"

The man nodded his head.

"Great!" Ari clapped his hands in front of him, appearing jovial about his situation while suddenly realizing that he really had no plan at all for what he was going to say. *How unlike me,* he thought, *first falling asleep on the sofa, now barging in on dangerous thugs like a rookie with no idea how to play the game, and getting all warm and fuzzy over some woman with a pair of long legs and a beautiful smile.*

Under his breath, he said, "Sheesh. I think I need a vacation," and in his mind, he heard Gray's voice say, "Brother, what you need is a girlfriend."

Ari laughed out loud. He really was losing it. And with that, he just let it rip.

"Well, my name is Stephen. I was a ... shall we say, friend? Sure, friend. I was a friend of Mr. Danshov. The man you killed in the restaurant."

THE EYES OF ATHENA

The man before him made a menacing noise in the back of his throat. Ari swallowed as if he were an intimidated civilian and told himself he wasn't really an intimidated agent.

"Anyway," he said, stretching the word out impossibly long, "Mikhail told me all about his little ... enterprise ... with your ... organization ... and I know you weren't very happy with him in the end, obviously, but I want a chance to pick up where he left off."

Ari smiled big again, looking hopeful for the man in the gray suit, who obviously only understood every fourth word.

"Oh, my. I think we've got a communication issue here," he said. "Is there someone else I could talk to?"

The man seemed to contemplate whether or not there was such another person and if that person should be brought into this very unusual situation. It was interesting to Ari to watch the battle going on behind the man's eyes as he struggled within himself to find the answer. He may not have been the smartest Suit at this little party.

While the man worked to make a decision, Ari chose to sit still, smile widely, and look stupid. He had found throughout the years that people rarely feared him and always underestimated him when he looked stupid. It had often proven useful.

Suddenly, the front door opened, startling the Suit enough that he nearly shot his partner next to him. Ari hid his snicker behind his hand as his tail walked in.

"What's going on in here?" the new Suit bellowed.

"Ah!" Ari said with his stupid smile in place. "You speak English."

"Of course Mossad dog."

The smile was gone. "Well, that's inconvenient," Ari said.

"Fazil, get some rope. Secure this idiot. Sadik, come with me. We need to ... speak to his associates."

"Yes, Adem." Fazil, it would seem, was the largest man who had stood behind Ari. As he moved left to grab Ari and reach for a section of rope on the table beside him, Ari shifted right and snagged the knife at his ankle, rolling across the floor and coming back to his feet in front of the still dumbfounded Sadik who had yet to move.

Before he could raise his weapon, Ari had him by the throat, his razor-sharp blade to the man's throat. Sadik dropped his gun without a word.

"You, too, Fazil," Ari said, backing toward the patio door and away from the three men facing him. When he heard it open, he was a little unnerved. At least until Katarina's melodic voice drifted inside.

"Gentlemen, if you don't mind, I think Mr. Cohen will be leaving."

Ari maintained his hold on Sadik and backed out into the alleyway and the waiting car.

With Sadik tucked between Katarina and Ari, Nestor sped away. Bullets pinged off the trunk lid and shattered the passenger-side mirror.

"Thanks for coming, guys." Ari used the zip ties Katarina handed him to shackle Sadik's hands and feet. The poor man had yet to really fathom what had just happened to him.

"Our pleasure, Mr. Cohen," Katarina said, but the glare Nestor gave Ari in the rearview mirror suggested otherwise.

"So, Mr. Cohen," Katarina said as she put a black bag over Sadik's still shocked face, "what is it you plan to do with your new friend?"

Ari had not really thought much about that.

"Nestor, if you would be so kind as to drop me at my car, I'll head back to the safe house. I'm sure I've caused you guys enough excitement for one day."

Nestor only grunted.

"Now, Nestor," Katarina all but purred at the grouchy agent, "do be nice. It would seem my American isn't quite a dead man after all."

Ari laughed heartily at that – the kind of laugh a doomed man bellows out when he barely escapes by the skin of his teeth. *Yeah,* he thought to himself, *I'm losing it.*

He shook his head. "I need a hobby."

CHAPTER TWENTY-FOUR

Ari tied his new friend to a kitchen chair in the safe house while he went into the bedroom to give Burke a heads up.

"You kidnapped one of the suspects and are holding him at the safe house?"

Burke was having a hard time wrapping his mind around Ari's plan. Ari thought that was probably a hard thing to do, since he didn't really have one.

"What exactly are you going to do with him?"

"Yeah, Tom, I really don't know. There's something there, something we're missing. I just... Yeah... I don't know."

"Ari, son, that's not some harmless old lady sitting in that kitchen. The man is a trained killer, even if he is a little slow. You better figure something out and figure it out fast. In fact, get whatever it is you need from him and get yourself on a plane back to the States first thing tomorrow. I'm not sure Moscow can take much more of you on the loose!"

"Yes, Sir."

Ari walked into the kitchen and looked at the man in the chair. He looked ... sad. Ari had gagged him, but there was little need. The neighborhood was deserted. He decided to remove the gag.

"Are you hungry?"

Sadik glared at him.

"Well, I am hungry. I'm going to cook, and you're in luck, because I am a very good cook."

Ari began to whistle again as he pulled out pots and pans, ingredients and spices for a real gourmet meal.

"I had planned on offering this wonderful repast to the lovely Ms. Katarina," he continued talking to the killer in his kitchen as if they were old friends. "But that's really not such a good idea. She is ..." he stopped then, the knife he was wielding held in suspension over a cutting board filled with fresh mushrooms.

"Distracting." As the word fell from his mouth, it hit him in the gut. He had not been himself since the moment he had seen her and now he was standing in this kitchen talking to a kidnapped Turkish killer all because he was distracted. With Jasmine, he had felt a need to protect. It wasn't the same with Katarina, but it was still something that overwhelmed his rationale self.

"Ah, Sadik," he said, as he resumed his chopping. "I think women will be the death of me some day. Be it love or lust or something in between. They either get into my heart or my head and cause me to lose something ... necessary."

He thought he saw Sadik smile.

"Women," the man said. "The beauty and the thorn."

Ari looked at him with real surprise. "Yes, Sadik. Like the rose, so complicated."

He turned back to his cooking.

"You are not so dumb as you let on, my friend."

Sadik looked up then. "Sometimes it is easier to be the dumb one in the room."

And at hearing the thoughts he had had in his mind only hours before, Ari stood and stared at the man in his kitchen.

"Alright, Sadik, speak!"

~

"Are you trying to tell me that you sat down and had a gourmet dinner with the Turkish killer you kidnapped, and then you simply released him?"

"It seemed the gentlemanly thing to do."

Ari was back in Burke's office. He had not gotten much in the way of Intel from Sadik, but whatever had been eating at him had been resolved and he felt a relief that allowed him to leave.

"Explain. From the beginning."

Ari sipped his coffee and took a moment to gather his thoughts.

"Turns out Sadik wasn't a Turkish killer after all. He was a Russian killer pretending to be Turkish to infiltrate a competitor Brigade. He wormed his way in as a Torpedo, which is their word for a hired assassin, and wound up on this Boyevik – or strike force – charged with taking out the realtor.

"It was a test of his loyalty, and he was given no knowledge of why the hit took place. Since he had only recently joined the group, he didn't know the background."

"So he was a waste of time."

"Not entirely. He did confirm that it was an Azerbaijani Bratva hit ... and we had a lovely dinner conversation."

Burke looked up from his files, his eyebrow cocked at that. "Excuse me?"

"I have to say, Tom. This one took a strange turn for me."

"You think so, Ari?" Sarcasm dripped from every word as Burke folded his hands on top of the mass of paperwork that always littered his desk. "You walked into a den of killers like they were a basket of kittens. I'd say there was something going on there."

Ari looked blankly at the wall for a moment. "Yes. Sadik and I had a nice long chat about all of that, and I was able to think it all through. It was quite cathartic really."

A small vein began to throb at Burke's temple, but otherwise he appeared unflustered. "You used the kidnapped Russian/Turkish killer as a sounding board while you self-analyzed yourself in the middle of a dangerous OP?"

Burke's calm voice belied the anxiety that was beginning to rise in the pit of his stomach.

At almost the exact same moment that Ari said, "I think I need a vacation," Burke told him, "Take a few days off, son."

The two of them laughed, and then Burke grew serious. "You've worked yourself day and night for Athena since the day you came on board, Ari. You have no life outside these walls other than your friendship with the Navy SEAL."

He walked around his desk and patted Ari on the back as he walked out. "Maybe it's time you got one."

CHAPTER TWENTY-FIVE

Inside the MOIS Military Complex, Tehran
January 3, 2009

"Karim, it is time." Mahmoud sat at his desk, glaring at his photo of the Liberty Bell, the most recent report on Baku spread out on the desk before him. Things were progressing quickly now. It could be weeks or months before the secret was in their hands, and then a few months more to build the weapons.

He looked up at his trusted assistant. Only Karim knew as much about this project as he did. "Get me Andropov on a secure line. We have much to discuss."

For the next hour, Mahmoud and Andropov plotted their next moves in half-code to be sure the foundation was laid so that things could move quickly when the breakthrough in the Stealth technology came.

Tverskaya Luxury Apartments, Moscow
January 5, 2009

A Zil limo with a Russian flag on its fenders pulled up in front of the Tverskaya Luxury Apartments and four Red Army guards piled out, followed by a Russian Army general.

The general unfolded out of the seat slowly, rising to an impossibly erect posture as if trying to extend his tiny stature, and looked around, chest full of military ribbons and medals. He straightened his hat and walked over to the main entrance. Entering the building, he moved toward the elevator and as he walked, he looked over at the building security guard.

In a high-pitched, demanding voice, he bellowed, "I am Major General Dimitri Andropov. Take me up to Boris Stanislau's penthouse."

THE EYES OF ATHENA

The mass of men piled into the elevator, not a word spoken. Arriving on the penthouse floor, the guards rushed out to secure the landing while Andropov strutted like a peacock out of the elevator and walked over to the apartment door, his highly polished boots clicking sharply on the tiled floor with every exaggerated step. Ignoring the ornate brass knocker and the electric door bell, he banged noisily. A butler opened it and looked down his nose inquiringly at the unscheduled visitor.

"Tell your boss that Major General Dimitri Andropov, the director of the Foreign Military Intelligence Main Directorate of the General Staff of the Armed Forces of the Russian Federation, is here to see him. NOW!"

The arrogant tone belied the diminutive stature of the man before him, and the butler, Edward Higgins, in his typical unflappable English clip replied simply, "Yes, Sir."

He escorted the General into an opulent ante chamber. Andropov strode into the apartment as if it were his own, and as the penthouse owner, Boris Stanislau, was a head taller than the general, Andropov looked around to choose the most imposing chair in which to sit.

"What can I do for the Director General of GRU?" Stanislau was visibly uncomfortable as he entered the room, fidgeting and moving his eyes around constantly.

"Do you remember nearly 10 years ago when you agreed to help the Kremlin?" Andropov absently handled the knick knacks on a nearby end table, casually tossing about priceless antiques while he seemed barely interested in the man before him.

Without waiting for a response from Stanislau, he continued, answering his own question. "We offered you the inside track on some oil leases that would propel you from millionaire status into the billionaire club?"

"Yes," Stanislau replied in a shaky voice. "I often wondered... Why did you choose me?"

"Because you were educated at Harvard and Oxford," Andropov said offhandedly, not even looking at Stanislau.

Stanislau simply nodded his head in understanding, but in truth he didn't.

Andropov looked up then. "You understand Westerners; that is always an asset to our political leaders, and now it's payback time."

"What exactly do you want me to do?"

"I have an important project that I have initiated, together with some associates of mine. All you have to do is follow my orders to the letter. Your first assignment will be to make a presentation to four people in New York. If you complete your assignments, more very profitable 'special' opportunities will come your way."

Menacingly, he added, "If not..." The fragile glass figurine in his hands fell with a crash to the floor, shattering. Once it had been worth a small fortune. Stanislau cringed.

"By the way, how is your son doing at school in England?" Andropov rose, pirouetted on his heel, and walked out without waiting for a response. Behind him, Stanislau had turned ghostly white.

Once the general and his entourage left, Higgins, who had eavesdropped on the entire conversation from the hallway, entered the room to find Stanislau still in a state of shock.

"Well, Mr. Stanislau, if that don't beat all?" He tried to calm his boss by downplaying the terrifying nature of the general as he busied himself cleaning up the mess. "Prissy little guy, wouldn't you say?"

Stanislau came back to himself at that. "As prissy as a coiled viper, Higgins. He is one person you don't want to cross, not if you want to see your next birthday!"

Higgins rose with the remains of the figurine in a dustpan. They both turned around, moving from the ante chamber back into the main library.

"I hope you have a bottle of Zyr on ice," Stanislau said as Higgins headed for the kitchen. "I think we might both need a shot of vodka after that visitor."

Higgins could not restrain his happiness at being able to share in some of his boss's excellent vodka. "I don't mind if I do join you, Sir!"

CHAPTER TWENTY-SIX

Washington, D.C.
January 12, 2009

Jade McQueen floated through the room, the consummate politician thanking her supporters and working the crowd.

Rocky McQueen was nowhere to be seen the day his wife accepted her appointment as Secretary of State for President Richard Klein. In truth, he had done little for his partner since the day Athena approached him about her recruitment. They had bought the home in New York State, and he had retired there at the end of his term. It was a large house with plenty of room for the two to avoid each other while they both lived there, and he was not unhappy to see her leave for Washington despite his jealousy over her rising career.

At the end of a very long day, Jade McQueen retired to her modest home in Georgetown, newly furnished and feeling slightly less lonely with the addition of a stray dog she had found wandering behind the White House of all places when she stepped out behind the kitchen area to hide for a moment of sanity and peace.

Her new Secret Service agent had picked up the scraggly mutt and put her in the car despite the smelly grime that came with her.

Smiling, McQueen thought to herself, "I think I'm going to like that David Gray."

He had come in with the little hound under his arm, likely ruining the crisp black suit he wore. He checked her home, all the while whispering to the dog to reassure her as McQueen followed behind. Once all was deemed safe and secure, he had taken his leave – but not before bathing the little dog in the kitchen sink with a liberal amount of dish soap.

"He got you all clean and pretty, didn't he, you little sweetie?" McQueen spoke to the small dog in a sing-song voice reserved for babies and animals. The big-eyed mutt watched her intently, licking the end of her nose.

McQueen had been assigned Gray for a reason. As the Secretary of State, she received her own Secret Service detail, but as an Athena Eye, that detail was hand-chosen and deeply vetted by the society. Gray had come with the highest of recommendations from Tom Burke. She knew he had been involved indirectly in an Athena operation, had an extensive military background and had been part of the Secret Service for nearly a decade.

She had worried that he would be stiff and reserved. Chances were good that the two of them would spend a lot of time together and she would have seriously reconsidered his appointment if he had been a bore.

Instead, she found him funny and charming, and the bit with the dog had sealed the deal.

She snuggled into bed with her new friend. "Yes, Sammy," she said, trying to avoid the dog's licking tongue, "I think we'll keep him."

CHAPTER TWENTY-SEVEN

David Gray tossed his ruined suit into a pile of clothes to go to the dry cleaners, but he was pretty sure Mrs. Lee was not going to be happy with him over that one.

He smiled as he walked back into his kitchen from the laundry area only to find Ari Cohen sitting at his bar eating an apple.

"And what are you grinning at, old friend?" Ari asked.

Gray was no longer surprised at having Ari suddenly appear inside his normally well-secured Georgetown townhouse. Since he had joined the Secret Service, he had had no time for anything but work – certainly no time for romance – so having a man barge in on him at all hours had not been much of an inconvenience.

"I think I need to get a dog," Gray said as he started rummaging through the fridge for something that might pass for dinner for the two of them. "A big one, with big teeth and a dislike for nosey, old Mossad agents."

He raised his head from the fridge shelves to grin evilly at his best friend. Ari simply crunched his apple in return.

"I am not old." He tossed the apple core into the trash bin and smiled at Gray. "And how was your first day on the new assignment?"

Gray's smile crept back into place as well. "It was good. McQueen is quite a character. I think it will make for some interesting moments."

"Oh, really?" The reappearance of the smile had not escaped Ari's attention.

Gray laughed now. "She rescued a dog."

"What is it with you and dogs today?"

"No really. On the day of her appointment, she heads out through the kitchen to hide and catch her breath and finds this mangy little yappy dog. Next thing I know, I'm carrying the grimy, big-eyed beast to her limo to hide it until we leave."

He laughed again. "She cleaned up good. Wish I could say the same for my suit!"

"On your first day of a Secret Service assignment for the Secretary of State, you washed her dog?"

Gray took a long pull of a cold beer as he chopped vegetables. "I told you. This one is quite a character."

He looked over at Ari. "So, you broke into my house to ask me about my day? I'm touched, dear, really."

A serious look came across Ari's face. "We have word of movement from Mahmoud. Something is coming to a head in Azerbaijan. Whatever he put in motion there nearly a decade ago is about ready to go live, and that means it's about time to take him down."

"And what about his little henchman, Heinrich?"

"We've had no word of a connection between them since the attempted hit, and Heinrich never resurfaced after Fairbanks."

"You know he has to pay." Gray's chopping was becoming more and more intense as the conversation progressed.

"Yes, David. They both go down, and you will be in on that, just as I promised."

CHAPTER TWENTY-EIGHT

Moscow
December 12, 2010

Stanislau had received instructions from Andropov that he needed to leave immediately for New York. With almost two years and little to no contact from the tiny general, he had become too relaxed for his own good.

All that had changed in a moment.

Higgins had been busy packing since early morning for the trip. As he was making his final preparations, he asked his boss, "Any special instructions, Sir? Will there be anything that you would like me to pack for you that I haven't thought of?"

"As long as you have remembered the present for my son, we will be alright. I am hoping that we have time to stop over in England on the way back so we can see Vondi."

"Then I think we are ready, Sir," Higgins said. "I will take everything down to the limousine and wait for you there."

The elevator opened on the underground parking level. Pulled up prominently was Stanislaus' favorite vehicle – a new Rolls Royce Phantom Limo, all white, shining brilliantly in the artificial light. As Higgins stepped into the garage, the chauffeur and another helper came to carry the suitcases and food hamper to the vehicle.

Some minutes later, the elevator came back down. The chauffeur and Higgins stood proudly between the limo and the elevator waiting on their boss. Higgins thought ruefully, *The life of the uber wealthy; not too shabby!*

In no time, the limo was leaving the underground parking area on its way to Sheremetyevo International Airport.

After the hour-long trip, the limo pulled into the private jet terminal, and Stanislau looked over at his butler. "I have a surprise for you, Higgins. I have just taken delivery of a new plane. It's the brand new Gulf stream G650; the best private jet money can buy."

The limo was maneuvering around a large hangar, and as it did so, the Gulf Stream came into view. "Good gosh, Sir. Is that it?"

Stanislau nodded his head, enjoying his butler's excitement.

"By golly, that's a thing of beauty. What did it cost?" Higgins knew his boss would have no compunction about being asked this nosey question; he loved gloating about his fortune.

"Sixty-five million dollars U.S. was the base price. It cost a little more, as I wanted some extras. It's the biggest, fastest and overall best private jet money can buy. Wait till you get on board. I'll show you around; she's perfect."

The limo pulled up alongside the gleaming plane. Higgins was so excited that he left the car and went up the ramp first, leaving the luggage to be stowed away by the chauffeur and the flight crew.

The captain was ready. "Mr. Stanislau, we have filed the flight plan and are ready to take off as soon as you are ready, Sir."

"I'm ready when you are, Captain; let's go"

Higgins was already in the cabin exploring; Stanislau called out to him. "Higgins, come and sit down and put your safety belt on; we are ready for departure."

Higgins hadn't been so excited for a long time, but dutifully came back to the seat next to his boss and sat down, tightening his belt. He remarked excitedly, "Mr. Stanislau, you have to tell me all about this plane; it's wonderful."

"As soon as we are airborne I will, Higgins."

Stanislau leaned back in his sheepskin seat, enjoying the view from the cabin's extra-large windows, and the Gulf Stream soon rocketed off the runway for New York.

"You know, Higgins, you can fly around the planet faster and higher in this plane than on any commercial jet. The light in this cabin is natural light so it makes you less tired. In fact, the cabin is filled with air that is actually richer than what you breathe in cheaper planes." Stanislau loved to talk about his aircraft.

THE EYES OF ATHENA

Higgins was like a kid in a candy store. "I can't wait to explore the galley."

"The galley is equipped with everything you need for serving excellent meals. I also had them install a special acclimatized wine storage system; we can't ruin the excellent food you serve with anything but the best wines."

"How fast does she go, Sir?"

Stanislau knew all the details. "She has two Rolls Royce engines, giving her a top speed of Mach .925, nearly the speed of sound, and much faster than commercial jets. We'll be able to fly 41,000 feet and go 8,000 miles without stopping, so New York without stops. Pretty cool, huh?"

"Now I want you to pay attention to this, Higgins." His butler stopped smiling and became serious, thinking there might be a problem. Stanislau leaned over toward a console in front of him, picked up a remote and pressed a button. A large flat screen TV rose from the console. The TV was on and provided the images from a camera under the plane's nose showing them what was below the plane.

"That's incredible, Sir."

Stanislau looked over at Higgins. "Wait till you see this."

The screen changed from the view beneath the plane to a recording of "Phantom of the Opera" playing in high resolution with the music being heard through a surround-sound system. It was Higgins' favorite musical, and he put his arm over on Stanislau's. "Thank you, Sir. That was very thoughtful."

United Nations Plaza, New York
December 12, 2010

Stanislau left Higgins at the Plaza Hotel, his favorite in New York City because of their impeccable white glove service. He loved old world luxury and elegance. As he left his suite, he reveled in his surroundings, enjoying every minute of it. He thought to himself, *Once you have enjoyed this level of lifestyle, there is no going back; that is why I must accommodate the general.*

As he exited the hotel, his limo entourage was waiting for him, much to the annoyance of several other guests. He entered his vehicle without bothering to acknowledge or apologize to those waiting. He did hear someone shout a little too loudly, "Impudent Russians!" although he didn't know how they knew that's who he was.

Stanislau thought to himself, *It's not as if I wear a scarf with 'Russia' scrawled across it; must have been one of the bodyguards that let it be known he was from there.*

His limousine took off from the recessed lobby entrance on Fifth Avenue and turned onto Central Park South. Before long, he was heading south in a procession on FDR Drive, on his way to the United Nations Plaza. At the U.N., they descended into the underground parking garage, heading straight for the elevators.

As soon as his limousine stopped, his bodyguards rushed out to form a defensive circle around the middle limo, and after receiving the all clear, Stanislau left the limo and headed for the elevator.

He was a very careful man. He didn't want his bodyguards to know about his business here. In fact, he didn't want anybody to know. This business with General Andropov had very little upside for him, but plenty of downside risk. He entered the elevator alone, pressed 39, and told his bodyguards, "Stay down here; I will go up by myself."

He continued his ascent, alone and silent. It didn't take long, but he did have time to think about the decision he had made nearly 10 years ago. He didn't regret it. When he had agreed to help the Kremlin, he was in a financial bind. Already a multi-millionaire, he had used too much leverage on one of his deals and therefore was very eager to gain the inside track on some oil leases. It gave him the collateral he needed to borrow more money and time to make his leveraged deal successful.

Andropov was right; it did propel his net worth into the stratosphere, although at the time, he did not realize that he was selling his soul to the devil – well not literally the devil, but the GRU, which was probably worse.

One of the smartest moves he had made was to employ the services of an ex-Navy SEAL as his head of security. He didn't want any potential problems with Russian bodyguards having dual allegiances. His bodyguard contingent was all ex-Navy SEALs or ex-CIA. He didn't trust his new Russian associates one bit.

THE EYES OF ATHENA

When the quirky little man from the Kremlin had finally called back to explain what the payback would be, Stanislau's shock was so evident that he had needed a few shots of vodka to steady his nerves.

He had given his first meeting with Andropov a lot of thought since then and had replayed every detail in his mind, from the uniform the general was wearing to the manner in which the man pranced into his penthouse, trying to assume control. Why would he come to visit a civilian with an entourage of four bodyguards? It could only be to intimidate. Stanislau thought that if intimidating him was so important, then this assignment must be very important to the general, which conversely meant it was also very dangerous for Stanislau.

Stanislau walked into the conference room. As with so many New York office buildings, the room was very drab, almost depressing. He strolled over to the windows and tried to look down on the East River. As was frequently the case in New York City, the clouds or mist hung so low that there was very little visibility. He could only see a few other office buildings around them. *Typical,* he thought. Why people liked New York, he would never understand; the weather was too unpredictable. *Ah,* he thought, *but the night life was superb – some of the best entertainment in the world.*

Stanislau was thinking that he needed to buy some tickets to "Phantom of the Opera" for Higgins, who would certainly get a huge thrill out of getting a night off here to go see his favorite musical with the New York City cast.

He turned his attention to the men in the room; they made him feel nervous. What a bunch of misfits – all of them short except the Argentinean Heinrich. *Fanatics of any variety,* he thought to himself, *are too unstable; they make very dangerous company.* The man closest to him was from Tehran and went by the name of Mahmoud. He wore a green sports coat, wrinkled slacks and dusty brown shoes with what looked like an old woolen tie. *A very strange combination,* Stanislau thought, *if you are going to wear a shirt and tie, why not shave?*

After a short time, he noticed a very bitter body odor that seemed to come from Mahmoud. The Iranian also kept flexing his upper cheek in a nervous twitch, which exaggerated his dark stubble and unkempt look, and the added scent of his Turkish cigarette was obnoxious.

Stanislau thought to himself he would have to remember if there was a next meeting to have one of his people come up to the room beforehand to put "No Smoking" signs in front of every chair. But then he did feel some pity for the guy, as he thought to himself that he would have a nervous twitch, too, if he had to answer to the Mullahs.

The man from Hamas, Ahmed, was also smoking, but he was calm, no sweat on his brow. He reminded Stanislau of a coiled snake. He was immaculately dressed in pressed slacks, blazer, starched white shirt, a tie and matching kerchief in his coat breast pocket. Stanislau assumed he was tall for an Arab, which wasn't saying much. He was clean shaven and perfectly groomed, not at all what Stanislau would have thought from someone who was the reputed head of Hamas' Izz ad-Din al-Qassam brigade – the military wing of the Palestinian Islamist organization.

The faint scent of expensive men's cologne must be coming from him, but even so, it was heavily overpowered by the Turkish cigarettes being smoked by Mahmoud.

The Hungarian, Konstantinos, sat next to Ahmed. The old man was reputed to be a ruthless businessman. It was said he had a penchant for destroying established democracies and showed no mercy. Nobody knew his motives; he just liked to control and decimate. Stanislau never trusted men he couldn't understand; this was one to watch, he thought.

Konstantinos was worth a bundle, but dressed like he just came out of the local thrift shop in a cheap creased jacket, un-pressed slacks and hair that looked like it was cut with sheep shears. His complexion was pallid, like diluted olive oil.

The last member at the table was the Argentinean, Heinrich. He was tall, blond, and almost military in his bearing. He held an expensive rose-colored handkerchief over his nose and mouth, which was not surprising considering the other aromas in the room. He also had a scar down the left side of his face, running from the outside of his left eye toward his nose. Stanislau thought the scar would normally give him that dashing look that many ladies liked if it weren't for the creepy vibe that emanated from him.

Stanislau didn't know Heinrich's history, but he was reputed to be well financed and had a reputation as a killer – not someone to cross. He noted with curiosity that the Iranian, Mahmoud, occasionally glared in Heinrich's direction, and that Heinrich seemed determined to ignore him.

Stanislau did not know why his "patron" in Russia had chosen these people for this enterprise. This affair was getting stranger by the minute, he thought, as he put his hand to the inside breast pocket of his jacket and pulled out the envelope he had brought with him. It was sealed, with a message stamped across the front that read 'Do Not Open,' and in smaller letters underneath, "Until instructed to do so."

He was beginning to get a bad feeling about this group, but he was not willing to give up all he had achieved for the sake of some doomed ideology.

"Gentlemen," he began, "I have with me instructions that I have been ordered to open and read to you."

He paused, looking around the room to see if everyone was paying attention, noting that only the Hungarian looked extremely disinterested.

"It is my understanding that you all have been contacted previously and have some familiarity with the proposed undertakings of this group. Is that correct?"

The four other members of the meeting nodded their heads in unison, and Stanislau began to read.

"For many years, our respective cultures have been bullied, cajoled, invaded, threatened and forced or tortured by the Imperialist leaders of the United States of America. More than a decade ago, we started analyzing the best way to take over and instigate a revolution in the United States. Our initial research indicated that the best way to accomplish our goals was to seize the country from within. Our objective is to simply bring the "Big Satan" of America to its knees and forever bring the U.S.A. under the control of the New World Order that we shall establish through the United Nations."

Stanislau thought to himself, after reading the note, *What type of a nut job operation have I gotten myself into?*

He looked around at his co-conspirators. There was absolute silence in the room. Mahmoud was now openly snickering. Ahmed lit another cigarette, sported an evil smile and looked even more venomous than before. Heinrich was impervious, no expression other than his obvious dislike of Turkish tobacco smoke. Likewise, Konstantinos was difficult to read; he looked like it was just another boring day at the office.

Stanislau looked down to his script and continued reading, his stomach releasing alarm bells of acid.

"As you all know, America has a formidable military presence, which includes several branches of intelligence services, both domestic and overseas. These agencies are not to be underestimated. Any breach of our security protocols will result in immediate termination of the parties involved. DO WE ALL UNDERSTAND?"

As Stanislau had significantly raised his voice when he read the last sentence, everyone realized the importance of responding and did so. All attendees nodded vigorously.

No one noticed the tiny camera inserted between the cross bars of the air conditioning vent. This meeting was being beamed directly back to Moscow. The unseen monitor in Moscow secretly said a thank-you to American technology.

Stanislau continued, "I will give you all an envelope shortly. You will take this envelope over to a private cubicle in each corner of this room. Please read and memorize your instructions, after which, you will all return to our conference table for a final briefing. Please leave your envelope and all contents in the ashtray in your booth."

He gave an envelope to each of the four conspirators, who retired to their corner booths. Each opened their envelope to read the opening missive.

"You are aware of our common objective to bring America to its knees and forever have it under the control of the New World Order. As we alluded, our initial studies indicated that the best way to accomplish our goals is to take over the country from within.

"In order to accomplish this, we must lay some structural ground work, which is presently underway, guided by one of the group. Additionally, in order to safeguard our project, individual assignments will be performed on a need-to-know basis. You will find a contact telephone number listed below; you will call this number weekly to simply report one of three things: On schedule, Meet, or Urgent.

"You will hang up without any further clarification, and you will be contacted."

Ahmed continued reading, "Your role will encompass three primary objectives: Supply the stealth submarines and training to Hamas as given to you; provide the self-propelled underwater shuttles that will deliver missiles and dirty bombs to the beaches of Gaza; and complete the design, building and testing of the long-range Stealth missiles that will reach the East Coast of the U.S."

Mahmoud pretended to read his scrap of paper. Having initiated this plan through his helpful little general, he decided to join the group in secret in order to keep tabs on them. He had even gone so far as to write out his "instructions" in case Stanislau got nosey. It would be bad that he knew all of the orders being directed to the components of the group, but at least he would not wonder why there were no orders for Mahmoud.

On his paper was written, "Your contribution to the revolution will be to put the resources in place for a massive strike against Israel. The ferocity of this attack must be of such intensity and be so well coordinated that it almost immediately must involve the United States. We feel that the threat of an attack against Israel, if it were to involve dirty bombs, would be very disruptive to the powers that be in Washington, D.C. This will enable us to implement Stage II of our campaign while the White House is distracted. If all goes according to plan, our goal will be achieved before the U.S. even knows what has happened."

Konstantinos, on the other hand, looked totally bored. He read through the preamble with no visible emotion. "As we know, one of the principal strengths of America has been the Declaration of Independence, which has put in place two or three temporary impediments that must be legislatively removed before our operation can succeed.

"As you are aware, we have been working diligently to alter the framework of the governing laws of the U.S. so that, after our takeover, we can forever control our enemy. Our objective is to accustom the voters of the United States to having third-party United Nations monitors in the voting stations so we can monitor, cajole, influence and, if necessary, intimidate voters. We must also repeal the 2nd amendment to the United States Constitution, which outlines the people's right to bear arms. Please provide an update as to who will champion this legislation for us and timeline for the removal of these obstructions."

Heinrich was worried, and when he was agitated, his facial scar turned vivid red. Although he loved the challenge of an intrigue, stalking a target for assassination was a dangerous business, and the U.S. Government had unlimited resources. Besides, his latest failure hung heavily on him – especially with Mahmoud glaring at him every time he looked up. His paranoia was intensified by having been in hiding since the Fairbanks incident and his great surprise that he had been contacted by Karim and ordered to appear for this meeting.

He read, "You are going to be our go-to agent, responsible for operational security and special assignments. Any breaches, leaks or assignments that require your special talents will be forwarded to you. We trust you will not fail us in this endeavor. In addition to the operational telephone number listed above, we have another number for you; this contact will be able to provide you with any special supplies that you might need while in the U.S. to carry out the assignments that we expect will come your way."

He memorized the telephone numbers, tore the instructions up and placed them in the ceramic ashtray.

They all returned to the conference table and waited for Stanislau to speak. He looked down at his instructions before continuing.

"Gentlemen, there will be no contact with each other during our preparations." He paused to make sure everyone understood. "Do you have any questions?"

All four attendees shook their heads as if to say no.

"You are dismissed."

CHAPTER TWENTY-NINE

December 12, 2010

By the time the attendees had left the meeting on the 39th floor of the U.N., the overcast sky had cleared up, and it looked like it would be a nice afternoon. Mahmoud took the elevator to the ground level. As it was such a beautiful day, he decided to make his way back to the Iranian Mission on Third Avenue by foot. He could always get a cab if he tired.

He was in such a jubilant mood; it looked like his plan was coming together and would propel his career much higher. He started his leisurely walk, leaving the U.N. Plaza and turning left on East 49th Street. As he walked, he thought how strange it was that he could come to New York City on a diplomatic passport and walk freely around town with no discernible problems even though he knew the Americans were aware he would destroy the U.S. in a heartbeat if he could. *These infidels,* he thought, *such stupidity; he couldn't understand it.*

Disturbed by how he could not understand his enemy, he decided to get a cab after all and get off the dangerous streets. He was beginning to think that the CIA or FBI must be following him; they would be crazy if they weren't. Better be safe and get a taxi. He waited on the corner of 2nd Avenue, but try as he might, no cabbie would pick him up. He would wave, whistle, shout; they all ignored him. The cab would slow down, look at him and take off for another fare. He even tried jumping up and down – it was actually to relieve his frustration – but even that didn't work.

Then a slow, misty New York City rain shower moved in from the east. Light at first, it increased in intensity until it was drenching everyone in sight. Mahmoud was getting soaked to the skin. He didn't have a raincoat, just his jacket bought in Tehran. A typical jacket purchased in a tropical climate, it was designed to let air flow through the material. In New York City, that also meant that rain would seep through and drench the wearer.

Mahmoud was getting angrier by the moment. *Arrogant infidels! Soon...* he thought to himself, fit to be tied. *Soon they will pay for their prejudice and egotism!* The longer he waited, the madder he got. Eventually, he decided to walk again.

It couldn't get any worse or him get wetter than he was. Mahmoud was fuming as he took off toward East 39th. Although it was only a few blocks, it was a humiliating trek. If he had had any doubts about his intentions after the meeting with Stanislau, he didn't anymore. He wanted to annihilate these New Yorkers and all Americans. He couldn't wait.

In fact, he decided, why should he? Since Iran had already captured a crashed drone and copied the technology, it would be interesting to ship Iranian drone components to a cell of new undercover operatives. He was going to get permission from the Ayatollah to set that up. It would be a little reminder to the American people that this country is not as invincible as they think.

Eventually, this thought helped him calm down. Imagine a cell of Iranian subversives, operating close to the capital of the most powerful country in the world, building drones right under the nose of the Americans. He almost had to laugh, priceless.

Twenty minutes later, he walked into the Iranian Embassy, looking for all he was worth like a drowned rat. He dripped his way across the expensive lobby rugs to the clerk at the travel desk, and screamed at her. "Get me on the first flight back to Tehran!"

It was always another major irritation for him that he could never get a direct flight back to Tehran from New York. U.S. State Department restrictions on a terrorist state meant he had to fly to Amsterdam or Frankfurt or even Moscow and then change planes, and then, after much wasted time, eventually arrive back at Tehran Imam Khomeini airport. If truth be known, he thought that was the only time he ever liked to see that name "Khomeini."

The travel clerk, trying to ignore Mahmoud's bedraggled state, responded mechanically without looking him in the eye. "You are on an 8:20 PM BA flight to London, then on to Tehran's Imam Khomeini Airport."

He had to hurry, so he ordered the Embassy car brought around to take him to JFK. The trip from Midtown to JFK in the early evening was always a challenge. He told his driver to get him there on time...at all costs.

The driver obeyed, but Mahmoud regretted choosing the limo for the trip. He had to grab the ceiling support twice to avoid flying to the floor and was only able to catch his breath after sitting back in his window seat on the British Airways flight to London.

He always bought two first class tickets so no one would be sitting next to him. *Now I can relax,* he thought. He leaned back in his chair and closed his eyes. His mind drifted back to the beginning – long before he joined MOIS.

I was so very young and impressionable when the Shah was deposed in 1979, Mahmoud thought. Joining the street fights and demonstrations in Tehran had been dangerous, but it at least it helped him get into the Republican Guard. All that shouting, he mused, surprised he had any voice left at all. "Death to the Shah!" and "Allah Akbar!" Ah, the populist chant.

Due to his height, he was directed to the Secret Police on joining the guard – the forerunner of the Iranian Ministry of Intelligence and Security. As a young officer rising through the ranks, he made frequent trips to both China and Russia; any foe of the "Great Satan" was a resource, and he had found a great resource in his little general there. He was still reminiscing in deep concentration when he felt the wheels touch down at London's Heathrow Airport.

CHAPTER THIRTY

London Heathrow Airport
December 13, 2010

Mahmoud arrived at Heathrow just before 9 a.m. London time, but he did not board the flight for Tehran. He had had a nice little chat with Andropov on the way to JFK and with hours on the plane to consider his options, he had come to a decision that quite excited him.

Heinrich Gosslau was no longer needed for this project. Andropov had found other ways to motivate his little scientist father, and Mahmoud was more than happy to be rid of the failed henchman.

He booked a flight to Buenos Aires and with this decision behind him, slept blissfully most of the 14 hour trip.

Buenos Aires, Argentina

It was 2 a.m. when Mahmoud landed in Buenos Aires. As he stepped out of the terminal into the night air, a dark man in a crisp linen suit approached him.

"Good morning, Sir. Welcome to Buenos Aires."

"Emilio, my old friend. It is good to see you again. I trust everything is in order?"

"Of course, Sir." Emilio handed Mahmoud a set of car keys. The car is parked at the curb. Everything you requested is in a bag in the trunk. Directions are in an envelope in the driver's seat. There is a disposable phone in the console with GPS to help in locating your target.

"The vehicle is untraceable, leave it wherever you like when you have finished with it and contact me on the cell phone. I will come for you."

Mahmoud smiled, and Emilio shivered at the evil that lurked there. He would never become accustomed to dealing with such men, but it paid handsomely.

THE EYES OF ATHENA

"You are a good man, my friend. I will speak with you soon."

Mahmoud walked to the nondescript black four-door at the curb and opened the trunk. He put his carry-on inside and unzipped the large black bag already laying there. Inside were the handgun, knives and axe he had requested.

"Soon, Heinrich, you will pay for disappointing me." He closed the trunk and slid into the driver's seat. Inside a small brown envelope he found an address and directions to the location where the coward had been hiding since he caught wind that the Secret Police were no longer protecting him. Mahmoud had stopped them from taking out the failed hit man upon his return to Argentina. Mahmoud had ... other plans.

Since he had detoured to London first, Heinrich had had plenty of time to return to his little hideaway. Mahmoud plugged the address into the GPS on the cell phone and listened as the electronic voice began to give directions. Pulling away from the curb, he found it hard to contain his excitement. It had been years working on this project with the scientists, keeping a low profile, staying out of the field, and he itched to take a man's life again.

It was actually a short drive into the countryside to a small, unassuming house outside of the city proper. Mahmoud parked, watching the house in the waning darkness. He would wait for dawn so that he could get a good view of his surroundings before making any moves.

~

As the sun began to rise, the small village-like neighborhood started to rouse to the sound of roosters and dogs and women beginning the day's chores. A young boy with sandy blonde hair and fair skin came bounding into the yard of the little yellow house that Mahmoud was watching. He was scattering feed for the chickens, scampering about as they pecked at his feet.

His mother called to him from inside, "Martin, hurry up, my son! Come and wash up and eat your breakfast."

Mahmoud was surprised to hear her thick Spanish accent speaking to the small white boy, who threw down the remainder of his feed and ran inside.

At the window, another fair-skinned face looked out – much older, much more wary.

"Good morning, Heinrich," Mahmoud said to himself with a smile.

He had parked some ways down the street from the house so as not to be noticed. Now he exited the car and retrieved his handgun from the bag he had switched from the trunk to the back seat. He slipped it into the waistband of his pants at his back and walked around the corner and back along the alley taking a long route toward the back of the little yellow house.

Mahmoud knew Heinrich was watching for anything out of the ordinary. *Always paranoid, the German must be half-crazed by now,* he thought.

From just up the alley and on a slight incline looking down on the back of the house, he could see the privy in the back. It was a good six feet from the house on a path full of chickens, dogs and even a pig.

"Such a noisy place you have chosen as your refuge, Heinrich," Mahmoud said aloud, watching the commotion of the village as it swung into full force with folks finishing their breakfast meals.

"How will you hear a quiet man like me?"

Mahmoud took a long hard look at the approach, like any good hunter would survey his surroundings. Where one might stalk deer through trees and brush, finding the best path to keep hidden, the same held true for stalking a man within in the village – a few steps this way behind that wall, turn that way behind that hedge ... Soon Mahmoud was well hidden right behind the privy Heinrich was bound to need at some point.

The stench was palpable, but Mahmoud was too elated by the hunt to let it bother him. Even the flies swarming around his face were ignored with glee. He sat patiently awaiting his target. So patiently in fact that he almost jumped when the back door slammed shut behind the tall, lanky Argentinian with the bad temper.

Heinrich practically launched himself from the back porch to the outhouse, wanting to put the security of some kind of structure between him and the world. Little did he know a snake sat coiled to strike behind his safety zone.

THE EYES OF ATHENA

Mahmoud waited until he felt certain Heinrich was indisposed inside the small wooden closet before moving around the building and throwing open the door.

Heinrich threw his arms in front of his face, expecting the Secret Police to gun him down where he sat. After a moment, he lowered them to see Mahmoud standing in front of him, empty-handed and smiling.

Heinrich's face was pure confusion as he stammered, "Mahmoud. What...? How...? What are you doing here? Am I needed?"

Grasping at the least dangerous possibility, Heinrich thought he must be needed for the project.

"Why did you come in person? Why didn't you call? This is dangerous ... you being seen here."

He seemed then to realize where he was and the position in which he had been found.

"If you don't mind ..."

Mahmoud stepped back then, still smiling. Heinrich seemed oblivious to the fact that he had not spoken a word.

Maybe it was the innocence on the young boy's face, but having seen the child in the yard changed Mahmoud's plan. He had intended to go in heavy and simply take Heinrich, leaving a trail of bloody bodies behind him.

All these years behind a desk and dealing with scientists and planners made you soft, Mahmoud, he thought to himself.

Heinrich emerged from the privy and headed toward the house, but Mahmoud stopped him. "There is no time. I have everything we need. You must go with me now."

He led the way toward the car. Heinrich hesitated, but Mahmoud turned with a look of pure malice then and said, "Now!"

In terror, Heinrich followed, hoping in vain that his fears were unfounded.

CHAPTER THIRTY-ONE

Heinrich and Mahmoud walked silently to the waiting car and slipped inside. Mahmoud turned the key, and they began to make their way out of the little village area and back toward the city proper.

"Where are we going? What are my instructions?" Heinrich was sweating. He was not a man who liked to deal with people face-to-face. His training had been in killing men quickly and without detection – usually from a distance.

Mahmoud, on the other hand, had learned every means possible to kill a man up close and personal, and he enjoyed it. Heinrich was disturbed by the smile on Mahmoud's unshaven face. It was unnatural and dark and spoke of thoughts behind his eyes that Heinrich did not want to know.

When the Iranian still did not speak, Heinrich's voice raised an octave with the rising fear in his gut. "I demand to know what is happening, Mahmoud. Where are you taking me?"

Mahmoud's voice was all too quiet, his tone clipped and precise. "Be quiet, Heinrich."

Terror gripped one of Argentina's most well-known assassins. He turned to face the windshield, watching the Buenos Aires airport come into view, gripping the edges of his seat with fierce intensity.

Heinrich had been raised by scientists at the table of both his grandfather and father until he was sent off to military school. He had never found a place in his heartless existence for God. It was a decision he questioned as the car bulleted into the airport parking area and around toward the private plane storage hangars.

These hangars were kept well away from the main traffic of the airport, where the rich and not always legal clientele kept their toys and their secrets hidden from view.

Mahmoud headed straight for the last hangar and stopped the car just outside.

He climbed out and retrieved a black bag from the back seat. To Heinrich he said only, "Come."

Heinrich wanted to scream. He wanted to run. He wanted to disappear. Instead, he simply followed Mahmoud into the hangar. Odd, now, knowing he was facing a viper coiled to strike, the assassin found no strength inside to fight back. It was if he were watching it all from outside his body – the pale, gangly man walking behind the strong, agile killer, doomed. Fear had robbed him of all senses, even the simplest thought of escape.

For his part, Mahmoud was not surprised. He had seen it often in the military leaders of opposing forces – so loud and full of fury from a distance, so meek and unassuming with the knife to their throat. He knew Heinrich could already feel the steel against his pulsing carotid.

Mahmoud pulled the door shut behind them as they entered the dark, empty hangar. It was dirty, unused for some time. In the center of the room was a single hanging light, a chair and a spool of rope.

"Emilio, my little efficient friend," Mahmoud said with a smile.

Heinrich jumped at the sound of Emilio's name. "Emilio? The Secret Police? They know I'm here?"

Mahmoud waved him away like a pesky fly. "Of course, you fool. Had I not ordered them to stand down, you would have been dead as soon as you set foot on Argentinian soil."

He pushed Heinrich toward the chair. "After all, what good is an assassin who cannot kill his target?"

"This ..." Heinrich fell to his knees as Mahmoud shoved him forward. "This is about that Mossad? He wasn't alone. I didn't have the proper Intel... I ... "

"Silence!" Mahmoud would not listen to the weak fool flounder for excuses. "You failed a very simple mission and were discovered. That is unacceptable."

"But you brought me in on your plan. I am part of ..."

"You are a fool. Your father was a necessary part of my endeavors, and you were kept alive until we were certain other arrangements had been made to ensure Hermann's loyalty."

"Other arrangements?"

"You need not concern yourself with that now, Heinrich. Suffice to say I was overjoyed to learn that you were never much of an incentive for your father, who finds you a great disappointment. Your demise will likely be a relief to the old man."

Heinrich looked up in utter despair. He could not speak because he simply had no words. He couldn't even find a good lie that would combat what he knew to be the truth in Mahmoud's words.

His head fell to his chest and he wept.

Mahmoud was disgusted. He grabbed the weeping man by his hair and threw him into the chair, binding him at the hands and feet.

Heinrich hardly even flinched at the tightening of the ropes, too consumed in his own private mourning of a father he had barely known. He raised his eyes now, and they flew open when they saw Mahmoud preparing for what would come next.

It had never occurred to the assassin – who always took the quick shot and ran – that there are those who enjoy the slow kill. He had not been taught the intricacies of torturing a man almost unto death – making him wish each moment for the grim reaper to come and take him – and yet not allowing him that respite.

Mahmoud whistled a happy tune as he laid out the knives Emilio had packed for him – an assortment of razor sharp blades in varying lengths for varying jobs. He noticed he had Heinrich's attention now, and he smiled.

"I see you have returned to the moment, Heinrich. Good, good." Mahmoud walked around the now gasping man, struggling against his ropes in vain. He stroked Heinrich's sweaty hair from his face, making sure it did not hide his eyes in any way.

"It has been oh so long, my little assassin, since I have had a chance to ... play." Mahmoud was fondling one of the knives just inches from Heinrich's face. "I've been very busy with your father and all of my planning. It will all be worth it, of course, when Iran has taken control of the world government and the capitalist American pigs are following our laws.

"He sliced across Heinrich's chest then, the knife cutting away shirt and skin with ease." Heinrich squealed more than screamed at the superficial but painful cut, and Mahmoud frowned.

"Such a woman." He sliced again, this time deeper, across Heinrich's flat stomach, and now Heinrich screamed. The sound echoed across the empty hangar, but Mahmoud knew no one was close enough to hear, and even if they did, no one in this part of the airport told tales about what they saw or heard.

Heinrich sat with his eyes closed, breathing hard, blood pouring from his wounds painting his blue shirt red. "Please, Mahmoud. Give me a chance."

"A chance for what, Heinrich? Yours is a job with no second-chances. The Mossad lives and continues to concern me. I lose sleep over him." Mahmoud was choosing another knife now. He looked up at Heinrich with a stupid grin. "I need my beauty rest, after all. No. You disappointed me, and put my plan at risk."

The knives were lying on the open black bag on the floor at Heinrich's feet. Mahmoud was kneeling, stroking their handles, choosing his next knife with care. He turned to remove Heinrich's shoes, as Heinrich again struggled against the ropes.

Without so much as a whisper's notice, he cut off Heinrich's big toe, then seemed to glory in the sound of Heinrich's pain as he held the bloody knife to his cheek.

"A thing of beauty," Mahmoud said, looking at the blade. "Emilio does know fine craftsmanship when he sees it. I imagine this blade remains as sharp as ever, don't you?"

Heinrich's head hung to one side and he gasped for air on anguished breaths.

"Let's see." Mahmoud reached down and removed Heinrich's little finger.

"Please!" Heinrich begged. "Please! No more!"

"Oh, but Heinrich, we haven't even begun."

"No. No, you monster. Just kill me. What's wrong with you?"

Mahmoud stopped in mid-stride toward Heinrich, cradling yet another knife. "Wrong with me? Oh, I would imagine there is quite a long list there, little assassin."

He leaned in close to Heinrich's face – tracing the scar with the blade of the knife. "Such a shame to have wounded your face at such a young age."

He moved the blade across Heinrich's chin and over to the other side, where he traced the scar's image again, this time with the knife blade leaving a blood-red gash behind.

"There, we've evened things up a bit," Mahmoud said with a hearty laugh.

"Ah, but somehow, I do not think the ladies would find both scars intriguing at all." He was standing in front of the wailing Heinrich, a bloody mess before him, striking the pose of the artist studying his artwork before making the next stroke.

"No. No it just won't do." He reached across with a smaller blade and removed the tip of Heinrich's nose.

"Please," Heinrich begged in barely a whisper. "Mahmoud, please. No more."

"Oh, Heinrich. You speak to me as if I have a heart for you. We are the same there, little assassin. A cold space where my heart should be.

"No. We have hours of fun left yet," Mahmoud said, turning to pull the axe from the black bag and set it at Heinrich's feet. "And once I'm done with you, I will chop up the big pieces that are left into little ones, and I will scatter them across the desert for the animals to carry off."

Heinrich screamed again, this time in pure anguish at the futility of his situation.

"Ah," Mahmoud said, choosing another knife with loving care, "sweet music to my soul."

CHAPTER THIRTY-TWO

Washington, D.C.
December 13, 2010

"I understand. Thank you." Jade McQueen ended her cell phone call and turned to John, her mentor and friend, the Eye from Massachusetts.

"Well that was certainly cryptic. What was that about?"

"We need to get to Athena OPs. I'll tell you on the way."

As the Eye from New York, former First Lady and now Secretary of State, McQueen had come into her own within Athena. She had made a point of learning all she could about the organization and its 200-year history of safe-guarding America and had become one of its strongest members. With her contacts, it only made sense that she would.

"I have a ...friend ...deeply connected to the more, shall we say 'radical' elements of the United Nations? He just called to tell me about a strange meeting that took place at the U.N. building yesterday with some unusual characters.

"From what he said, these players have no business being in the same room together, and I want to know why."

Athena OPs Center, Bethesda, Maryland

McQueen pulled up to a non-descript building on the outskirts of Bethesda. She entered the gate code and passed through to the parking area.

She and John approached the glass double doors, and she swiped the microchip in her forearm across an access panel to enter. The lobby was plain. A receptionist sat at the desk ostensibly to greet and direct visitors. No one needed to know the unassuming young lady was trained to kill a human being a hundred different ways.

McQueen was always impressed by Athena OPs. Having been privy to the inner workings of the National Security Agency (NSA), she knew the organization had been intercepting phone calls and Internet communications at least since the 1990s and maintained a facility at a major underground complex just outside that not only monitors cell phone conversations, but most digital Internet traffic. She had to chuckle to herself thinking of their motto, "More times than we can count, we've made history, without history even knowing we were there."

She knew the operation was impressive, and yet, Athena's OPs Center also had a credo, but not for public dissemination, "More times than we can count, we've helped the NSA make history, without the NSA even knowing we were there."

John caught that impressed gleam in her eye. "Always amazes me, too."

"If only the public knew that every so called "master" spy agency in the world was, in fact, being hacked and data mined every minute of every day."

The volume of data taken in by the NSA alone was so vast that it could not all be analyzed by human technicians; computers had to be programmed to flag certain key words. Athena had encountered the same growth of information as the NSA, but in the early days, it had devoted significant resources to the development, storage and processing of information. Consequently, Athena had a processing center that would make the NSA green with envy.

The Athena board had decided in the 1980s to invest significantly in the companies that manufactured the hardware and designed the software of the future. Most of those investments were made in Silicon Valley and Tel Aviv. They realized that this strategy was risky, but if successful, it would guarantee Athena access to the best brains and intelligence hardware in the world.

They built their nondescript OPs center in the NSA's backyard outside Bethesda, and this was the heart of Athena's intelligence-gathering effort. The principal directive behind Athena's existence for more than 200 years had been to uncover any attempts or conspiracies that meant harm to the way of life intended by the nation's founding fathers.

THE EYES OF ATHENA

Creating the OPs Center had been a massive endeavor of hand-picking personnel who would stand for those beliefs and protect them – and the secret of the center. They operated on a need-to-know basis to protect Athena at its core. But in order to analyze the amount of data brought into Athena OPs, key personnel were a necessity.

All information coming into the center was classified by source and then assigned a priority code. Foreign embassies and the United Nations, as well as known terrorist cells, were assigned the top priority. These communications were translated if necessary then given a "key word" scan.

McQueen walked past reception and straight to Tom Burke's office. His door was open, and he looked up, surprised to see two of the 13 board members standing in OPs.

"I have a feeling this is not a social call," he said with no humor, indicating the two should take a seat.

"Hello, Tom. I think we better go straight into the Situation Room and put the analysts to work," McQueen said, declining the seat and turning quickly to head across the hall.

"Good afternoon, Tom," John said. "She's a bit wound up. Perhaps we should follow."

Burke and John followed McQueen across the hall and into the Situation Room, where she was already asking an analyst to look for data on the U.N. meeting.

"Excuse me for asking, Madam Secretary, but what gives?" Burke asked, more than a little perturbed to have someone taking over with his personnel.

"Sorry, Tom. I'm a bit more than curious about a tip I got earlier. Do the words 'New World Order' mean anything to you?"

"We've been picking up some chatter on that here and there," Burke said cautiously.

"Well, I've got a contact on the inside at the more extreme end of the U.N., and I'm hearing more than chatter. He told me there was a meeting yesterday of some unsavory characters and that phrase was mentioned. I want to know why."

Burke turned to the analyst. "Janet, have we had anything come across in the last 72 hours regarding the U.N. or 'New World Order'?"

"We did pick up an encoded signal from a U.N. meeting room to a location somewhere inside the Kremlin. It was encrypted, and just decoded about five minutes ago. I believe that key-word phrase had it flagged Omega 3, Sir."

Priority code Omega 3 was the highest code that a key-word scan could initiate. If, after a preliminary evaluation, the intelligence staff concurred with the alert, it would be elevated to an Omega 2. The protocol for an Omega 2 was for it to be transcribed immediately. If appropriate, it was sent to the Voice Recognition team. An Omega 2 would go to the head of the line for identification. The transcript and recording went immediately to the senior officer on duty and, if necessary, an immediate briefing could be ordered.

"Bump it to Omega 2 and get me IDs." Burke turned to McQueen. "Good work, Madam Secretary. It's rare that anyone gets a tip before we catch it in here."

Thirty minutes after elevation to Omega 2, the VR team had identified three of the four attendees at the U.N. meeting.

"Boris Stanislau." Burke pointed to a man in the frame of the video showing at the front of the room. He was reading from the Voice Recognition report. 'As a very successful and wealthy Russian businessman, he frequently shows up in the media, but until this alert, he hasn't tripped a single intelligence flag. If it weren't for the company he's keeping, I'd say this was an anomaly, but we'll open a surveillance file on him.

"Next up, Ahmed Ahad. This one is on the Intelligence Watch List." Burke was beginning to have a bad feeling about this; it didn't pass the smell test. He asked Janet to check INS records to see when Ahmed had arrived in the U.S. since all persons on the IWL were flagged by immigration whenever they entered or left the country. Ahmed had not re-entered the U.S., at least not using his standard passport or a diplomatic passport.

That feeling in his gut was sounding alarm bells. When someone on the IWL was trying to hide his itinerary in the U.S., it typically meant he was trying to hide something else.

Burke wasn't keen on the idea of ordering a full facial recognition scan at all points of entry on the east coast, but it was beginning to look like a necessary evil. Chances of a security leak – and alerting the enemy – increased exponentially, since enemy intelligence services had been known to put a "flag" on the photo files that recorded their operatives illegally entering the country. But Burke thought he had to know, so he forwarded the request.

"Cletus Konstantinos." Burke again pointed to the screen. "This guy is bad news. He has a reputation for meddling in a lot of foreign affairs and leaving nothing but carcasses behind."

"Just what was his connection here?" Burke wondered.

"And this guy." Contempt dripped from every word. "Mahmoud. We've been watching him since the Stealth crash in Bosnia. He entered the U.S. two days ago, everything legal, flew out last night."

He pointed to Heinrich. "No voice ID on this one, but they called him Heinrich and his connection to Mahmoud leads us to believe this is the assassin Heinrich Gosslau that killed an innocent war vet while trying to take out one of ours. We've been looking for him ever since."

Burke turned to the Eyes. "Madam Secretary, Sir, this is a scary assortment of no-goods. I'd sure like your blessing to elevate to Omega 1."

Omega 1 meant a full-blown investigation that had all the resources of Athena available until the threat was deemed to be a false alarm or had been neutralized.

With Mahmoud and Gosslau involved, Burke was hoping for neutralized.

CHAPTER THIRTY-THREE

December 14, 2010

Burke had two Code Reds flashing on his screen as soon as he logged on. Both were on Ahmed. He had been identified two days ago entering the U.S. through Atlanta's Hartsfield airport on a U.K. passport in the name of David Hassan. Then, due to the "All east coast FR alert," he was flagged last night driving thru US-Canada customs on I-87, probably on his way to Montreal's Trudeau International Airport.

Burke tried to gather his thoughts. Yesterday afternoon had started with the Omega 3 text: "More than a decade ago, we started analyzing the best way to take over and initiate a revolution in the United States. Our initial research indicated that the best way to accomplish our goals was to take over the country from within. Our objective is to simply bring the "Big Satan" of America to its knees and forever bring the U.S., under the control of the New World Order that we shall establish through the United Nations.

Add in the Bosnian crash connection with Mahmoud and the immediate departure of all concerned, and Burke was nervous.

He dialed the direct extension for the Secretary of State. "Where do we stand, Tom?"

"Running in-depth background checks on all these suspects, Madam Secretary. I want to know why Moscow is using them or what it has on them and I want to find the connection between these players." He added, thoughtfully, "there is something else really bothering me, Ma'am."

"What's that, Tom?"

"What's the link with Tehran? We know the Iranian was at the crash site with the Russians. Now he surfaces in the middle of a Russian-U.N. plot? What does Iran have that Russia doesn't have? We know he's been working in Baku for a decade on something related to the crash. We suspect weaponry. He's had years to implement something really nasty, Ma'am.

"Moscow likes to use Tehran for political advantage against us, but it has never been an OPs partner before, and they have no reason to collaborate now officially – not unless there was a big advantage we know nothing about."

"Where do we go from here, Tom?"

"Aren't you having dinner with the Russian President tonight?" he asked.

"Yes, I am."

"If I send you a transcript of the transmission, could you bring it up with him to see what his reaction is? This could be quite serious; seems like some Jihadists might be involved."

McQueen hesitated, thinking over the ramifications of the situation.

"Alright, Tom, send it to me; I'll talk to him tonight."

"Excellent. One other thing, Madam Secretary, I'd like to send one of ours with you."

"I have my own security, Tom. You vetted him and he's quite capable."

"Yes, Ma'am. Gray is top-notch, but I've got a bad feeling about things these days, Ma'am. I'd feel a might better if you had a little extra muscle along for the ride."

"Who do you have in mind?"

"Cohen, Ma'am. He's fully briefed on this OP, having been involved since the beginning, and he has worked with Gray."

"Fine. But he stays with the Limo, Tom. I'm not barging into the Kremlin with a dozen armed men at my beck and call. No matter how appealing the thought might be.

CHAPTER THIRTY-FOUR

McQueen had never particularly liked the U.S. Embassy in Moscow. Despite her favorable treatment by Russian officials, she tried to limit her time in Moscow as much as possible.

As she put the finishing touches to her ensemble for the night's dinner engagement, she lamented her uneasiness to her shadow waiting just outside her bedroom door.

"This place just doesn't feel secure," she told Gray, who sat in the living area waiting to take her down to the limo. Ari had opted to wait with the limo and keep an eye on things from outside.

He laughed. "Considering they halted construction of the original Embassy by Russian contractors because the place was totally bugged, I'd be hard pressed to think that just because an American company built this one with American materials that it's a solid fortress of impenetrability."

What an embarrassment that had been to the State Department. The Cold War had ended, and the U.S. was showing its belief in the new USSR by using local contractors. That was 1985. It wasn't' until 2000 that they started over on the new construction.

The two countries had a long and tumultuous relationship of course. Russia had recognized the still-fledgling United States of America in 1803. By 1809, the two countries had exchanged Ministers, and in 1898, the U.S. staged its first Embassy in St. Petersburg. Then came the Bolshevik Revolution of 1917, and it wasn't until 1933 that the U.S. opened a new Embassy in Moscow and officially recognized the new government of Russia. Then came the tensions and distrust of the Cold War, and when the Soviet Union dissolved in 1991, the United States recognized the new Russian Federation and began diplomatic relations afresh with the new Russian government.

Gray looked up as the bedroom door opened and McQueen swept through in a soft green dress just feminine enough to catch a man's breath without giving away an ounce of the natural strength and confidence she carried in her position.

She was pleased to see him smile as he rose and to offer her his arm to lead her out. Her attire earned her another approving smile when they met Ari at the curb.

The black limo with U.S. Flags flying on the fenders drove through the snow to the Kremlin Palace, its occupants a little more tense than usual inside.

Dinner at the Palace is always an interesting event, as even the choice of the room is an indication of the 'esteem' with which the guest of honor is held.

As McQueen's limo pulled up at the Palace, she was greeted by an official.

"Good evening, Madam," he declared flamboyantly. "I am Gregor, a caretaker of the fabulous Kremlin Palace, and I have been asked to escort you to the President. I thought I might show you some of our history on the way."

"Thank you, Gregor. That would be wonderful."

She turned to Gray with a sly smile that showed she knew how much he loathed the historical tours. "Come along, David; you don't want to miss this guided tour."

Ever charming, he moved up to accompany her. "Yes, Ma'am."

Again, Ari stayed with the limo, as promised, and kept watch on the outer perimeter, he smiled devilishly at Gray as the couple sauntered off behind the effervescent tour guide.

"On this occasion, we are going to dine in the Golden Chamber of the Tsarina Irina Godunova," Gregor said with great pomp and circumstance.

He added in a confidential whisper, "The President chose this room for you himself. This was the official reception room of the Russian Tsarinas, where they held formal celebrations of Russian monarchs' weddings, meetings with Russian and foreign clergy, and receptions for relatives of the royal family and for ladies of the court."

As McQueen's guide led them through the Kremlin Palace to the Private Golden Chamber, he continued with his history lesson. "The chamber was part of the palace complex built in the Kremlin in the late 15th century and modernized in the mid-19th centuries. In the 1580s, it was rebuilt as a ceremonial reception room of Tsarina Irina Godunova, the wife of Tsar Feodor I of Russia.

"It is in the style of Italian Renaissance architecture," he continued. "These are some of my favorite art pieces in the palace. You will note that the walls of the chamber are decorated with paintings on a golden background."

Gregor turned to point out some paintings on another wall. "The paintings on the vault show episodes from Christian history associated with Emperor Constantine of Byzantium and his mother, Helena."

Pointing to the eastern wall, he added, "That is where the Tsarina's throne used to stand. You can still see the paintings depicting the conversion of Princess Olga, the first Russian Christian Princess.

"The paintings on the western wall feature scenes from the life of Empress St. Theodora," he concluded.

As they were shown to the dining table, Russian President Igor Bronsky approached. "Ah, Gregor, have you given our guests a guided tour?"

"Yes, Sir, as you requested," replied Gregor graciously.

The President responded in an appreciative tone, "Thank you, Gregor. That will be all."

Gregor bowed slightly to his President. "Thank you, Sir."

McQueen and Gray both said at nearly the same time, "Thank you, Gregor."

Bronsky turned to his guests, waving toward the room expansively, "I chose this room especially for you, Madam Secretary. I hope you approve."

"You are too kind, Sir."

"Not at all, Madam," he replied, kissing her hand, "just a slight indication of the esteem with which we regard you."

Changing the conversation, he added, "Your press is very efficient; they know what you are doing almost before I do!"

He laughed heartily at his own humor and began reading a newspaper headline he brought with him. "MOSCOW - U.S. Secretary of State Jade McQueen on Saturday opened two days of talks with Russian leaders on nuclear arms control and other security issues and on the outlook for bringing Israel and the Palestinians back to the peace talks."

McQueen added ruefully, "Misdirection by us, I'm afraid, Mr. President; these are strange times we live in, strange times indeed."

She moved over to the chair being held for her by a waiter and sat down – followed by the two most powerful people in Russia – for a typical Russian dinner at the Kremlin. Gray stood behind her, waiting in case he was needed. Due to his military training, he was on full alert, watching, ready for whatever.

Each person at the table had their own personal waiter. Gray was watching one server attentively, focused on his every move. Every time the Secretary said something, the waiter would pause what he was doing, not noticed by most, but seen by Gray.

As Gray moved to McQueen's side to give her copies of a briefing for her hosts, he whispered in her ear, "Your waiter is pretending to pay you no attention, but he is listening to and understanding every word."

She nodded. "Thank you, David."

After the meal, hot tea was served. "Is it safe to talk in front of the staff?" she asked Bronsky, wanting to be sure no other ears were privy to her next words.

He nodded. "They are all vetted by GRU."

Having been reassured, she continued, "Gentlemen, it has come to our attention that a covert operation is underway that could jeopardize international stability and even, perhaps, our relationship."

Gray watched Bronsky; he had not changed his demeanor at all during the first part of McQueen's statement, but as she added the last statement, he visibly tightened his posture, indicating he was unaware of any plot and certainly not happy with that potential. The reaction from the waiter attending Gray's boss was abrupt. He tried to recover quickly, but his reaction had been noted.

She handed them a copy of the U.N. Omega 3 alert. After a few minutes, both the President and Vice President looked up. The Russian leaders shared faces of total surprise and utter shock.

"Who is the Russian?" they asked almost in unison.

"We are not sure yet, but the signal was transmitted directly to GRU headquarters in Moscow."

Looks of surprise were replaced by consternation as each frowned at one another, almost as if they were in possession of some secret information.

"It is an unfortunate conclusion," McQueen said, "but we can only surmise that the Director General of GRU, Dimitri Andropov, is involved."

Bronsky's posture had stiffened in his seat. The previously relaxed, carefree attitude gone, now he was sitting almost in a stiff, military manner. "If the communication went to GRU, General Andropov is either involved or incompetent. Either way, he must be dealt with."

Unnoticed by all except Gray, the Secretary's personal Russian waiter did a double-take again and quickly tried to recover his composure. The waiter removed a plate from in front of the Secretary then walked back to the kitchen entrance.

"In order to eliminate this threat, we are going to need your help," McQueen continued. "We don't know yet exactly what they are going to do, only that they intend to do us harm."

Gray interjected, "Could you excuse me for a minute?"

All three people at the table looked at him, not understanding. He added, "If you don't mind, I need to go to the kitchen for a moment."

McQueen, as innocently as could be because she had total confidence in Gray, said, "Of course. You might want to try some of the roast goose we ate; it was excellent."

Gray left the room. He entered an area where the staff waited to be called. McQueen's waiter was not there, so he continued on to the kitchen, bustling with activity. No waiter. He looked around to no avail, so he asked, "Where is the Secretary's waiter?"

Only one worker in the kitchen seemed to understand his question, responding in very heavily accented English, "He said needed go outside for smoke maybe minute ago."

"Thank you. I think I need a smoke as well. What direction did he go?"

The worker pointed to an exit from the kitchen area, "That way. You see stairs. Go down stairs and out door on ..."

THE EYES OF ATHENA

He did not know the word for left or right, so just held up his left hand, adding, "Door on this side."

Gray thanked him and hurried out after the waiter. As he found the staircase, he went over to a window trying to see out, looking for the glow of a cigarette. Instead, he found the waiter talking on his cell phone. Gray watched, unseen, from the window for a few more moments.

He used his wireless radio earpiece to call for Ari's attention at this location, filling him in on the details. "I've got a fishy waiter on the south corner down from the kitchen. He's talking to someone on a cell phone. Need you to recon the area."

"I can be in three," Ari replied.

Before Ari could round the corner, the waiter finished his conversation, pocketed the cell phone and turned back toward the building. Gray alerted Ari and walked quickly and silently back toward the kitchen where the helpful worker looked up and asked him, "You no smoke cigarette?"

"I left my lighter in my bag in the dining room. Thanks for your help," Gray said, slapping his head in mock exasperation.

As he entered the dining room, the Secretary, the President and the Vice President all looked up at him.

"Everything ok, David?" she asked.

"Just fine," he answered. "You were right; that goose is excellent."

McQueen and Bronsky turned their attention back to their conversation with the Vice President. "That's the plan, gentlemen," she concluded.

Both men started to smile. "That is a wonderful strategy," Bronsky remarked.

McQueen leaned closer to him, whispering close so no one else could hear, "If we can't find out from our sources what they plan, we might need to arrange for a personal interview with Andropov and one of our specialists. Is that OK?"

The Russian laughed. "Just let me know when you want us to start on this end."

She smiled deeply now. Just to make sure, she added, "We are in agreement?"

She looked over at her hosts, to gauge their reaction, and they nodded, smiling in unison. Then as an afterthought, "We need to make sure that no one is alerted prematurely..."

Gray watched as McQueen's waiter came back into the room and went up to the wall to stand ready in case he was called. Gray sidled over to him, took a deep breath and said, "Everything ok?"

The waiter did not budge or respond, but Gray had achieved his objective, there was no smell of cigarettes from the man.

McQueen, still seated at the table, was giving her thanks to her hosts, "Gentlemen, this has been a wonderful evening, and the honor of you choosing the Tsarina's Golden Chamber to host our meal was very special."

The President responded graciously, "You are welcome; that is how we view you, as America's Tsarina."

The eyes of her waiter, standing patiently behind her, flickered again, forehead frowning, understanding every word, still watched unseen by Gray.

CHAPTER THIRTY-FIVE

Darkness had fallen over the Moscow sky as McQueen sunk comfortably into the rich leather of the Embassy limo seats on its way to the airport. She was exhausted and it felt good to have changed into a pair of jeans and a sweater for the trip home.

If there had been more time before they arrived at the airport, she might have taken off her shoes. But she decided to wait, and try to focus on the goals that had been accomplished on her trip.

Gray sat beside her on her right, Ari to her left.

"Do you think the Russian President believed everything you said at dinner?" Gray asked.

Without hesitation, she replied, "I think so."

"You need to be very careful. That waiter was paying way too much attention to everything you said. By all accounts, he should not have been able to understand English at all. I think it's safe to assume he was there on someone's behalf, most likely Andropov..."

Gray paused as the vehicle entered the restricted area of the airport.

As they began to move again, McQueen asked him how much he thought the waiter heard.

"I don't think he caught the key information – the plan. Most of what I heard, which is what he heard, was information he already knew. At best, Andropov will know that we know, but he won't know what to expect."

"Actually, I don't think it will be a problem." Ari seemed very sure of his assumption. "As you were coming out to the limo, I caught sight of a small group of the President's men escorting one of the waiters into a waiting military vehicle. I suspect that they were not fooled by David's sudden need for goose ..." He smiled then.

A few minutes later, McQueen, Gray, Ari, two assistants and one other Secret Service agent boarded the USAF Boeing 757. Everyone was hoping for a smooth flight with no turbulence.

About an hour later, when the plane was somewhere over Western Russian territory, McQueen was suddenly awakened from a deep sleep by Gray.

"Madam Secretary," he said as he tapped her lightly on the shoulder.

It took her about a minute to finally open her eyes and focus on reality. "Yes, David, what is it? Is something wrong?"

He took a deep breath. "The pilot wants you to fasten your seatbelt. Two unidentified planes are approaching our air space at a high rate of speed. This area is meant to be a no-fly zone, and the pilot is unsure of their intentions."

"Are we going to try and outmaneuver ..." she was cut off in mid-query when the 757 took a sudden plunge and a hard right to port.

The instant change in course caused Gray to lose his balance, and he landed on top of her. Before she could say anything, they both heard a tremendous thunderbolt of noise and saw very bright lights pass by outside their window.

Twin jet afterburners were raging at full throttle as the MIGs roared past. Needless to say, there was a look of panic in the eyes of almost everyone on board.

McQueen quickly composed herself. "David, what the heck is going on?"

At that exact moment, the pilot came over the intercom and started speaking very quickly. "Madam Secretary, we have two Russian fighter jets clearly harassing our plane. The last one came directly toward us at Mach One speed, and if we hadn't evaded as we did, we would have been hit."

McQueen picked up the phone so she could have a direct conversation with the pilot. "What is the Standard Operating Procedure under these circumstances?" she asked with an air of confidence. As always, it only took her a few seconds to digest and recover in an emergency.

"SOP calls for fighter jet support from the nearest USAF ba..." Before he could finish, the pilot had to execute another sudden plunge and, this time, hard turn to starboard.

THE EYES OF ATHENA

Suddenly, McQueen could hear the rat-tat-tat of gunfire and explosions coming through the intercom.

"I'm hit! I'm hit!" the pilot yelled as pain shot through his body at warp speed. "They have strafed the flight deck, and we have all been hit..."

She could hear the pain in his voice and felt totally powerless. Looking up, she saw Gray and Ari moving toward the cockpit as one.

The pilot continued speaking as best he could between gasps. "It looks like all of our electronics are hit; the damage is pretty severe..." He started to slur his words as if he had had too much to drink.

By some miracle, the pilot was able to say a few more words before passing out. "We're all hit; I am putting the plane on automatic pilot....call Rammstein..."

SecState1 was now in a full tailspin as oxygen masks fell from overhead and papers flew around the interior of the cabin because the pressurized seals near the flight deck had been broken.

Thankfully, the airplane finally stabilized at 10,000 feet and the pressure subsided.

McQueen called out to Mark Scully, her additional Secret Service agent, "Find the alternate pilot, and meet me on the flight deck."

She raced up the gangway with her steward only a few steps behind her. Ari and Gray were already moving bodies within the cabin. It only took a few seconds to realize everyone was dead.

At that moment, Scully rushed in to say he could not locate the other pilot. "Can't seem to find him..." But he stopped mid-sentence as his eyes focused on one of the corpses. "Oh, there he is..." and he pointed to the other dead pilot.

"You mean he's dead too?" McQueen asked with a tone of horror in her voice. "There's no one who can fly the plane?"

The plane's emergency warning system started beeping noisily, as a computerized voice began shouting: "WARNING, WARNING, STALL SPEED, STALL SPEED"

Gray told McQueen to have a seat. "I need to try to fly this bird."

Scully and the Steward headed back into the cabin to calm the other passengers.

Gray quickly pulled the dead pilot from his position and took command of the airplane. Without a word, Ari slid into the seat beside him.

As Ari put on the headphones and was about to call for help, McQueen interrupted him. "Call Rammstein over our secure network and tell them we have an emergency. But not over the public emergency bands, understand?"

She took a deep breath and continued speaking. "Scramble the transponder signal so whoever is responsible doesn't know whether we are going down or not."

Ari did as he was instructed, Gray struggled to increase air speed of the 757, and within a few more seconds, as the plane accelerated, the nose finally inched skyward. He took a heading to Rammstein.

Switching the radio frequency to the secure bandwidth, Ari spoke calmly into the headset, "Rammstein, Rammstein, this is SecState1, do you copy, over?"

A voice replied, "We read you five by five, over."

Ari took a deep breath and continued talking to the voice on the radio. "This is SecState1; we have an emergency; need clearance for an emergency landing and also scrambling transponder code blue, over."

The voice on the radio replied instantly. "Transponder code blue, acknowledge; receiving you on blue. Continue on heading 240; maintain current altitude, and we will clear all traffic for you. Twenty minute ETA... Let us know when you have a visual. Over."

McQueen watched as Gray was finally able to get the plane under control. He turned to tell her, "Madam Secretary, we are now under control and flying normally. Well, as normally as we can, considering the circumstances."

Just then she bent down toward Gray and kissed him fully on the lips. "David, you know, if you were a few years older, you could have been the President of the United States!"

As he savored the kiss for as long as he could, Gray tried to hide a look of utter surprise on his face. He caught the look from Ari out of the corner of his eye, cleared his throat and said, "I really am much older than I look, Ma'am."

THE EYES OF ATHENA

The Secretary of State of the United States winked at him and left the flight deck.

CHAPTER THIRTY-SIX

Athena OPs Center, Bethesda

Burke seemed to live at the Athena Ops Center nowadays. He was trying to get a handle on Operation Boris. As far as he was aware, none of the official government agencies had any clue as to what was happening or about a potential plot against the US.

To his knowledge, the only employee of the government that had any inkling about what Athena was calling "Operation Boris" was the Secretary of State, and she was betting on Athena rather than taking their limited information to the President.

Well, he thought, *if he had to have one person on his side in case he needed to call in the 'heavy guns,' that would be the Athena Board Member from New York.*

The idea originated by the Board Member from Massachusetts to invite her into Athena was working out to be an extremely good choice for the security of the country. *The founding fathers would be very proud,* he thought, his musings interrupted by an analyst who proclaimed quite loudly, "Sir, we are getting a Code Red from Rammstein AFB concerning the Secretary of State's plane!"

"Good heavens, son! The Secretary of State's plane? What the heck happened?"

"SecState1, made an emergency landing last night at Rammstein Air Force Base in Germany. Her plane was peppered by two MIG fighter jets. All the flight crew members were killed."

Burke's thoughts immediately went to his last conversation with McQueen. Had he inadvertently put her in danger? Burke was fuming. *It must be connected,* he thought. "What about Cohen?"

"All other personnel were accounted for, Sir."

"And just where in the sam hill was the fighter escort she was meant to have?"

The analyst busied himself at his computer then lifted his head from the screen indicating he had the answer. "Sir, apparently the fighter escorts have been pulled off from all cabinet members due to the spending cuts at the Defense Department."

Burke was getting very agitated. "Who was the danged fool at the Defense Department that made that decision?"

The analyst replied, "Sir, is that a rhetorical question or do you want me to find out?"

Burke responded, "As you were, son, a rhetorical question. This government has been making a lot of danged fool decisions lately. Who landed the plane?"

"Checking, Sir, won't be a moment. Got it, Sir. Her Secret Service agent is an ex-Navy SEAL pilot, one David Gray."

Burke was showing his evident relief. "Of course."

Rammstein Air Force Base, Germany
December 18, 2010

Since his emergency landing at Rammstein Air Force Base, Gray had been trying to figure out what had happened to cause the attack on McQueen's plane. The only thing that made sense to him was the suspicious behavior of the waiter at the Kremlin. He had been held over for minor injuries, while Ari escorted McQueen home by military flight.

It was just as well. Gray had questions. After a good night's rest in the officers' quarters, he decided to walk over to the maintenance hangar where SecState1 had been taken to see if he could get any more information from the crew working on the plane.

As he was about to leave, he thought it would be a good idea to pull up some information on the MIG's armaments; he needed to know what to look for when he got over to the hangar. If there was one place he was sure he could find that information, it would be at the European tactical headquarters of the United States Air Force.

After getting permission to use a computer at the officer's mess, he delved into the Air Force database for Russian-made MIG's. He didn't know whether it was a MIG 15 or even the more modern MIG 23, but he learned that the plane's performance and aerodynamics had advanced considerably with each new model. Still, the basic armaments had not changed. For air-to-air armament, the Russians had internal guns and externally carried rockets and missiles. It had either three 23 mm cannons or two 23 mm cannons and one 37 mm cannon. The 23 mm cannon had a firing rate of 800 rounds per minute with enough ammunition carried for six seconds of firing. The 37 mm cannon had a firing rate of 400 rounds per minute and carried enough ammunition for five to six seconds of firing.

The MIG-17 was capable of carrying two Atoll missiles on external pylons. These were exact replicas of USAF Sidewinders. *Thank heavens they hadn't launched any sidewinders at us, we would have been history if they had,* he thought. It only made sense that the attackers thought that if they killed everyone on the flight deck, the plane would crash.

One last thing he needed to know, what countries had MIGs in their air force? No sooner said than done. In no time, the computer had listed all the countries that had bought them – a rogue's gallery of terrorist states from the Syrian Air Force and the Libyan Air Force to the Yemen Air Force and the Bulgarian Air Force.

Gray was ready. He logged off the computer, went out to the main lobby of the mess and asked them how he could get to the aircraft maintenance area. He accepted a ride and was soon walking into the hangar. He walked over to the nose section of SecState1 and stood in front under the plane looking up to try to see the damage.

It wasn't long before a maintenance worker came and stood beside him, both of them just looking up at the airplane.

"Pretty amazing isn't it?"

Gray looked over at his new friend. "Yep, sure is."

After a few more moments of quiet thought, the worker added, "Difficult to imagine that anything this big could actually fly isn't it?"

Gray had to chuckle, he looked down at him. "I thought you were talking about the bullet holes in the body and wings."

THE EYES OF ATHENA

"Well," said the worker, "there certainly is that, too. They don't know how lucky they were; some of those slugs missed the electronic brain of this bird by a hair."

Gray started his walk around the plane, the mechanic just following. He looked at the wings and whistled to himself, adding, "Boy that sure was close. I don't know how they missed the fuel tanks."

The maintenance worker looked at him. "Yeah, you're right. We thought the same thing when we saw the holes, but lucky for them – at least for some of them – the angle of the plane when the gun was fired was sufficiently off so that the bullets went through the wing, missing the tanks."

"Yeah... real lucky," Gray said out loud. "Did they ever find out what caliber the shells were?"

"Sure did," replied the worker, "23 millimeter."

"That's just what I was afraid of."

After lunch, Gray boarded a military plane back to the U.S. He found a window seat and sat back to enjoy the flight. In no time, he felt the pull of the jet as it took off. In the seat back in front of him, he pulled out a magazine titled "Welcome to Andrews Air Force Base." Inside the front page, he started reading, "Welcome to the Courses at Andrews, reflecting a military presence, classic sense of style and gracious hospitality, the Courses at Andrews Air Force Base carry an air of true timeless elegance. High-end amenities, exceptional facilities and an unforgettable golf experience are the standard at this military resort.

"The envy of many golf courses located in the Maryland and Northern Virginia area, The Courses at Andrews boasts three 18-hole championship courses that are created from an extraordinary design and provide an enjoyable challenge for golfers at all skill levels.

"Our distinguishing attribute extends beyond just the three golf courses. It's reflected in everything we have to offer at The Courses at Andrews, including our golf tournament, operations, food and beverage signature outlets, the only military resort resale golf shop, our complimentary practice facilities, and our state-of-the-art fitness center. Moreover, we are committed to making The Courses at Andrews AFB a place of warmth, hospitality, and operational efficiency. To us, that means prompt, courteous service, and genuine responsiveness to your needs.

"We hope you enjoy your experience at The Courses at Andrews and will use the facilities often."

He had to laugh under his breath; only in the U.S.A. would you have a military base that had a golf course, let alone three golf courses. He was beginning to wish that he was posted to the Tactical Air Command at Andrews, until he reminded himself that he had retired from his unit years ago.

In no time, he fell asleep. It was a quality a lot of his mates envied; he could get on a plane, close his eyes and be asleep in five minutes, even if he just got up. The pilot talking over the intercom woke him, and he tightened his seat belt for landing. He looked out of his window at, sure enough, the biggest expanse of golf courses he had ever seen.

After landing, the plane pulled up close to a terminal, and a ramp was pushed up to the plane doors so everyone could disembark. As Gray climbed down the ramp, a black suburban pulled up next to the plane. When he reached the bottom of the ramp, the door to the suburban swung open, and McQueen called his name, warmly waving him over, "David, come here."

He ambled over, a big grin on his face at seeing her.

As he got closer, she thanked him again. "I would not be alive today if it wasn't for you." She added, in retrospect, "The next time you tell me someone is acting suspiciously around me, I will pay more attention."

Gray had one of those million dollar smiles, and he flashed one at his boss then. It was the smile of someone who genuinely liked the person he was sworn to protect. He remembered the Secret Service adage, 'Worthy of Trust and Confidence,' and he didn't think that quite depicted the Service's deep commitment, but it would do for a start.

"I'm glad I was there, Ma'am; the world needs more people like you."

She looked deeply into his eyes before replying, "No David. We need more men like you. Get in the car; we need to talk."

Gray slid into the black suburban and sat next to McQueen. The driver started the drive back to DC.

"You are familiar with our security protocol when cabinet members fly overseas aren't you?"

"Yes, Ma'am," he responded.

"An attack on my plane is not meant to be possible without counter measures, right?"

"Yes, Ma'am."

"David, the $64,000 question is, are you sure those were MIGs?"

"No, Ma'am, I'm not. We were in Russian airspace, so I assumed they were. Many other fighters have twin after burners, including some of ours. All I saw was the glare of the afterburners, and I assumed."

"But I did check out the plane after you left Rammstein," he continued. "The maintenance people told me that the slugs they recovered were from a 23 millimeter cannon, which is what the MIGs fire."

"Is it possible for some other air force to have masterminded this plot in Russian territory?" she asked.

"Theoretically, yes. We have – and the Russians have – sold planes to many countries. They all have the technology to fly sub-sonic under radar without detection. If they also were able to get your flight plan... The Soviets have sold MIGs to a bevy of terrorist states, Libya, Yemen, even Iran has them."

McQueen looked somewhat crestfallen. "So that is no help," she said. "It could have been any number of terrorist states that tried to take us out."

"It would be fairly easy to find your plane, wait for a signal, then, when they detected your transponder, accelerate up to 50,000 feet and attack from above."

McQueen looked worried. "I'm scared, David. I have been getting pressure within the States to discourage me from any political run in 2016 and from delegates to the U.N. who know I am against any power grab by foreigners wanting to subjugate the U.S. constitution to the U.N."

"What about your husband, can't he help?"

She was quiet for a moment, then replied, "We have been living separate lives for quite some time now. Besides, he is a politician. Even with the connections he once had, I'm not sure that he could do anything." Changing her tone, she added with a sly wink, "Well, perhaps he could talk them to death!"

Gray was honored that she was being so candid with him. He put his hand on top of her hands crossed in her lap, looked into her eyes and said, "Ma'am, you know I will do anything for you. I'll be there for you."

He patted her hands and went to move his hand away, but she quickly turned her hand and held onto his, looking into his eyes. Softly, she said, "I know you will, David. I know you will. There are so few people I can trust. Thank you."

They both turned after the emotional revelations, trying to recover their composure and were quiet.

Immersed in their own thoughts, they entered the Woodrow Wilson Memorial Bridge on the Beltway back to Georgetown. Gray spoke first. "You have created some very dangerous enemies."

She was still looking outside the suburban at the Potomac. "I just ... I just don't know who to trust... Except you; I am going to request that you be assigned to me 24/7 until we sort this out."

"Hummh, 24/7... This sounds like it could get very interesting," Gray said with an impish grin on his face, trying to lighten the mood.

McQueen lightly punched him on the shoulder. "David, I am being serious."

She sighed then, knowing she was about to walk a fine line with the President. She was, after all, his Secretary of State, and he was due a full report. She had managed to keep a lid on the whole incident, and they were keeping the affair under wraps for now – no Congressional oversight, no military intervention, no media and so far, no change in the nation's DEFCON defense level.

"The Air Force is going to know about as much as we do." She was thinking out loud now, but would welcome Gray's input. "I won't be able to keep their findings from the President's desk, and his first leap will be just like ours – Russian. I'll have to counter that, and that means bringing him in, to some extent."

She was hitting a well-worn speed dial number now and soon heard the Member from Massachusetts on the other end of the line. "John," she said, diving in with no preamble. "I'm formulating my thoughts for a meeting with the President tomorrow. Everything he's got coming in will point him to Russian MIGs in yesterday's attack, but I don't buy it.

"I believe Bronsky, and I think I need to give the President enough on Operation Boris to at least keep him guessing right along with us. Do I have your support?"

Gray could tell the answer she got was one she had been seeking. She smiled as she disconnected the call just as the black suburban pulled up in front of McQueen's house in Georgetown. As usual, Gray walked in ahead of his charge, checking the house for safety and determining it all clear. Sammy nipped at Gray's heals the whole time, until he picked her up to rub her soft ears. He nuzzled her absently and handed her to McQueen as he readied to leave. She hurriedly grabbed hold of his arm, worried. He glanced back at her, saw the look of panic and realized just how frightened she really was.

He said in his sincerest tone, "It's OK. I'll come back here. First I have to get some stuff from my townhouse. I have an old friend staying there I need to talk to, OK?"

McQueen looked over at Gray. "Is this the old girlfriend variety of friend or something else?"

She immediately felt foolish for the question. What had made her ask it anyway? It was none of her business. Gray noted the crimson rising in her cheeks, and he smiled.

"I'm sorry; that is none of my business," she stammered, turning away.

He looked over at her and said, "I'm glad you asked. No, this is not an old girlfriend. I don't have one at the moment. This is an old boot camp friend who was visiting the capital. I told him he could use my place, since I don't seem to spend much time there nowadays.

He touched her arm, turning her back to him. "I'm glad you asked."

Gray headed for his car, still parked in the service lot from their little trek to Russia.

Georgetown is a historic place, located in northwest Washington, D.C., situated along the Potomac River, viewed more as a high-end shopping and dining area, rather than a crime area. Still, as Gray left McQueen's house, he was on high alert. Over many years, on dangerous assignments with the military, he had almost developed a sixth sense, and it had saved his bacon many times.

That sixth sense was sounding alarm bells now. His subconscious had seen something; he was worried but didn't show it. His normal relaxed manner was gone; in its place a soldier in civilian clothes.

He stopped on the curb, opened a bottle of water he had taken from the kitchen, and looked down the street as he took a swig. The residential areas of Georgetown were filled with quaint, historic buildings, making it easy to spot people, things or cars that were out of place. His eyes stopped as he checked out the street to the south; a new four-door, large, silver car sat at the next corner, four Suits inside, completely out of place.

He watched the car out of the corner of his eye, wondering why it was there.

Is it a rental? Can I see the plates; find out who they are? he asked himself.

He was sure it didn't belong, but this was crazy, could he be imagining it?

Gray turned around, deciding to go in the other direction, just in case. He walked to the corner, made as if to turn left... the silver car with the four Suits had moved to follow him; it was down the street at the next intersection. He crossed the street, and pulled his cell phone out to call McQueen.

"Ma'am, this is David. Do not leave your house; keep your security detail there."

Her deep concern showed in her voice. "David, what's up? You're scaring me."

While he was talking on his cell phone, his eyes were scanning the street. "Ma'am, I have possible enemy contact in the area. Stay put. I'll call you later."

If Gray thought his phone call would give McQueen any type of comfort, he was wrong. She was scared out of her wits. He pocketed the phone, reached inside his jacket, and pulled the breach back on his gun. He crossed the street, walking toward the silver car.

He was moving fast now. He approached the car, and one of the Suits looked over at him. Gray noticed that now there were only three Suits in car. The driver had, by now, also seen Gray approaching their position.

Gray was on ultra-high alert, ready for anything. As he got closer, he heard tires screech as the car swerved down an alley to avoid traffic and escape his approach. The alley was clear. They were able to speed down its expanse, turn a corner and disappear from view.

Gray pocketed his gun again, thinking to himself that their reaction to his pursuit confirmed that he was under surveillance. He retrieved his cell phone and hit re-dial.

As soon as the phone was answered he was speaking. "Ma'am, danger confirmed, keep security team inside. No one in or out, confirm?"

McQueen's voice still showed her anxiety. "Save us, Lord! David, what is happening here?" She pleaded with him, "Please be careful, David. I need you here."

His mind was already thinking about his next move. "I'll be back as soon as possible," he said absently.

CHAPTER THIRTY-SEVEN

Gray's townhouse was only a short distance from McQueen's but he took the long way around, constantly checking for pursuit. An hour later, he approached his home from the north instead of what a surveillance team would have expected – the south.

As he drove, he made the call to Secret Service. When his supervisor answered, Gray's report was short and sweet. "Sir, we've got a situation at the Secretary of State's home. She was under surveillance. Silver four-door, late model. Four occupants, all white males in gray suits, dark hair, pale complexions. One exited the vehicle before the vehicle left the area. I instructed the Secretary to stay inside with her detail. No one in or out."

"Where are you Gray?"

"Sir, the vehicle seemed interested in me. I am checking my residence. I had a friend staying with me. I need to know that he is unharmed."

"Understood, Agent Gray. I will send backup to your location as well as reinforcements to the Secretary's home. Keep me apprised."

Gray turned onto College Street to find a parking space still a good distance from his home. He wanted to be on foot, not make an easy target getting out of his car in front of his house. He found a suitable parking space, got out of the car and started the walk toward his house.

He considered waiting for the cavalry to arrive, but his worry for Bob wouldn't let him. He couldn't have a repeat of Fairbanks.

Gray put his gun inside his jacket, but held it in his hand, safety off and ready. No need to alarm some sweet little old lady walking her dog.

THE EYES OF ATHENA

That sixth sense was ringing alarm bells again, and he asked himself what his subconscious had seen. He stopped and looked around, trying to appear as normal as possible.

"What is it, Gray? Think."

He knew that something was wrong; the hairs on the back of his neck were bristling. His training kicked in again and he shifted into automatic mode, his movements mechanical. He still could not make his brain recognize what his eyes had seen. He squinted, as if focusing intently as he looked around would do the trick. He could almost feel his brain melting with the effort.

And then, like a bolt from the blue, there it was; his front door was not closed properly. Someone had forced the door, leaving the door jamb damaged, but closed. It wasn't obvious from the street, but it was there.

Gray took a second to walk down the street on the same side as his house, all the time trying to scan the houses and roofs across the street. He couldn't see anything suspicious so he turned around to walk back to his townhouse. He was still checking the roofs as surreptitiously as possible. As he approached his home, he cautiously sidled up the steps to the front door, trying to make himself as small a target as he could.

He peeked through the window by the door quickly. Nothing; he saw no movement. In one swift, sudden move, he crashed through the door, dove head first, hit the floor, and rolled to one side. He scrambled forward along the same side, scurrying like a sidewinder in order to be an impossible target.

His gun was drawn, and he was frantically looking for some sign of Bob. A pool of blood just feet inside the door set his heart racing.

A voice from the corner of the hallway made him jump. "Well, that sure was a heck of an entrance."

Bob leaned against the wall, concealed from all windows and doors, bleeding from a shoulder wound and looking very pale with oncoming shock.

Gray crawled over to his friend. "Good to see you alive and well, Bob."

"You think some foreign brawler in a cheap suit is gonna take me out?" But it was obvious Bob was fading.

Gray grabbed his cell phone and dialed the numbers for his supervisor again. In a city like D.C., the Secret Service was more likely to respond faster to his emergency than any ambulance. He grabbed his first aid kit from the hallway closet. An avid sportsman, his kit was heavily stocked for all sorts of traumatic injuries.

He situated Bob prone on the hallway floor as the first detail of reinforcements arrived to keep watch for any wayward Suits. Raising Bob's knees and covering him with a blanket to help ward of shock, he applied pressure to the shoulder wound and tried to keep him talking.

"Sorry about this, pal."

"No worries, Gray. I've seen worse."

"Can you tell me what happened?"

"I was making a pot of chili in the kitchen when I heard the front door go. Sad to say I was not expecting your home to be invaded, so I was not properly armed."

"I would think that awful chili you make would be weapon enough," Gray said with a laugh.

Bob scowled at him. "Kick a man when he's down why don't you. Anyway... Big, ugly guy comes stomping through the hall. I clobbered him with the cast iron frying pan. Dang sure I broke his nose. But he got a round off as he backed out, and I happened to be right in the way of the bullet."

"So they left without knowing if they were successful in taking you out?"

"It's a good hit," Bob said. "They saw me go down."

Sirens sounded in the distance. "Think I'll rest just a bit, Gray. And don't go thinking you don't owe me for this one."

He closed his eyes as the paramedics came through the door.

Gray needed time to think. Of one thing he was sure; it took an incredible amount of organization to mount an operation to take out the Secretary of State's plane and then have a car full of assassins watching her house and another team watching his townhome.

There was one other thing that was bothering him – who could get access to all the information necessary to know that he was the agent in charge for the Secretary of State? They also planted a waiter in the Kremlin. This took the resources of a large organization. It was looking more and more like whoever was trying to kill them was top-level brass with government resources available to them.

"But why?" Gray paced his kitchen as Bob was loaded into the ambulance and he waited to brief his supervisor.

After telling the Secret Service hierarchy everything he knew about the incident – except the fact that he and McQueen weren't sure the MIGs were Russian or some other terrorist state or even home-grown – Gray was finally alone in his house. A detail guarded the exterior.

Because the Suits had left without knowing if they were successful in their hit, the decision had been made to stage Gray's death.

After the townhouse cleared, he gathered some things, and headed down to his garage to get Bob's car, got in and drove off.

The question on his mind now was would the Suits think they had killed Bob, and if so would they think he was Gray? What would be the reaction of his new enemy when they heard the police report that Gray's body had been found in his townhouse – surprise? He guessed he was going to find out soon enough. He decided that driving around his neighborhood was not a good idea; he needed to find a very public place to stop and think through his next steps. While he was sure his face would not be making the nightly news with any report of his untimely death, if it turned out the Suits new his was alive, he would just as soon be safe in the bosom of a large, protective crowd.

A little while later, he pulled into a truck stop off the highway, got out of the car and went inside the restaurant. He watched the parking area from the lobby for a while and didn't see anyone following him.

Gray found a back booth and sat with his back to a wall with a good view of the front of the restaurant. Above him, he had a clear line of sight to an overhead television tuned to a local channel. He ordered breakfast, since by now dawn had come and gone, and waited. He knew he needed help, and while the Secret Service guys were good, one name came to mind – the only person he could think of that he really trusted.

After he finished his meal, he saw the news station switch over to an urgent news flash. The camera showed a yellow ribbon cordoning off the outside of his home, emergency lights flashing from police cars and emergency vehicles. Two medical examiners were maneuvering a gurney with Bob's blanket-draped body on it down from his house and into an ambulance.

"I'm gonna owe him big time for this one," Gray said to himself, chuckling as he remembered the look on Bob's face when they had asked him to play dead for the cameras.

"What are you getting me into, Cowboy?" is all he had said with that stupid sideways grin he always had.

Gray got up and walked to the television to turn up the volume. He listened attentively to the announcement.

"We have a news flash from the D.C. Police Department. Secret Service Agent David Gray, a former Navy SEAL, was found shot to death in his home this morning in what authorities believe may have been a murder-for-hire. The unknown assailant left Mr. Gray to bleed to death of a serious shoulder wound. Police say the suspect entered by breaking through the front door. Officers are presently searching adjacent properties for any clues."

Gray sat down again. In no time, his cell phone began to vibrate. He looked at the caller ID and nodded in recognition. He walked over to the store area of the rest stop to look for a prepaid cell phone. Locating one, he walked up to the front, paid for it, then returned to his seat in the restaurant.

He took out his old cell phone, removed the battery and used the table knife to rip an electronic circuit away from the phone, totally disabling it. Then he picked up his new phone to dial McQueen.

She answered on the first ring.

"Ma'am, its Gray."

"David Gray, I thought you were dead! Did you see the news?"

"Yes, Ma'am I know. It was a ruse. They tried to kill my friend, Bob, the one I was telling you about, though I'm sure I was the target."

McQueen began to sob, emotionally ripped apart. "David, will you get over here?"

He felt deep concern for her. In fact, he was surprised at the depth of his concern. He knew she was safe and had planned to work the case from outside the agency now that he was a dead man, but he couldn't stand the fear in her voice.

"Yes, Ma'am, I will. When I'm close, I'll call you to tell you to let me in the back door. When you get that call, it might be a good idea to tell the Secret Service agents to stand down and take positions on the outside. It might be wise for everybody to think I'm dead for the time being while we work this out."

He disconnected the call, pocketed the phone, pulled out a twenty and walked over to the register to pay his bill. He left the restaurant and walked toward Bob's car, still scanning every movement around him, checking the shadows for anyone who might be watching him, hidden from view. He saw nothing.

Gray climbed into the car and started the engine then pulled out his new cell phone. He punched in Ari's number and waited, as soon as Ari answered, he jumped right in. "Ari, David. I need help, need someone I can trust. I've got a code red here in D.C."

"I was just thinking about you." The note of anxiety in Gray's voice surprised him Ari. "I heard the report that you were dead, had, in fact, been murdered," he said.

"A rumor of convenience, friend. I'll explain everything."

"So I surmised after a quick call. I look forward to the explanation. Where shall I meet you?"

Gray gave him the Secretary's address and instructions on what to tell the detail when he arrived.

"There's a suspicious Suit in the neighborhood around the Secretary's personal residence, not one of ours. I lost track of him. Can you come in the back way, find him and ID him?"

"Be my pleasure. Shalom"

Gray resumed driving toward Georgetown, still scanning the traffic around him, alert for any tails. Knowing that Ari was on his way to McQueen's home gave him an instant sense of peace.

As Gray got closer to McQueen's townhouse, he pulled out his cell phone and dialed her number. When she answered, he said, "five minutes," then hung up.

At the appointed time, McQueen separated the shutters on her front window, cautiously peering out until she saw Gray then rushed to the back to quietly open the door.

"Did the Secret Service leave?" he asked as he entered.

She was so relieved to see him, her impulse was to jump into his arms to hug him, hold him. She wanted the kind of hug that her Daddy used to give her, for him to tell her not to worry and that everything would be OK.

Instead, she responded calmly, "A few minutes ago."

They both walked into the parlor. "In a few minutes, we are going to have another visitor," Gray warned her.

Instantly alarmed, her voice betraying her concern, she asked, "Who?"

He turned and flashed a calming smile, "Relax, Jade. It's Ari."

He had never used her first name before. Neither felt it inappropriate in that moment, and she was reassured and calmed.

As she sat on the sofa, McQueen asked how he knew Ari.

"He saved my life on an overseas mission, a jump behind enemy lines that went bad. The whole team was blown out of the sky. I survived because of Ari."

"That's when you left the military?"

Absently, Gray answered, he was still on full alert, his attention mostly elsewhere. "Yes. My leg was torn apart in the gunfire. I was no good for the kind of military missions I preferred, so I retired and took an offer from the Secret Service."

"And now you're here."

He looked at her then, warmly. "And now I'm here."

CHAPTER THIRTY-EIGHT

Athena OPs Center

Ari practically barged into Burke's office. Burke was, as usual, buried in work. "Up to my alligators in elbows, Ari," he said, smiling at his own humor. "What's up?"

"Just got a Code Red call from Gray."

Burke's good humor faded. "Fill me in."

They walked out of his office into the Situation Room as Ari told him Gray's story. Immediately, the staff was on full alert, knowing their boss and recognizing from his stride and demeanor that this was not a time to screw around.

"Pull up satellite recon of the neighborhood around SecState's house, looking for somebody out of place," Burke commanded.

A big screen opened up on the wall in front of a team of computer operators. The screen showed a satellite view of Georgetown, and as coordinates were inputted into the computer, the view narrowed down to a residential district, the clarity amazing. The eye in the sky was viewing, scanning the neighborhood.

Moments later, "Got him, Sir."

Burke looked over at Ari. "How do you want to handle it?"

Ari gave it a few moments of thought then said, "I'll make the approach. Can you get transport to the safe house ready?"

"You got it." Burke replied. Intuitively, they knew what needed to be done and Burke knew what Ari was planning.

Then an idea occurred to Burke, and with a thoughtful expression he turned to his counterpart. "Ari, have you heard anything from your old Mossad contacts recently? Especially about a 'New World Order" or conspiracy?"

"Might be a good idea to talk to my old station chief in Tel Aviv," Ari replied.

From his tone, Burke knew that something was going on but that Ari wouldn't betray a confidence.

"Why?" he asked. "Connect the dots for me, Ari."

"No can do, Sir. That will have to come directly from Ben Rosenberg."

Burke was overjoyed. Had he been alone, he might have hollered, "Come to Daddy!" or some such other expression of delight. Ari had just confirmed that Mossad knew something was going on. He made a mental note to talk to Rosenberg as soon as possible.

McQueen's Georgetown Neighborhood

A parking attendant was walking down the street in front of the Secretary of State's home in Georgetown, stopping at every car and checking meters to see if the time had expired. The attendant walked up to a silver car with the Suit inside. The meter person checked the meter, walked the few feet over to the car window and knocked.

The Suit inside lowered the window. "Can I help you? I filled the meter." He had a heavy foreign accent.

The parking attendant replied, "The parking meter is fine, Sir, but you are taking up more than one parking place." As he said this, he was pointing down at the curb.

The Suit opened the door to look down at the curb, and Ari stepped to the side so the door would open freely. As the Suit leaned over to see, Ari's hand touched the Suit's shoulder, and the man's reaction was to jump in surprise, but before he could do anything else, the syringe full of ketamine took effect and the Suit slumped over.

Ari was all efficiency now as he pushed the man back into the car. He turned his hand over to push the syringe back into the ring, then pulled out his cell phone and dialed the Athena number programmed into its memory.

As the call was answered, he said simply, "Bring the ambulance up."

Seconds later, an ambulance screeched up alongside the car, and two paramedics ran to the back, pulled out a gurney and loaded up the Suit. Ari retrieved his raincoat from the ambulance and pulled it on over his uniform. He removed his hat, threw it in the ambulance and walked toward the home of the Secretary of State.

Gray was waiting. He opened the back door for Ari and they embraced, then walked over to the kitchen table and sat down. McQueen joined them.

Without any preamble, Gray launched into the story, "Ari, at the moment, it looks like someone is trying to take out the Secretary of State."

Before they could get into any details, both Ari and McQueen reached for their ringing phones. At the same moment, neighborhood emergency sirens started sounding. Something's hitting the fan, Gray thought.

Ari answered his phone to hear, "Ari, this is Athena OPs. This is an evac order; we have two drones moving into D.C. airspace. Military says they are not ours."

He asked no questions and immediately disconnected, looking toward McQueen as Gray watched her.

McQueen answered her call. "Ma'am, this is Secret Service dispatch, we are sending a team over for an emergency evacuation."

"What in heaven's name is going on?" she asked.

"Ma'am, all cabinet officers are being evacuated. D.C. is under attack. We have two unidentified drones over D.C. This is not a drill, Ma'am."

Gray was the only one without a phone alerting him to some danger. "What the heck is going on?" he asked anxiously.

"It looks like we are under attack," Ari responded.

"Ari, you go with her..." Gray said, but his face showed confusion; something didn't add up. "Why didn't they shoot the drones down?"

"They can't. Not until they know what the payload is." Ari turned to his friend. "I think you'd best come with us, David." He looked to McQueen and back to Gray. "We need to fill you in on some of the puzzle pieces you're missing."

CHAPTER THIRTY-NINE

"We?" Gray was genuinely confused now. He was riding in the back of McQueen's suburban headed toward Bethesda, and he still didn't know why.

"Since when are you and Jade a 'we'?" he asked Ari, both noting a hint of jealousy in the question that he hadn't meant to put there.

"Since we both work for the same organization," Ari said ignoring the tone.

Gray sat looking from one to the other uncomprehending. "You work for the State Department? I thought you were CIA?"

"I am more than just the Secretary of State," McQueen tried to explain. She looked at Ari. "Maybe we should just wait. This will all make more sense at Athena."

"Athena? More than Secretary of State? I think somebody better start from the beginning and better start now."

McQueen took a deep breath. "Alright, David, the beginning was more than 200 years ago..."

Gray's head rotated slowly toward her, his mouth hung agape. "You have got to be kidding me."

He turned back to Ari, who said, "Trust me, brother. The explanation will make more sense in about twenty minutes."

They rode in silence then until they reached the nondescript gates of the Athena OPs Center. They parked and entered the secure lobby area. Gray was slightly taken aback when McQueen raised her forearm to the key access scanner and was buzzed in.

No mild-mannered receptionist greeted them. Today, she stood in full military gear, a fully-automatic rifle in her hands, guarding the doorway to the bunker, which housed a second, fully-functional Situation Room.

"Ma'am. We've been expecting you. Agent Cohen." She turned her gaze on Gray and waited, for what he had no clue.

"He is with me," McQueen stated simply. The woman stepped aside so that McQueen could again swipe her forearm across a panel to gain access to the stairwell.

"Handy," Gray said, still totally befuddled by everything around him.

Gray followed the pair down a well-lit set of stairs to a second scanner-access door and into a bustling room full of computer equipment and personnel.

"Hello, Tom." Gone was the frightened woman Gray had known in McQueen's kitchen. She was all business now. "Ari and I will need a few minutes alone with Mr. Gray to make some things clear."

Burke looked questioningly at McQueen, but didn't say a word. He simply pointed her toward a quiet room off to the side.

The three took a seat, but Gray's attention was on the room outside. "What is this place? CIA? FBI?"

"This organization is outside the parameters of the U.S. government," McQueen said.

That got his attention. A lifelong military man now proudly part of the Secret Service, Gray was all about God and country. If he was about to hear how he was falling for a woman who was part of some secret conspiracy against his nation, well, this had already been a really bad day.

"Relax," Ari said, sensing his rising distrust. "We're not here to overthrow your government; we're here to protect it."

"As I said, the beginning goes back more than 200 years to the nation's founding fathers," McQueen was looking him dead in the eyes now, keeping his focus and willing him to believe what might be an unbelievable tale.

"The 13 original colonies created the Eyes of Athena to keep watch over America from outside the realm of the formal government – to safeguard the founding principles of this nation from all threats, foreign or domestic.

"Those 13 original representatives recruited their own replacements, and for the most part, each has recruited his own replacement down the line over two centuries. Until the last Eye from New York State up and died suddenly without passing the torch. In absence of a replacement, the decision was made by the entire group to add some new blood – make some real changes – and you're looking at her."

Gray looked incredulous. "I see. And you?"

"I was recruited as an agent after the incident in Bosnia," Ari explained. "I told you I was being loaned out by Mossad. When you assumed CIA, I let you believe that because I had not been cleared to tell you anything else."

"Wow. You've managed to keep that cover for 10 years. Impressive." Gray wasn't sure if he had a right to be hurt, but he was. He understood the need for their secrecy, and looking at the Situation Room outside, this was an organization that took secrecy very seriously if no one had found out about it in 200 years.

"And you're telling me now because ..."

"Because we couldn't very well leave you in my townhouse while we hid out here from the drones and we couldn't very well bring you here without letting you in on what you're seeing," McQueen said.

'Besides, I think it's time you got the full scoop on this whole affair. You'll be a much more effective resource for solving it."

Burke knocked on the open door then. "Madam Secretary, we've got news on the drones."

McQueen led the three of them back into the Situation Room.

"Give us the report, son."

An analyst who didn't look much older than Gray's well-worn boots began to read from the screen in front of him. "We've tracked the drones from satellite images of their entrance into D.C. airspace. The reason they haven't targeted anyone or anything is because they can't, Sir. They carry no payload."

"You're 100% sure of that, son?'

"Sir, I'd bet my life on it. These are dummies sent to distract military intelligence."

"You better be right, son, because you're betting more than your life here." Burke turned to McQueen. "I suppose it's up to you, Madam Secretary, to make that call."

THE EYES OF ATHENA

"Open a secure line, please, Tom. I'd like to speak to the White House bunker. Get me the President."

CHAPTER FORTY

Athena OPs Center, Bethesda, Maryland
December 20, 2010

Burke sat in the Situation Room at Athena OPs going over Intel. With the President alerted to a possible foreign operation in play even before the drones attack, it had taken quite some doing to get things under control, convince him of the true nature of the drones get them disposed of and get the nation's military might refocused.

Now no one was sure what they had missed in the meantime. While every covert government agency in America scrambled, Athena analysts were pouring through data trying to figure out the answer to why someone had wanted to distract everyone in the first place.

In the meantime, there were other fish to fry.

"Ari, how are you going to handle the Suit? He hasn't said a word since we locked him up."

"He's only been in our safe house for a couple of days – not enough time to crack a pro. Seems like a real tough guy; no body markings, finger tips burned off with acid," Ari added thoughtfully. "It will take more time. We'll see what he is made of."

Ari paused a moment. Something had been niggling at him since they took the man into custody. Burke saw the questioning behind his eyes. "What is it? Something about this isn't sitting right with you?"

"You remember the Moscow shootings about six years ago? The bankers in the restaurant?"

"Russian mafia, sure."

"Azerbaijani Bratva," Ari corrected him. "The accent when he spoke to me in the car, facial features, suits, all of it …"

The light went on in Burke's eyes then as they both grasped the connection Ari's mind had finally made. "You think this guy is part of that crew?"

"He sure looks like it. It fits, Tom. My gut is screaming at me."

"But what does the ...er... Bratva have to do with our Iranian plot in Baku?"

"That's what the Suit is going to tell us."

~

The safe house was an old Victorian home with a concrete ground floor. Ari had left the Suit in a room with only a creaky, old, metal-framed bed and a bucket. A single low-wattage bulb hung from the ceiling.

Two guards approached the cell door. One held it open while the other emptied the contents of a bucket at the prisoner.

"Here, catch!" The first guard shouted loudly. Inside the bucket were two copperhead snakes that landed on the floor in a loud, angry heap.

The guards closed the door, listening for any reaction. When they didn't hear anything, the first guard put his ear to the door, expecting some noise. He turned to his mate, "I don't hear much commotion in there. In fact, I don't hear a blessed thing. It ain't natural to not react when someone throws a couple of snakes in your cell."

They opened the tiny hinged door within the door to take a peek. Nothing; no sound, no movement. The guard looking through the door slit turned to his mate. "He's on the bed, not moving. He better not be dead or Cohen will kill us."

The second guard who still hadn't looked into the cell asked, "Where are the snakes?"

"I don't see them," his cohort said mystified, adding, "We'd better go in."

He moved back from the door to retrieve a key from his belt. Unlocking the door, they opened it slowly, and the first guard entered. He hesitated a moment in the doorway. The Suit on the bed looked disheveled. The guard looked back at his mate almost questioningly, and they nodded to one another, deciding to enter. Both crossed the threshold gently, closing the door behind them, and a furious chaos was unleashed.

In one swift movement, the Suit rose up on the bed and threw the snakes he was holding by the heads at each guard. Copperheads normally don't want much to do with humans. In fact, they would much rather scurry in the opposite direction. But having been hunted up outside the D.C. area, carted around in a bucket for a day and a half and then thrown unceremoniously at the ugly galoot in the cell, these two were not particularly happy.

Now, snakes that much preferred slithering in the undergrowth were once again airborne and headed for humans. Terrified, the guards were stunned as one snake landed on the shoulder of one guard and one at the feet of the other. Standing one behind the other, the second guard fumbled for his pistol, but he was in such a panic that he couldn't get his weapon free from its holster.

Unfortunately for both of them, his mate in front of him, horrified by the snake around his neck – who, to be honest, was just as terrified by him – slipped into full retreat, backtracking into the fumbling guard and knocking him off balance, which only further hindered the guard from getting his pistol out of his holster.

The Suit was all action now. He jumped up, turning from the bed, and landed on the floor. All his weight moved in a single flowing motion toward the guards – a low circular kick that took out the retreating guard in front, who fell, still with the snake around his neck, struggling to either get away or get in striking position. A second kick wiped out the guard behind him, still trying to get his gun out.

The Suit swiveled to the closest guard, pummeled three bone-jarring punches to his jaw and the guard was out cold. Not satisfied, the Suit delivered a quick twist to the neck, snapping it. Meanwhile, the snakes, more scared than the guards, tried to slither away to the side of the cell frantically seeking shelter from the crazy humans they had encountered.

The guard behind recovered his wits and tried to sit up, only to find himself in the high-beams of the Suit's attention. He let off two vicious jabs to the guard's chin, sending him down again then slammed his head onto the metal bed frame on his way to the floor. Blood sprayed out from back of the guard's head. The Suit reached down and secured the guard's head, one hand under chin, the other behind his neck, with a sudden, violent twist, his neck snapped.

Both guards were dead; silent. The Suit searched each body, looking for anything of use to him. He removed their pistols and cell phones. He double-checked the cell then simply walked out.

Once out the door, he was cautious, listening for danger, the sound of more guards, anything, but all was clear. He turned back to the cell door and locked it, the poor snakes entombed at least temporarily with the dead guards, then moved to the stairs.

The Suit walked up the stairs toward the kitchen. The staircase was hidden from the view of the guard above. He emerged into the kitchen gun in hand to find the third guard still reading his newspaper, unaware of the commotion downstairs although he heard the footsteps coming up. The guard was paying no attention to the staircase and, without turning around, asked, "Well did he talk?"

"No, I did not," The Suit's thick accent startled the guard who was only half listening.

The guard looked around in total panic to see the Suit walking toward him. He tried to recover his wits, reaching for his pistol, but it was too late.

The Suit, pointing a gun at the guard, said, "No. I would not even think of it." He walked over and instructed the man, "Give me your car keys."

The terrified guard picked up his keys from a shelf on the wall and handed them to the Suit. As the guard pulled his hand back, the Suit cold cocked him with the butt of the gun. The Suit, with amazing speed, caught the guard's head on the way to the floor and, with a vicious twist, snapped his neck as well. The Suit let the body fall to the floor. He looked over the kitchen, alert for any further danger or anything that might be of use to him, then walked out after wiping the blood from his hands on a kitchen towel.

He reached the curb and paused to scan the neighborhood for danger, checking out the buildings across the street from him and looking up and down the street. His eyes totally alert, he pulled out the guard's cell phone, dialed a local number and listened as the call made the noises of being forwarded.

Soon, a voice answered in Turkish. "You have failed."

"We took out the Secret Service Agent, but could not have known the Iranian would unleash his ridiculous drones on the city."

"Are you giving me excuses for your failure? You were captured."

"They learned nothing. I left a trail of death and silence behind me."

The voice was unimpressed. "Regroup. We will come back to the little American princess. Go after Ahmed in Paris then Stanislau. I will have your team meet you. Do not fail me."

The line went dead.

CHAPTER FORTY-ONE

Paris, France
January 10, 2011

Burke looked out his first class cabin window on his flight to Paris' Charles de Gaulle Airport. Beneath the plane, he could see the mammoth expanse of land dedicated to France's largest airport – nearly 8,000 acres, if he remembered correctly. He could see in the middle of this vast area the central building that had the famed skylight in its center. He remembered spending a few weeks there on the upper floor trying to track some foreign terrorists with the "Surete" – the French version of police special operations.

Burke felt the gentle bump as his plane landed and settled back to wait for the all clear to disembark. As he didn't have any checked baggage, so he was one of the first people in line to get a taxi for the trip to the center of Paris to meet his counterpart from the Mossad. The trip from Charles De Gaulle Airport always took way too long in his opinion; it was only about 25 kilometers, but the traffic in Paris was awful, as it always seemed to be.

He was always amazed that there were so many cars on the road in France when gasoline equated to nearly $10 per gallon here. (Euros didn't make any sense to him.) The taxi headed for his hotel and drove past the Tomb of the Unknown Soldier, down the Champs Élysées to Avenue George V. The taxi made a sharp turn and pulled into the hotel. He paid the driver 175 euros. *Dadgum*, he thought, *that's more than $200.* He couldn't understand how the French survived financially; these prices were astronomical.

Burke entered the ornate marble foyer heading for the check-in counter. This hotel also had many fond memories for him of happier days with the one love of his life. His beloved was taken from him so unexpectedly, but they had spent their honeymoon here. *So many memories,* he thought, *he really shouldn't come back.* Her not being with him anymore made the memories almost too painful, but he couldn't resist being here if he were in Paris; it would almost feel like betrayal if he didn't come back to visit the place of his fondest moments.

The tapestries that adorned the walls were the same, and fresh flowers filled the lobby. *There was something timeless about the George V, as with most of Europe,* he thought, *things don't change that much.* He left his carry-on bag with the concierge and walked out of the hotel.

It was time to stop reminiscing. When on a mission, that type of sentimentality could get you killed. Burke focused to control his thoughts. He put on his "mission" face; it was time to work, he thought. He started his walk toward the metro station, but before leaving the hotel entrance, he tried to scan the street outside to see if there was any danger. Paris was as it always was – busy, noisy, full of activity, honking horns and smells – making detection of unwanted attention difficult.

He turned to the right on Avenue George V to walk toward the metro, passing many people, none paying him too much attention. He looked at his watch and noted he had 35 minutes to get to his appointment at the Gare du Nord. He picked up his pace. Walking past Fouquet's restaurant on his way to the metro, he looked longingly at the fresh bread and pastries in the window. As he passed, he inhaled the Parisian aroma – a mixture of coffee, pastries, fresh bread and Gauloise – always the Gauloise, the French would never give up the almost Arabic smell of their cigarettes. He even noticed the cigarette smoke lazily wafting out of another corner cafe.

Burke quickly reached the metro, entered the station and walked down to Metro Line 1 to wait for his ride. He stood with his back to the wall, as no self-respecting operative would wait for the train close to the edge; it was way too easy for an assassin to gently prod you to lose your balance as the train approached. He had read many times of people being killed that way.

After a few minutes, he felt the "whoosh" of air being pushed in front of the oncoming train. Passengers began to edge forward, except Burke; he always waited until the last few seconds to board. At the last moment, he pushed his way into the waiting train for the short ride to the Gare Du Nord.

At Strasbourg St. Denis, Burke changed trains to get onto the line for the Gare du Nord, still being very careful and watching his trail. He got off the metro at his stop and decided to follow protocol, knowing that Rosenberg would be watching him as he approached their rendezvous. He kept walking up the escalators as he arrived; it was much easier to spot a tail if the tail also had to push past other stationary travelers.

He spotted no danger, but as a precaution, as he reached the main concourse of the train station, he decided to walk a parallel course in front of the restaurant where they would meet, the Chez Clement. Burke spotted Rosenberg without actually looking at him, seated with his face toward the main concourse, watching.

Burke moved swiftly, designing his speed and his route to expose a tail. He arrived in front of the restaurant where Rosenberg was sitting over in the corner nursing a cafe au lait. Rosenberg nodded imperceptibly to him, indicating that it was safe to approach, that he did not detect any tails.

"Hi, Ben," Burke said.

"Good to see you, too, Tom. Would you mind telling me what all the panic is about?"

Burke could tell when he was being played. "Let's cut the crap, Ben. I need to know what is keeping Mossad operatives up at night."

Rosenberg was playing the innocent patsy now. "Like what?"

Burke was getting annoyed with this charade and decided to dive in. "Two MIGs try to shoot down our Secretary of State in Russian air space after a meeting in Moscow with the President of Russia. How's that for starters?"

He watched Rosenberg for any reaction. None. Burke thought to himself, *its danged tough questioning another professional, particularly one as good as Ben Rosenberg; they don't give much away.*

He decided to try again. "We intercept a U.N. communication going to the Russian Secret Police talking about a 'New World Order.'"

Again no reaction. Burke continued, "A terrorist member of Iran's delegation is in New York for a U.N. meeting. He leaves town before his scheduled meeting at the same time we intercept this message."

Burke was getting angry. This was turning into a one-way conversation, a monologue. "Ditto a reputed member of Hamas, who is a member of the Palestinian delegation to the U.N. – chooses to enter the U.S. on forged papers then turns right around to leave after this meeting. Both are on the IWL."

This finally cracked the concrete veneer that Rosenberg had assumed, and Burke decided to pursue this line of questioning. "Does that smell funny to you, Ben?"

He waited for a response. Finally, Rosenberg decided to speak. "Tom, you know that new natural gas field discovered off the coast of Gaza?"

"Yes, of course."

"We intercepted chatter that Iran intends to attack our off-shore oil rigs and install medium range missiles capable of delivering 'dirty' bombs to Tel-Aviv."

Burke looked amazed. "I find that difficult to believe. That would be an act of war; the Mullahs know what you would do if provoked. Tehran would cease to exist. How are they going to do that?"

"We don't know yet. Terrorist chatter is alive with talk about the 'Arrows of Islam.' Have you heard about that?"

"That's a new one on me," Burke replied. "What in sam hill is that?"

"We don't know; all we have is chatter and the date, January 24th, the date of the Prophet Mohamed's birthday."

Burke was getting frustrated. "Dang it, I come here for answers and just get more problems."

Rosenberg decided to hand Burke some information. "By the way, I hear you had some scary stuff in D.C. with drones in restricted airspace?"

"Yeah, we're looking into that, too. Looks like a truck making a delivery to the Air Force was high jacked."

This time, Burke could see the look of surprise on Rosenberg's face. "Check your information again, Tom." After a pause, he said, "You do know Iran has the capability to build operational drones don't you?"

"What... In D.C.? You got to be kidding." It was Burke's turn to be surprised; he didn't know what to say.

"Check it out for yourself," Rosenberg replied. Then he added another thunderbolt. "And by the way, that second operative, Ahmed, member of Hamas you mentioned..." Burke looked up; Rosenberg had his undivided attention now. "He's one of ours, hands off. For your ears only, OK?"

Burke looked around at Rosenberg, and nodded. "Why didn't you tell me earlier?" He was offended.

"You want me to trust the same people that sell F 16 Fighter Jets to the Muslim Brotherhood?" Rosenberg asked, adding, "Sometimes I wonder which side you guys are on...."

"Not my gig," Burke said, but he understood Rosenberg's position, sometimes he didn't know either. He got up, turning to walk away, almost sulkily, then he added, "Thanks, Ben. Let's keep in touch."

Ahmed's Apartment in Paris

The Suit stood across the street, waiting in the dark. He saw Ahmed arrive in a taxi escorted by a slinky female. He watched and waited. He saw the date get out of the cab, turn to hug Ahmed and say a little loudly, "That was so much fun; I've never been to the Crazy Horse Saloon before."

Ahmed and his date walked over to his building, where he pressed a button on the electronic entry pad, then keyed in some code, and the double doors swung open for them to enter. The elevator took them up to his apartment. As Ahmed opened the door, he gave her a slow kiss, and as they kissed, walking into the apartment, he untangled himself long enough to say to her, "Go to the bedroom and wait for me."

She turned and walked into the bedroom. Ahmed continued down the hallway to the main room, walked through and went into the kitchen. He took off his jacket and hung it close to the window. As he did so, he heard a faint "beep" from his computer.

He walked over to his desk, sat down at his computer, and went through his security protocol. He thought to himself that these people in the Mossad headquarters need to get a life, asking me for an update at this time of night. He went into the kitchen to make himself some strong coffee, then returned to type his report.

The Suit outside watched the lights go on in Ahmed's apartment. He was all business now. Undetected by anyone, he stealthily crossed the street, fiddled with the security system, and entered the apartment building.

He paused inside the entrance to see if anyone noticed him enter. He heard a door opening and he pulled out his silenced Glock, waiting until the door was open enough for him to see inside. A nosy neighbor stood in her doorway; the Suit aimed his silenced pistol, let loose one shot to her forehead, and watched as she fell back in to her apartment. He followed, pushing her dead body back inside.

The Suit looked past her into the room, seeing what he assumed was her husband, snoring contentedly in his armchair. He leveled the Glock again, aimed and fired one shot into the husband's head; he would never wake up again. After a quick search of the apartment to make sure no one else was inside to set off an alarm, he headed back to the front door. He looked cautiously into the hallway, and seeing no one, he exited, closed the door and climbed the stairs.

The Suit ascended the stairs effortlessly, reaching Ahmed's apartment, three flights up, without even raising a sweat. He paused outside Ahmed's door, pulled a lock picking kit from his inside jacket pocket, examined the lock, and chose a pick. Quickly, he jimmied the lock, entered the apartment silently, and closed the door with his back to it. He heard noises close to him coming from someone in the bedroom. He opened the door just enough to see inside and pointed the silenced gun through the crack. The Suit saw Ahmed's date getting undressed. One shot to the back of her pretty head, and she fell to the floor dead.

He retreated noiselessly from the bedroom, walking down the hall, and saw Ahmed typing at his computer. The Suit had been told Ahmed was Hamas and well-trained; he would not be an easy target.

Unknown to the suit, one of the reasons Ahmed had his computer on this desk was so that he could see a reflection of what was behind him in the window. From the corner of his eye, Ahmed saw the Suit walking toward him with pistol and silencer raised, not quite aimed at him but close.

Ahmed braced for a quick evasive move to get some cover when suddenly and surprisingly, the noise of a very loud Parisian police siren not only broke the silence but startled the Suit, who looked up. Ahmed made a dive to his left to get behind the sofa. As he moved, he saw the Suit's surprised face in his reflection in the window. The Suit fired off one shot, missing Ahmed's head, but hitting his shoulder. Ahmed pulled his gun and waited absolutely still behind the sofa, silent, daring not even to breathe.

The Suit was also silent as he recovered his wits. He waited a few more seconds, thinking his target must be incapacitated and gaining confidence. He walked forward, peeked around the sofa, and, to his great surprise, looked into the barrel of Ahmed's gun leveled at him. Ahmed fired two rounds, and the Suit dropped his gun, one hit in the shoulder, the other in his chest – fatal. He was dying; Ahmed rose and recovered the Suit's gun. He put his heel on the Suit's wounded shoulder.

"Who are you?"

The Suit kept silent, but Ahmed put more pressure on his wound. The Suit groaned loudly and painfully now, as Ahmed increased the weight of his foot on the man's destroyed shoulder.

"Why?" demanded Ahmed.

The Suit struggled with his pain. Ahmed glared down at him. "Why?" he demanded again, but the Suit's eyes glazed over and his jaw went slack.

Ahmed shoved the corpse away with the foot that had been standing on him. Angrily he stormed into the bedroom to assess the situation he knew he would find there. As he returned to the living room, he was dialing his superiors. He would need a clean-up crew and an evacuation plan. It was time to pull him from this OP.

On the street below, two other Turks in dark gray suits waited for some sign from their group leader. When they saw a car pull up and Ahmed climb in, small suitcase in hand, they simply climbed back into their own vehicle and sped away, making a report of their failure as they went. It was lucky for Demir that the target had disposed of him before he was forced to face the Pakhan.

CHAPTER FORTY-TWO

Athena OPs Center, Bethesda, Maryland
January 12, 2011

Ari was back in the board room of the Athena OPs Center in Bethesda with Tom Burke. "I just got off the phone with Ben Rosenberg in Paris; he thinks you are responsible for the attempt on Ahmed's life."

"Me!" Burke exclaimed. "I hardly had time to get on a plane, let alone leak the information."

Their faces betrayed their concern. "Just what is 'The Arrows of Islam'?" Burke asked.

"I don't know."

"So just what do we know?" he said as much to himself as Ari. "Mahmoud and Andropov have some kind of connection over the Stealth crash in Bosnia in '99. Mahmoud has been working some secret plan – most likely weapon-based technology centering around that stolen Stealth – in Baku, Azerbaijan, for more than a decade, but we can't get more than a whisper of exactly what he's doing or what he has in mind.

"Ten years go by quietly with little contact between Mahmoud and Andropov," Ari chimed in. "Then a clandestine call on a secure line from MOIS to GRU is followed by this meeting of strange bedfellows at the U.N."

"I don't suppose your good friend Ben Rosenberg shared anything new that he learned from debriefing his plant, Ahmed?"

"Not with him thinking you nearly got his agent killed," Ari said. "But we do know part of the plan involved Ahmed planting dirty bombs to destroy oil fields in the Gaza strip. Of course now that Ahmed has gone missing from Stanislau's little merry band..."

Burke simply nodded. "Things are gearing up, Ari. I need you to take the next plane to Baku. Find out exactly what that monster is up to so we can figure out how to stop him."

Baku, Azerbaijan
January 16, 2011

Ari walked out of the terminal at the Baku Azerbaijan International airport looking very tired. The flight from New York to London was an eight-hour haul; the flight to Baku, another five-plus hours. That, plus layovers, meant his internal clock was all screwed up. He looked around for a taxi. London-style purple taxis were everywhere. The line was short, so he was able to get a ride pretty quickly. He settled into the back of the cab grateful to be off his feet. "Jumeirah Beach Hotel, please."

The taxi ride took him through a surprisingly modern city; he even spotted an Apple retail outlet. After a 30-minute trip, he arrived at his hotel. He checked in, dropped off his stuff in his hotel room, and sat in the hotel lobby impatiently awaiting the arrival of his contact. His eyes constantly moved toward the entrance, betraying his anxiousness. He spotted his contact, Michael Cahil, entering the lobby and got up to meet him.

Cahil was a low-level civilian clerk with no field experience, but was the best contact Athena could come up with on such short notice. Ari was clearly tired and also irritated, barking at his contact in a manner most unlike him, "You're late; let's move."

Cahil seemed unflustered, and Ari decided this must be one of those cultures where punctuality is not a concern. The young agent shook Ari's hand and said, "Good to meet you. I trust you had no issues with your flight?"

"What have you learned, Cahil?"

"Mahmoud is at the Airport Sheraton. His only contact has been with his assistant, Karim Khan, who we have discovered owns a house in Zabrat. I checked the house out. No one lives there but an old man. OPs is trying to ID the old man now."

"Take me to the house." On the way, Ari was quiet, trying to figure out the puzzle of the old man. They arrived at 7:30 A.M. and Ari told Cahil, "Park at the end of the block so we can see the entrance."

Five minutes later, a car drove up – an older, large Mercedes. An old man had obviously been waiting for the car, and as soon as it pulled up, he came out wearing an overcoat and a fedora and carrying a briefcase. The driver got out of the car and went into the house to bring out an old leather suit case. He put it in the trunk, walked around the car and got in behind the steering wheel.

Ari tried to focus the long-lensed camera on the old man. He wanted to get some good photos for identification purposes. The car left the old man's residence, turning into the road where Ari and Cahil were waiting. As he passed them, Ari asked Cahil, "Have you had any experience tailing a car?"

"Just in training, Sir."

"Of course." Ari cursed his luck under his breath, wishing he had a more experienced agent with him.

"Follow them; stay about 100 yards back and keep a car between if possible."

They followed the car with the old man into Zabrat, where the car continued on its way, turning into the Azerbaijan Ball Bearing Plant on Suth Street in a very industrialized area of the city. Ari tried to get a handle on this new location. The plant covered nearly four blocks with chimneys extending skyward bellowing dirty smoke. Workers crowded the entry ways, clocking in for their shifts. Loud noises abounded so that it was difficult to hear. There were noises coming from the factory, noises of the forklifts loading and unloading trucks, noises from every angle.

"This place is huge," Ari said.

He looked across the street from the factory, noticing a little cafe that was no doubt frequented by the factory workers. "Cahil, walk over to that small cafe and ask some of the workers about the factory. See what you can find out."

Cahil nodded his head, got out of the car and walked over to the cafe. Through the glass window, Ari could see him talking to some workers. He was obviously jovial and instantly well-liked and stayed in there for a good twenty minutes, after which he returned to the car.

He opened the driver's door and got in, letting in a fresh wave of factory smells, diesel and sweat with him. "They all were eager to talk," he reported. "Good money they say.

They don't know who owns the company, but it runs three shifts a day, 24/7."

"Do they know who the old guy is?" Ari asked.

"They say he is an old German named Gosslau who has been working there for ten years or so."

Gosslau, Ari thought. Heinrich's last name. Ari did not believe in coincidences. The old man must be Hermann Gosslau, the jet propulsion expert. He had had the political influence to get his son into Russian military school from the bowels of Buenos Aires and now was deep in the anonymity of Baku, Azerbaijan, working for the Iranian, Mahmoud. That in itself set off all kinds of red flags.

"They don't know much more about the old man," Cahil was saying when Ari refocused. "They say he works in an area that is off-limits to workers."

That feeling in Ari's gut was really twisting now; he was on full alert for any clue. "What else?"

"One curious worker tried to look into that area," Cahil said, "you know, that area where the old man worked? He turned up dead the next day.

"They all said they were afraid to go anywhere close to that area ever since. Most workers have taken wide detours around that part of the factory since that happened. Besides, they said they now have some kind of foreign military patrolling the area, and they are extremely mean. One man said he thought the guards were Iranian."

Bingo, Ari thought to himself.

They were both quiet for quite some time. Then they saw the old man get into the same car and take off again. "Follow that car, Cahil, but be really careful; they mustn't learn that we are following them."

Cahil slipped the transmission into drive and edged into traffic to follow the car. It was still relatively early, so they had to drive through thick rush-hour traffic to Zabrat airport. The car they were following entered the area that was for freight and cargo.

The old man's car passed through a security gate and continued on to stop in front of two Ilyushin Il-76 cargo planes that were being loaded with crates from the Azerbaijan Ball Bearing Plant, according to the company name stenciled on the side.

As Ari watched, the trucks moved away, having finished loading, and the planes' engines started to warm up. Gosslau got out of his car and boarded one of the planes. Both planes' engines were running at almost full throttle, and slowly they started to roll down the runway and get into take-off position. Ari watched as the planes, one after another, gathered speed ever so slowly. They must have been close to full-weight capacity because it was only as they approached the end of the runway that they got enough speed going to gradually lift the nose up, followed painstakingly by the rest of the plane, just before the runway ran out.

Ari looked at Cahil, "Go inside; see if anyone knows where those planes are going."

Cahil got out of the car and headed toward the cargo terminal. Ari stayed behind, casually glancing occasionally at the terminal while he finished writing his report on his smart phone.

After he finished his report, he started to get nervous. Cahil was taking way too much time. He kept his eyes glued to the terminal but was fidgeting, getting impatient. He didn't like not being in control of the situation, especially with someone who had no field experience. He was regretting his decision to send Cahil inside, but it had seemed a simple task at the time.

Ari's attention was diverted by a commotion on the top floor – an observation deck – where he heard someone screaming in terror. He looked up to see a body go flying over the railing and land to the screams from passersby on the concrete below. Panicking people scrambled out of the way in all directions.

He resisted his first reaction to run over there to see what he could do to help. He knew there was nothing he could do, not after a fall like that. He also knew it must be Cahil lying broken on the concrete, dead and innocent, dark blood spreading from underneath his motionless body.

A crowd was gathering around Cahil's body now – rubberneckers and people pointing up to the observation deck. Police sirens became audible in the distance as other people ran out to the street to see what had caused the panic. The sound of sirens coming closer should have had Ari moving, but he continued motionless, waiting, resisting the urge to run into the cargo terminal.

The police sirens were screaming painfully now at full volume as people rushed over to Cahil. An ambulance arrived. Ari watched, knowing that he could only avenge Cahil if he kept a cool head. Against his better instinct, he waited, hoping to identify the culprit slinking away in the confusion.

There was movement now from the front entrance of the terminal, just beyond the gathered crowd. In the confusion, Mahmoud was sneaking out, surrounded by four military-type people dressed in suits. They made their escape unnoticed by all except Ari, their faces burned into his subconscious. He swore to himself that there would be a day of reckoning.

As Ari watched, a Mercedes limo pulled up, and Mahmoud and his cohorts climbed in to vanish into the Baku Airport traffic.

CHAPTER FORTY-THREE

Baku, Azerbaijan
January 16, 2011

Mahmoud was in a foul mood. He had had to kill that nosey American at the airport – undoubtedly some spy with the CIA or FBI, bumbling fool – and Karim had briefed him on the disappearance of Ahmed.

The plan was falling apart before things even got started. Who were these strange men plaguing his efforts just as they finally came to fruition? His only consolation was that everything else was a façade for the powers that be. His only real objective was the missile launch against the United States and Tel Aviv.

"Nothing else matters," he told himself, as he watched the progress on the factory floor below him. "The launch will proceed. The American dogs will learn our power. They will bow."

Karim heard him mutter these words, but remained silent. He had finally learned even he was not truly indispensable to the man he both revered and feared at once.

~

Only blocks away, a group of men in gray suits met in the back of an old man's café to discuss the clandestine affairs at the Azerbaijan Ball Bearing Plant.

"We have failed in our attempts to end the American's investigation into the plan." The youngest of the men spoke with his head down. "We lost the Hamas agent in Paris. The assassin Gosslau was killed by the Iranian."

He looked up now. "Demir is dead. What are your orders?"

THE EYES OF ATHENA

"We will have the prize in that factory, my son, but your tactics have been too ... extreme, and so we will change our focus.

"The Hungarian's part in this plan is harmless. The American democracy has been on shaky ground for decades, he will not topple it before we realize our goals. He is a nothing in this scheme; let him be.

"As for the Iranian and his little Russian general, their work must go on. The prize must be completed, but their plan must not. We will use the Americans to keep these two in line. Let them continue their investigation, but do not let them get so close that they stop construction in the factory."

He stroked the young man's face, as only a father would. "The prize must be completed, son, but our ... enterprises ... depend on the capitalist excess of America going forward unhindered. Do you understand me, Adem?"

"Of course, Papa."

"Once all of this ugliness with the Iranian is over, bring the little scientist to me."

"And what of the others then, Papa?"

"Anyone left standing in our way ... will not be standing long."

CHAPTER FORTY-FOUR

Bethesda, Maryland
January 18, 2010

The executive board of The Eyes of Athena rarely met in full session.
Portraits of the original 13 founding members adorned the wall, Benjamin Franklin, John Adams and Thomas Jefferson among them. On one wall, hung a large frame with the charter of Athena: "To protect the independent colonies from the intrigues of oppressors plotting to subvert the will of free men." Underneath, it read, "Founded 1776" and was signed by John Adams and Thomas Jefferson.

Members of the current board sat around a conference table. Conversation was light, but the mood was tense. A gavel called the meeting to order, and following roll call by the Secretary, McQueen announced, "Gentlemen, the first order of business should be an update on our current Omega 1 alert.

"Before we hear a situation report from Colonel Burke, I want to remind the members of this organization that I have become the target of a conspiracy. My life has been threatened twice now, gentlemen," she said.

"And lest we forget the magnitude of that statement, may I remind you that not many people have the ... shall we say fortitude ... or connections to order a hit on the U.S. Secretary of State in flight over Russia."

The Eye from Massachusetts asked, "Who is on your suspect list?"

She gave that some thought as, to herself, she wondered who wasn't on her suspect list? But to the Member from Massachusetts she responded, "I don't trust anyone except David Gray. He saved my life. Everyone, including Athena,

THE EYES OF ATHENA

is on my list. Are we sure we don't have a mole in here?" she asked.

There was a gasp from the membership. Burke rose to his feet. "Madam Secretary, no human being on this planet undergoes a more strenuous background test than those who enter Athena – at any level."

"Be that as it may, Tom, someone out there wants me dead and has come darned close once. Either somebody doesn't want me to run for any additional offices or follow my path to the Presidency or somebody doesn't like my position to limit the authority of the U.N. within the United States. Regardless, someone is terrified of me." Then, trying to lighten the mood, she added, "other than my husband of course."

Burke stood up to give his report. "Since we initiated the Omega 3, we have lost four operatives, and our member from New York, the Secretary of State, has had an attempt on her life – and possibly more attempts thwarted.

"We know Iran and Russia are involved. We think the masterminds are a Russian general – the head of their GRU – Dimitri Andropov and an Iranian member of the MOIS, Hamid Mahmoud. We also know the conspiracy involves a 'New World Order' under the guise of the United Nations and something called 'The Arrows of Islam,' which is tied to the Prophet's birthday on January 24th."

"That's not much to go on, Tom," McQueen said.

As if to reaffirm what Burke had said, she added "Gentlemen, if it weren't for my Secret Service agent, I would be dead."

"Didn't I hear that your agent was killed by an unknown assailant?" the Member from Virginia asked.

McQueen nodded. "It's a pretty complicated tale thus far, Sir. Gray's death was a ruse. He's been too close to an assassin's bullet twice now – once in the path of bullets intended for one of our operatives, Agent Cohen, and once with a friend shot in his place. That last one the Secret Service let go to the media as a confirmed kill to get the target off his back.

"Add to that being on the SecState1 plane with me when it was nearly shot down in Russian airspace. He's had a long ride with this OP already."

190

Virginia having been brought up to speed, Burke resumed, "Mahmoud was seen leaving the airport terminal in Baku after one of our operatives was thrown off the observation deck."

The Member from Massachusetts stood up, his military bearing unmistakable, to address Burke. "What happened in Paris?"

Burke took a deep breath; he was getting a little defensive. "Bear with me, please," he responded, before continuing. "I went to Paris to talk to Mossad's Chief of European operations and learned that Mossad had someone on the inside.

"The Suit that we arrested outside the Secretary of State's house the night Gray's friend was shot escaped from us in D.C. and tried to take out the Mossad agent in Paris. We think it was a coincidence that they tried to take him out so soon after the Mossad chief told me about him, but now Mossad thinks I leaked the confidential information."

"So who is the Suit?"

"We don't have any solid evidence on that, Sir," Burke responded. "He had his fingerprints burned off and didn't say a word in custody prior to his escape. What we think is based on some very good gut feelings on the part of a long-time field agent."

"Let's hear them, Tom," McQueen interjected.

"Ari Cohen worked a case six years ago that sparked recognition when he saw these men. He noticed similar patterns – suits, accents, skin coloring and cultural ticks." Burke glanced at the details in his notes.

"The suspects in the mass shooting at a Russian restaurant took out two of our contacts as collateral damage just to kill a realtor with whom they had been doing some shady business. They were Azerbaijani Bratva – that's the Russian version of the mafia – operating in Moscow and elsewhere. At the time, we thought the hit was retaliatory for the realtor taking on too much spotlight for deals being used to launder money for the mob.

"In digging into the details now, we find that there was a real transaction that took place during all of those paper-only real estate purchases – one ball bearing plant in Baku, Azerbaijan, by a shell corporation that traces back to somewhere in Iran."

"And the mob was involved?" McQueen sounded incredulous.

"No. Danshov made that transaction happen outside of his relationship with the Bratva, which was apparently a bad idea. We suspect they figured out whatever it is the Iranian is really up to and want in on it. They seem to be killing off all of the players – not just those on one side or the other."

"So what do we know about Baku, Tom?" McQueen asked. "What was in the Russian transport planes? Do we know where they are going?"

Man this is a tough case, Burke thought, but at least going over these leads, one by one, helped him clarify in his mind the connection between them. He had to remind himself as the board became more and more agitated that they were all on the same side.

"We still don't know what was in the planes," he said, resuming his report. "The planes are multi-purpose four-engine commercial freighters; max load is 80,000 pounds with a max range of 5,000 miles."

Then, after checking some of his notes, he added, "They took the northern route over Russia to Irkutsk."

"What about the scientist in Baku?" Massachusetts asked.

Boy, oh boy, thought Burke, *here we go.* He took a deep breath. "I'm sure you are familiar with the V1 and V2 bombs used on London toward the end of World War II?"

Everyone nodded; you'd have to be a real youngster to not remember the stories of those weapons of mass destruction.

Burke continued, "The chief designer for the Germans was a Berliner by the name of Fritz Gosslau. He died in 1965, but he had a son born in 1946, called Hermann. After his father died, Hermann moved to Argentina. What is very interesting is that Hermann is a better scientist than his father. He is probably the best brain in the world when it comes to pulse-jet-powered weaponry."

Massachusetts wasn't one to beat around the bush, and he probed with another question to clarify in his simple language the point Burke was making, "Do you mean missiles?"

"Yes, Sir."

Massachusetts was hopping mad. "Jiminy Cricket! Are you kidding me? This is a potential major disaster. How was that involved in the drones incident over D.C.?"

"We have no idea, Sir. We have yet to find a connection. In fact, if I didn't know better, it would seem the whole drone thing was just a joy ride of some sort – a childish prank by someone with serious issues against the powers that be in Washington."

Burke tried to turn the report back to point.

"Our agents confirmed an elderly man living in the Baku home of an Iranian citizen – Karim Kahn, assistant to Mahmoud at MOIS – is Hermann Gosslau. He spends his days inside that ball bearing plant in Baku. Recon of the plant shows a section is off-limits to all but authorized employees and seems to be patrolled by what we believe are Iranian Republican Guards."

Massachusetts was on his feet again, pacing. "Is there anything else, Tom?"

"The attempt made on the life of one of our agents back in '99 afforded us a rare chance to gather prints at the scene. The good Heinrich Gosslau is rarely so careless, but then, being a sniper, he is rarely chased by the people he is sent to kill."

"Gosslau?"

"Yes, the son of our reclusive scientist. He apparently did not inherit the family brilliance and opted to take a much different career path. We lost track of him after the failed attack on our agent until he resurfaced at the U.N. meeting, after which he disappeared again. We believe he is hiding somewhere in Buenos Aires."

"Let me see if I have this right, Tom. So, one, we have a major threat to subjugate the American way of life to a 'New World Order.' Two, we can't be sure who is pulling the strings or exactly what they are planning or even how many different factions are involved. And three, we have assassins running around killing our people and then hiding from the most heavily connected organization on the planet."

The big man sighed heavily, rubbing the space between his eyes. "Sounds like we don't know squat, and, on top of that, we have enemy drones flying over D.C. for no apparent reason."

Massachusetts stared accusingly at Burke. "Did I leave anything out?'

Burke ignored the barb. "I said we don't know how the drones are connected to the 'Arrows of Islam,' Sir. That doesn't mean we know nothing about them."

Massachusetts was still glaring at Burke. "This better be good news, Tom."

Burke took a sip of water, wishing uncharacteristically that it was bourbon. "The drones were not ours, as previously thought – stolen from a delivery to the Air Force. These were Iranian-manufactured, but assembled over here."

The member from Massachusetts was apoplectic. "Are you kidding me? This is the U.S. of A. By all that's holy, I want an action plan on my desk by lunch tomorrow!"

Massachusetts suddenly remembered another question he had. "Where on earth is Cohen?"

"On his way back from Baku," Burke replied.

Massachusetts looked over at McQueen. "Madam New York, as you have some insight with the Russians..." He turned back to Burke then, "We do believe the Russians are involved somehow, Burke?"

Burke nodded, and Massachusetts continued with McQueen, "Would you mind chairing a strategy meeting to devise a plan of action?"

"Be happy to, and I want David Gray brought in officially, now."

Massachusetts was only too happy to oblige. "I'd say he's more than earned it. You'll have to do the intro..."

There was no dissension from the other members in the room.

"Done."

CHAPTER FORTY-FIVE

Athena OPs
Tuesday, January 19, 2010

Burke sat at his desk at the Athena complex, Ari across from him. They had been looking over new Intel, and Burke looked up now.

"I hate to do this to you, Ari, but it looks like you're on the next flight to England. We've got Intel that Stanislau left JFK last night headed for Bristol. It seems Vondi, his son, is the team captain of a Rugby game on Wednesday. It is possible that Stanislau is the weakest link among all these players and maybe the most vulnerable."

"I haven't even unpacked my bag from Baku yet. You want me on another plane?"

"If you haven't unpacked your things, you'll have plenty of time to make your flight," Burke said, attempting a bit of humor.

Seeing Ari's stone-faced response, he added quickly, "I want you on the next plane to the UK. Go down to this game at Vondi's school. He attends Millfield in Street, Somerset. Go to the game, make their acquaintance and get on their radar screen. Evaluate Stanislau and see if you can find out what he is up to."

"I was just in bloody London returning from Baku," Ari mumbled under his breath. "I should have just stayed there." At Burke's icy glare, he responded, "Yes, Sir."

"I have sent a team on ahead of you in one of our planes in case we need to bring him back here. We have to know what his connection is to this intrigue."

Later that day, Ari was seated in the First Class cabin of his flight across the Atlantic, reading his briefing. "The senior rugby team plays Portsmouth on Wednesday morning; kick-off is scheduled at 10:00 AM. at-home for the Millfield

Rugby field. Stanislau is staying in Glastonbury at the George Hotel."

London Heathrow is always a zoo, one of the few places in England where armed guards are out in force, submachine guns held in patrol mode, ready for any terrorist shenanigans. Ari was relieved when he finally made it to the car rental desk and retrieved a car to start the drive out west to Somerset.

Later that morning, he arrived at the game. He had never been able to get Gray into Rugby, which was first introduced in Israel by the Brits in the 1920s.

Ari looked over the field, typical with goal posts at each end, just like Football, he mused. He had tried to dress like any other parent. It was a normal English late fall day – misty, chilly and raining lightly.

There were no bleachers; all the spectators were standing or walking on the sidelines. Most people were wearing boots with mud everywhere. He had brought an old trilby hat and a raincoat. He picked up a program from a vendor standing inside what looked like a miniature firework stall. After perusing the program, he learned that Vondi was not only the team captain, but also the scrum half.

At the appointed hour, the two captains lead their teams onto the field and started a warm-up. Within minutes, the referee called the captains over for the coin toss. Portsmouth won and elected to receive the ball. The Millfield team would kick off to start the game.

Millfield kicked the ball to Portsmouth. The Portsmouth player was situated perfectly, and he looked ready to catch the ball and launch off up field, but to the player's amazement, the muddy ball slipped through his outstretched hands, rolling unpredictably like a drunken sailor from side to side down the muddy field.

Suddenly, both teams caught up with the ball. Everyone jumped on the mass of muddy players, trying to recover the ball. Ari laughed to himself. This is where he would lose Gray, who would have no idea what was going on, and often commented that it looked like mud wrestling only much more violent.

The whistle blew, and order was restored. The muddy players lined up again facing each other, the ball was thrown in and the teams started a new free-for-all. Back and forth they went until a muddy mass of sweating bodies seemed to be charging directly at Ari. At the last moment, the Portsmouth player leading the group dropped the ball, followed by bellows of anger at the lost opportunity.

In the confusion, 10-15 players suddenly tried to change direction. The leaders couldn't retain their balance and went sliding, followed by the laggards tripping up on them. It dawned on Ari with horror that he would have no time to dodge the mass of humanity hurtling straight for him. He had on his brand new and now very muddy Johnston & Murphy's and he couldn't get any traction, even if he tried to get away.

The lead player skidded over the sideline into him, and Ari's hands flew out of his coat pockets up into the air, as if trying to balance on a teeter totter. He just managed to keep his balance when another mud-soaked player careened into him. This time he had no chance and landed underneath two players as if he was one of them.

Maybe Gray was right, he thought, sitting on his rear in the mud. Then three smiling teenagers, also covered, in mud with seemingly only their white teeth and eyes shining through, asked loudly, "Sir? Sir? Are you all right, Sir?" Ari's muddy demeanor was soon forgotten at the grins they offered him.

He assured them he was fine and managed to get to his feet after they left. He looked over as play resumed and saw Vondi had the ball and was charging back up field. He was passing the ball to his teammates running behind him. Side to side they went up the field, then with 5 yards to Portsmouth's goal line, the ball was passed back to Vondi, who dove over the goal line and landed in a pile of mud and arms and legs.

He had scored a try, which Gray would swear looked just like a touchdown. Vondi got back up and looked over at his father and smiled. Stanislau was hysterical with excitement, clapping and shouting, "That's my boy! That's my boy!"

As Stanislau jumped up and down, Vondi was beaming with pleasure, and Ari found himself secretly wishing he had a boy like that.

After the game, Ari made his way back to the hotel where he knew Stanislau had also made a reservation – the

George Hotel in Glastonbury. As he turned away from the game and got into his car, he wished he could stay for the celebration, but he needed to scope out Stanislau's room.

It was about a forty mile drive from the rugby field to Glastonbury. The area around the game was typical English countryside, emerald green fields and chin-high hedges alongside the tiny English country lanes hardly big enough for two cars to pass. Every mile or two, he came across an old tavern and a historic stone or limestone church dating back more than 500 years. Eventually, the wide-open countryside yielded to a more urban setting still full of public houses and churches, but now interspersed with homes instead of open fields.

Ari arrived in Glastonbury and drove through town until he found the intersection with High Street, then turned left toward the George Hotel and Pilgrims' Inn, built in the late 15th century to accommodate visitors to Glastonbury Abbey. Glastonbury, itself, was one of the oldest abbey ruins in the world, having been built in the seventh century. The George is the oldest purpose-built public house in the South West of England, having once been the Pilgrims' Inn of Glastonbury Abbey. By the mid-nineteenth century, the building was known as the George Hotel.

As Ari drove up High Street, he recognized the front of the three-story building from the briefing he had read. Above the archway entrance to the hotel, hung the coats of arms of the abbey and of King Edward IV.

He parked his car and walked in to the reception desk. He couldn't help but think of the stark difference between the hotel in Baku and this monument to stability and history. After checking in, he decided to go up to his room.

He was bushed; he rested on the bed, but before he let himself fully relax, he picked up the phone to call room service. "Could you send afternoon tea up to my room, please?"

The receptionist at the front desk, more than happy to oblige, said, "Yes, Sir. Would you like a traditional English afternoon tea with scones and clotted cream, Sir?"

Trying to use the local vernacular, Ari responded, "That would be splendid."

"Fifteen minutes, Sir."

Ari decided to think through his plan as he enjoyed his scones and tea. He thought it was time to act, so he left his room and walked down the wooden, creaky-floored corridor to Stanislau's quarters. After listening for any sound of approaching guests, he put his pick into the lock, twisted and went inside.

He looked around and checked the suitcase, which was expensive but no help. Soon, he heard a noise coming from outside the room. Cursing himself for having taken time for tea, he looked for a place to hide, but before he could react, the door opened.

Vondi Stanislau came charging in. He stood close to the door, looking at Ari, his face full of innocent surprise. Vondi was confused; he stammered, uncertainly, "Must be in the wrong room." But then he saw his father's suitcase.

Ari followed his eyes and saw where he was looking. "You are in the right room, Vondi."

Then Vondi recognized Ari. "Didn't I see you at the game today? What are you doing in my father's room?"

"Yes, you did see me at the game." Ari turned to see a chair behind him, and followed with, "May I sit down?"

Vondi nodded his head, as Ari tried to explain. "You love your father, don't you, Vondi?"

Vondi nodded again, and Ari nodded as well to reassure him. "Your father is in big trouble. I'm here to see if we can help him."

Vondi, sharp as a tack responded, "Who is WE?"

Ari instantly liked the kid and his straight forward attitude. "That's complicated," he said. "I am with a special American organization that secretly protects the country from outside threats."

"The CIA? FBI? Something like that?"

"We are not part of any government agency you have ever heard of." He had decided to tell the boy the truth – at least as much of it as he could. "What you are going to hear now is very 'top secret.' You cannot discuss this with anyone but your father and me.

"I need to get your father in here," Ari said. "It would not be appropriate for me to ask you to go get him. So will you please wait here while I go get him?"

Vondi asked only, "Are you going to hurt him?"

Ari thought this kid would go far; he was very smart. "No," he assured him.

Vondi seemed happy with Ari's response. "Then I will wait."

Ari left Stanislau's room and went downstairs to the Pilgrims Bar, a traditional and quaint pub with an access from inside the hotel as well as from the street. The serving bar was forty feet long with bar stools and there were tables in front of that area, as well.

He walked into the bar, smelled the age-old aroma of hops and began looking for Stanislau. He found his target in the midst of quite a crowd, so Ari fought his way through to stand beside him.

Ari noticed the bodyguard was sitting against the wall in front of the bar trying to watch his boss as Ari approached. The bodyguard tensed, as Ari whispered into Stanislau's ear. "Your son needs you. Please follow me."

Stanislau turned to look at the stranger in total alarm, shouting back at him loud enough for the bodyguard to hear, "Who are you?"

Ari had to think fast, his name would mean nothing to the man, so he responded equally as loudly, "Three names, Boris, just three."

Stanislau was still alarmed, and he turned to his bodyguard, trying to catch his eye.

Ari continued, "Mahmoud, Ahmed, Andropov." Then Ari added to see his reaction, "'The Arrows of Islam.'"

Stanislau reacted immediately to the three names, but remained blank at the mention of the latter. Confused, the Russian jerked up from his bar stool. His bodyguard, alerted where he sat at a table behind his boss, also reacted, standing up suddenly. Beer glasses crashed to the floor from the sudden movement and patrons in front of the table scattered trying to avoid the mess splashing on the floor.

This also had the result of scattering the people who were close to Stanislau as well, leaving him out in the open. The bodyguard now had an unobstructed line of sight to both Stanislau and Ari. He reached inside his jacket to place his hand on his concealed revolver.

Unnoticed by all, a solitary figure stood in the doorway, dressed in an overcoat and trilby hat. His right hand was hidden inside the left section of an unbuttoned coat, held closed by his left forearm.

Stanislau was nervous; there was gentle, anxious laughter from the patrons standing around him, but his bodyguard was on full alert, eyes focused on Ari, who likewise stared back.

"Sorry, everybody!" Stanislau shouted. Comforted that his bodyguard was now watching Ari – hand on his revolver – Stanislau returned his attention to the stranger.

Ari continued in a quiet, unassuming voice, "You and Vondi are in great danger; Andropov is covering his tracks."

Over by the front door to the street, the unobserved hit man went into action. In one fluid movement, he pulled the gun from inside his coat, crouched slightly, steadied his right hand with his left hand and aimed. He fired, and the bodyguard went down, a single shot to the head.

Ari pivoted as the crowd panicked at the sound of gunfire and the sight of blood gushing from the bodyguard's head wound. Everyone and everything became confusion and hysteria.

Ari pushed Stanislau just as the hit man fired again, but he was seconds too late. Stanislau clutched at Ari's arm as he fell. Ari waved for his team, swiveled his head to look at the man now lying in his arms. He knew Stanislau was dying, blood pouring from a neck wound. The Russian must have known it, too, as he pulled Ari closer. He felt at the man's neck, the carotid artery pulse getting weaker and weaker.

Outside, it was dark – pitch black. On this moonless night, someone lay prone on Tor Hill, the light of a luminescent watch face revealing a mask-covered visage, eye held to a telescopic sight. Silently, he adjusted his scope. The only sound is his faint breathing, alone, intent on his mission.

Tor Hill lies across the street from the George up behind the shops on High Street. It has been a fixture overlooking Glastonbury since before Roman times.

In the pub below, Stanislau took his last life's breaths, looking at Ari, trusting him, and hoping. "Save Vondi," he gasped.

Ari watched him die, released him and laid him gently to the floor. Then his demeanor changed from the sympathetic caretaker of a dying man to a soldier, intent on catching up to his enemy. He swiveled just in time to see the hit man turn to leave the pub.

Ari shouted to his team at the other end of the bar, "Get Vondi out of the hotel!"

Then he turned to chase the gunman. The pub was still full of people, and the people were confused and in disarray, blocking his path.

Ari shouted loud enough for all to hear, "Everybody get down! Don't go outside!"

He jumped over the remaining obstacles, reaching the door, and turned to look left and right. He caught sight of the hit man and headed out.

The shooter up on Tor Hill paused, eyes closed for a moment then he refocused through the scope. The hit man was walking away from the doorway of the Pilgrims Bar, trying to blend in, an easy, unsuspecting target. The view of the rifle scope was centered on his head.

The hit man had waited, motionless, as if he expected a car to pull up. The shooter had watched through his scope as everything exploded into motion. The hit man moved out when he had heard pursuit coming from behind him. When he heard Ari shout he had moved away from the entrance to the pub and he was moving quickly now, constantly looking all around him for danger.

Just as the shooter was about to fire, the hit man moved again, that movement turning a fatal head shot into a survivable wound. He lurched to one side just as the shooter fired. The bullet caught the hit man somewhere in the side and spun him around. He crashed to the sidewalk but only for a second. Very quickly, he was back on his feet, running uphill. He moved across the street, eyes attentive, searching for the shooter.

Ari heard a second shot, saw the hit man go down again and reckoned he was finished when the man didn't move. Staying in the shadows, Ari tried to locate the shooter, but the hit man was faking. Ari realized he didn't even know if the second shot actually hit the man. He watched the hit man get up and noticed he didn't seem to be suffering any physical trauma from the second shot.

Ari kept to the shadows then, slowly following the hit man, whose attention was now diverted by the shooter.

Unflustered, the shooter pulled the trigger for another shot. The hit man went down again, and this time he stayed down. The shooter waited, watching through his scope. When he had confirmed there was no more movement from his target, the shooter calmly left the rifle where he was laying and walked down the hill toward town. He knew his fingers left no prints, and he had left nothing else with which to identify him.

As the shooter reached the bottom of Tor Hill, he started to hurry. His ride – a Mercedes – pulled up, tires screeching to a halt. The shooter swung open the door and jumped in as the driver asked, "Mission accomplished?"

The shooter responded, "Yes, but I think I saw that Mossad agent leaving the pub. He is becoming too much of a problem. Pull around to the front; I'll see if I can take him out, too."

The Mercedes started moving, driving conservatively up High Street toward the George Hotel.

Ari located the hit man and waited, not wanting to become another target for the shooter. When he felt it was safe, he approached the man, reached down and felt the life ebbing out of him from his carotid artery. Looking around for danger, Ari was low to the ground, searching the man. He turned his hand over to see the finger tips burned off.

Ari's sixth sense told him something was wrong. Suddenly, he jumped back as two silenced shots ricocheted off the sidewalk where he had been kneeling. He tried to move back into the shadows. Looking up, he saw a man moving toward him and reaching inside his coat to grab a knife.

Ari barely had time to pull further back as the knife sliced through the air in front of him. The shooter lost the knife in his zealous swipe at Ari and it fell to the sidewalk. Ari grabbed it, looked at his opponent, and waited.

The shooter approached within hand-to-hand combat distance another knife in hand, striking and striking again. Skilled, professional, obviously martial-arts trained, Ari thought quickly, as he dodged the man's swiping knife, blocking each strike. One hit connected, only a flesh wound, but Ari lost his balance and crashed backward through a display window. The shooter leaped at him with two knives now. Little did he know that Ari had been conserving his energy, assessing his attacker to determine his weaknesses.

Ari stumbled backward, blood spreading on his arm. He removed his raincoat, ready now. He knew what strategy to use, and anger surged through every fiber of his being. He worked to control it, determined. He took the offensive, swinging under a thrust by the shooter, and impaled his thigh. His attacker was stunned, not expecting this. Ari marched forward as doubt spread on the shooter's face. He swung again, just missing, but still the shooter fell to the ground, and Ari jumped onto his attacker, forcing his knife into the shooter's neck.

Tires screeched outside the shop the duo had fallen into as a car pulled up. Ari's team ran in, and one pulled a gun. He aimed at the assailant and in a split second, shot the shooter dead, blood spreading from his wound. Ari moved to recover, letting the adrenalin return to normal levels.

"Come on, Ari!" his team member yelled. "We've got Vondi. Stop playing around will ya? We need to move."

Ari looked up, nodded his head slightly and grabbed the shooter's hand. He turned it over to see the prints had been burned off.

Ari's team left the shooter in the shop. Their vehicle was waiting outside, engine running. With the faint noise of police sirens getting louder, the car took off and drove within the speed limit going out of town. All the team members were beginning to relax when the driver noticed a car speeding up behind them, approaching aggressively.

Ari's driver maintained his speed, but he was becoming more concerned, and his tone betrayed his anxiety. "I think it's the Mercedes that guy got out of."

Ari tried to see in the rear view mirror, but the headlights of the pursuing Mercedes were switched to high-beams. Maintaining his calm, he said, "Try to stay cool. There are a ton of cops driving to the scene; they would be crazy to try anything here."

As his team drove out of town, multi-colored lights of police cars passed them, sirens wailing. As soon as the emergency vehicles were out of sight, the Mercedes got aggressive, flooring the accelerator and driving into the back of the team's four-door. Everyone was thrown forward.

As Ari's driver noticed the change in behavior of the Mercedes, he increased speed, minimizing the effect of the bump. Now there was no hiding, the Mercedes was trying to push them off the road. The cars jockeyed for position, with the super-powered Mercedes trying to pass and both cars swerving into the opposing traffic lane.

Ari's driver tried to stop the Mercedes from overtaking them as the two cars hurtled down the highway, weaving in and out of the other traffic on the road. His driver expertly steered the car, braking, accelerating, and swerving to block the Mercedes.

The Mercedes was driving more erratically, going for broke and dangerously leaving decisions to the last moment. The pace quickened and he swerved the Mercedes right at the bumper of Ari's car.

Ari realized he was going to have to do something. He pulled his Glock, turned around and aimed at the Mercedes' driver through the rear window. Just as the Mercedes was about to speed into their car again, Ari fired, the first shot shattering the window, the next shots hitting their target, and the Mercedes slowed, swerved and crashed into an oncoming truck.

The team headed back to the hotel. Ari settled back in his seat in the car, opened his smart phone, and began his report to Burke, "Mission blown. Team will work evidence and clean up. On my way back to D.C."

CHAPTER FORTY-SIX

**Del Rio's Restaurant, Washington, D.C.
January 19, 2010**

Del Rio's in Washington, D.C., normally had a two-month waiting list to get a reservation. That is, of course, unless you were one of the privileged few; the lucky diners in that category could call up Mario, the Maître D, and get a table pretty much whenever they wanted. The problem for the lucky few was that it was difficult to let your hair down in such a public location. The Secretary of State was not only one of the lucky few who knew Mario and could get a table whenever she wanted, but she had found a solution to the problem of having a good time in such a public place.

Gray walked cautiously along the terrace, looking toward the courtyard. He was on full alert, as he passed restaurant guests, scanning them all, watchful for any danger. Those in European clothes got more scrutiny than others.

Gray descended the steps into the lobby and said to the restaurant's Maître D, "Reservation for Gray." He spoke confidently since the lobby was crowded with people who had arrived early for their table, not wanting to be late.

The Maître D' looked down at his reservations and smiled, "Ah, there we are, Mr. Gray. This way, Sir."

The aromas coming from the kitchen in the restaurant were very appetizing, and Gray could feel his stomach talking to him in response. The Maître D led him past the kitchen area where open fire grills were glowing, covered with large, thick, juicy steaks, all sizzling. They continued to his reserved table. The restaurant was already full of diners, some watching him. Gray was nervous; it had been a long time since he had a date, and this felt like a date.

Finally, he decided the eyes watching him were just curious and no threat and he began to relax.

After seating Gray, the Maître D pulled out his napkin from the water glass on the table, shook it slightly, and gave it back to him.

"Can I get you a cocktail, Sir, while you wait for your company?" Gray ordered a scotch.

"Any special blend, Sir?"

"Your standard scotch will be fine." Gray did not plan on drinking it anyway; he wanted to be fully alert, just in case.

"I hope you find this booth suitable, Sir." The Maître D finally left Gray to his own thoughts. As he waited for his guest, he watched the restaurant. When his eyes drifted over to the entrance, he saw the Maître D escort a tall, exquisitely dressed brunette to his part of the restaurant. When they kept coming toward him, Gray smiled. Finally, the Maître D delivered the brunette to his table, pulling back a seat for the guest.

Gray smiled conspiratorially at his guest as she slid into her chair. "Brunette tonight?"

After years on her detail, he was familiar with all of the crazy disguises McQueen used when she wished to just blend in and have a normal outing. Usually, he was the lone Secret Service agent to accompany her, but she had requested that he meet her tonight and had had an agent drive her to the restaurant instead.

Despite having divorced her husband late last year for his many very public indiscretions, McQueen and Gray had not acted upon the mutual attraction they felt for one another. They were people of quality, as Gray's grandfather used to say. McQueen would not have left Rocky if it weren't for the fact that he was so obviously miserable in their marriage – turning their home into a drug-crazed orgy every weekend and preying on the vulnerability of young women who were impressed by his power and money. She still prayed every day that he would find his own peace in this world somehow.

"Let's get business taken care of first then we can get down to having some real fun." McQueen shook off thoughts of her ex-husband and his sad life.

"Now that you are aware of my ties to Athena, I need to ask if you would be willing to join forces with our organization – continue ostensibly as my Secret Service agent, but be privy to the Intel, assets and responsibilities that come with being an Athena agent as well."

"I wondered when you'd ask," Gray said, sipping the scotch after all. He had thought about the possibility since the night the drones attacked, had been eager to be on the inside, but now that it was presented to him, the weight of what was being asked sat heavy on his shoulders.

"Is that a yes?" She was leaning toward him now, her big brown eyes staring into his own.

"Of course, Jade. How could I refuse?" He gave her the million dollar smile then, and she reached across the table to touch the back of his hand, a smile on her face as well.

"Wonderful. I think you will be a great asset to the organization."

"Asset?" Gray said, his smile turning sly. "Never been a woman's asset before."

McQueen laughed. The waiter came by to take their order and for a moment, they contented themselves with small talk – not first date conversation, because they had practically lived with one another for years now as he protected her day in and day out, but the comfortable conversation of old friends or a couple who had been together for ages.

McQueen turned serious. "Agent Gray, we do have some business to discuss."

Gray put his fork aside. They had been sharing a piece of chocolate cake that dripped with calories both would regret later.

"Before I go on, as your introduction to the organization, is there anything we didn't tell you the other night that you want to know? Any question still lingering?"

Gray, who had lived for years in a military program of need-to-know, felt he was sufficiently briefed on the background of Athena and would learn what he needed to know as each situation developed.

"No, Ma'am. I believe I'm good to go."

McQueen smiled. "Of course. We have received some new Intel on the Mahmoud situation and his ties to the Russian government. After discussions with our Russian connections, I need you to go back to Moscow and interrogate Dimitri Andropov."

To his credit, Gray took the statement in stride, as if it were everyday he received instructions to interrogate a high-ranking official of one of the most feared entities in the Russian government.

"Andropov ... Won't be easy to get near him." Gray was already thinking.

"We have already made ... arrangements."

CHAPTER FORTY-SEVEN

Athena OPs
Wednesday, January 20, 2010

Ari sat across from Burke with a sour look on his face. He was not one to take the loss of a mission lightly.

"Any idea what went wrong?" Burke asked in as non-judgmental a tone as he could muster. He had been in Ari's shoes, had lost men he sought to protect – good and bad – and it was always hard to take.

"You tell me, Tom. I can't for the life of me fathom what was happening at that pub. Did you get an ID on the hit man in the doorway?"

Burke smiled then. "Craziest thing, actually. We had this young pup analyst straight out of college, never been farther than the California coast, but he loves the finer things in life. He's got a real thing for pouring over the crime scene photos, evidence details, all of it. Wants to be one of the big boys in the field one day."

Air looked unimpressed. "Don't they all?"

"Anyway, this kid spots the hit man's shoe knocked off when he fell. Sees the maker's mark on the inside, and he recognizes it from his study of the finer things. Turns out there's only one place to go in Moscow if you want the best in fine footwear, and that's this little old man in the village. Makes his mark on the inside leather of every shoe."

"The kid traced this guy by his shoe?" Ari sounded unconvinced.

"I kid you not, Ari. The man makes a handful of shoes every month for a very select clientele. So, we knew Moscow. Sent the guy's photo to your ... friend, Katarina," Burke had to smile here, "And she got us the scoop. He's Bratva."

Ari sat up a little in his chair. "Bratva? The Azerbaijani?"

"That's the wrinkle," Burke said with a sly grin. "Straight up Moscow. They are a rival Brigade. Katarina made some inquiries and discovered the hit had nothing to do with your new friends in the gray suits. This was all about some unsavory partnerships Stanislau had made with the Moscow mob!"

Ari almost laughed then. Stanislau had gotten himself mixed up with characters bent on a plot that could mean world destruction if it all went really wrong, and instead he got himself killed over a bad deal with some really bad guys.

That had him wondering, though, "Hey, Tom, not to get too far off subject, but what about Vondi?' Ari really did like that kid.

Tom's smile faded. "He took it all hard. He's a good kid. Back in school. Turns out most of Stanislau's billions are quite legit and quite safe in offshore accounts all over the place – and he left it all to Vondi and the butler as his guardian."

"Higgins ..." Ari said absently. They had questioned him at the scene before Ari left.

He snapped back to point then. "And the sniper?"

"That one is trickier. We got nothing from the sniper other than knowing he obviously had military training.

Burke was pacing his office, reading from a report he picked up off his desk. "The guys in the Mercedes were another story. Anyone you left alive was long gone before our team got on scene to take over for police, and there was no identification on any of them, but we found enough superficial evidence and enough in witness interviews to ascertain they were Russian."

"So the little general opted to take out his Russian contact."

Burke nodded in agreement. "Looks that way."

Ari was thoughtful for a moment. "And he shot the hit man just because he got in the way of doing his job and may even have cost him his fee if he was rogue military or freelance."

"That was our bet," Burke said. "And you they want dead just because you're becoming a real pest."

Down the hall, McQueen was in her Athena OPs office on the phone with the Russian President.

"Ah, Madame Secretary, how is our Tsarina?"

"Mr. President, you are a flirt!" As he laughed delightedly, she turned the conversation to a more serious subject. "Mr. President, I think it is time to implement our plan. We need to interview Andropov."

The Russian President turned serious, as well. "I will have him picked up tonight."

"Our man is on his way and should land tomorrow morning."

"Tell your agent that my man, Viktor Arkady, will be calling for him after we have had time to make Andropov more ... receptive to answering our questions."

~

Gray leaned back into the opulent leather seat of the official vehicle, closed his eyes, and enjoyed the feel of the plush leather of the limo taking him to Andrews Air Force Base. After a short while, his solitude was disturbed by revving jet engines. He opened his eyes to confirm why the limo was slowing down. It pulled up alongside a 757 on the runway, prepping for takeoff.

He grabbed his bag and made for the ramp. He climbed the stairs and ducked as he entered the plane, where a steward relieved him of his bag.

"This way, Sir." The steward led him to his seat.

Gray followed and settled into another plush leather seat. Gray had asked McQueen why she wanted to use SecState1 for this mission.

"You know as well as I do, David, this is a chess game. We're being watched, and I want to keep whoever is on the other side off balance."

He smiled, remembering how she had moved closer to him in the limo then, placing a hand on his chest and looking full into his face. "But just so you know, you will have two stealth fighters following you ... 20,000 feet above you, just in case." She had paused then. "I'll be as sure as I can that nothing ever happens to you."

SecState1 touched down at the Moscow Airport the following morning. Gray was awakened by the sharp bump of the 757's wheels hitting the runway. The day was so overcast and gloomy that he could not see anything until the airport runway appeared under the plane. As the plane taxied down the runway, he watched from his cabin window to see the buildings he was passing. It looked cold, wet and frigid, and icicles dangled from the gutters of the hangars they passed.

The plane did not go to the regular terminal but to a small, secure building that he guessed must be the private plane area. As they taxied in, a cavalcade of black limousines chased them through the thick snow. Gray walked down the aisle toward the exit.

As he approached the front of the plane, the cabin door swung open and an avalanche of bone-chilling air invaded the cabin. Gray walked to the open door, and a new flurry of fresh snow started to fall.

This is certainly the way to travel, Gray thought. *A convoy of black suburbans sure gave one a sense of self importance.* After 30 minutes, the procession drove into the embassy compound, the flag waiving high above asserting this piece of Moscow real estate as the domain of the United States of America. It was strange, he thought, how arriving inside this compound made him feel more American than he did when he was home.

CHAPTER FORTY-EIGHT

While Gray enjoyed his flight, Victor Arkady, on the orders of his President, took three Ukrainian guards to the general maintenance area of the building General Dimitri Andropov used as his Moscow apartment. After some minutes, they identified the air supply intake to the General's apartment. They added a sleeping gas and waited the required time to put the General into a deep sleep. A little later, they went up to General Andropov's apartment, equipped with a gurney.

Whether anyone saw them or not, no one was foolish enough to interfere with three guards and a colonel dressed in the uniforms of the Kremlin's very exclusive Kremlin Guards. Arkady and his guards jimmied the lock and entered silently. He went over to the bed, looked at Andropov and lifted the man's eyelid to make sure he was heavily sedated.

Having confirmed that status, Arkady turned to his helpers. "Gas in the ventilation system works every time," he said with a smile.

One helper, a loyal Ukrainian Guard responded, "Ja."

Arkady withdrew a syringe and injected Andropov in the shoulder with more drugs. Sleepily Andropov rubbed his shoulder, turned over in his bed and continued sleeping.

What seemed only minutes later to Andropov, he awoke, or did he? Was this a dream or was it real? He was having a hard time differentiating between the two. He was in a haze, in a dream, or was he?

He could see three men are in his room, or did he? What are they doing in my room? This must be a dream, his confused mind thought. The Kremlin Guards picked him up, put him on the hospital gurney and strapped him down. They turned to their boss, waiting for the go ahead to leave the apartment. Arkady was checking out the area outside the apartment, and as soon as he verified it was safe to move, he signaled his men to leave Andropov's apartment.

Arkady was hoping they didn't run into any of the ultra-loyal GRU agents. If they saw their boss being wheeled out on a gurney, it might have proved difficult to explain. They entered the elevator. Andropov was still in a deep-sleep dreaming stage. *This can't be,* he thought, *I am in my apartment in Moscow.* He was so tired, but he felt the gurney moving him. He felt exhausted, wanting to sleep, but he was sleeping, wasn't he?

Later that night, after a long trip through the Moscow streets, Andropov opened his eyes, shaking his head as if trying to wake up from a bad dream. He was being pushed through a tunnel – a dark, humid, medieval tunnel – following a man holding a lantern. His eyes were wide open, but he was having trouble seeing. *This absolutely cannot be happening,* he thought. *I am going down a tunnel into a large cavern.* Bookshelves covered one side and books filled the shelves. On the other side, boxes lined the walls. Stenciled on the outside was the word "bucher," (book). Other boxes were stenciled "manuskript" (manuscript) and others marked "olgemalde" (oil painting).

Andropov asked in a faint, scared voice, "Where am I?"

The guards ignored him. Andropov could not understand what the guards said when they spoke. He tried to listen intently. He asked weakly again, "Are you talking about secret underground tunnels? But this isn't the Lubyanka, our Moscow headquarters."

He continued being wheeled down the bumpy, cold, uneven passageway, entering a smaller cavern, and with horror, he watched as the guards shackled his ankle to a huge metal stake hammered deep into the middle of the rock floor. Andropov saw the guards retrace their steps, about to leave him alone and in darkness. It was awfully cold, with only a night shirt to warm him. He was waking from his fog, realizing that this was not a dream.

Desperate now, he shouted, "What are you doing? Why are you leaving me here? Do you... Do you know who I am?"

The Ukrainian guard looked back at Andropov. "I know who you WERE, old man. I know who you were."

Andropov tried again. "But why are you doing this?"

THE EYES OF ATHENA

The Ukrainian guard, in a thick guttural accent, said only, "Orders." Then the guard uttered with total contempt, "Prepare to meet the ghosts of those you sent to the bowels of the Lubyanka, old man."

Liquid started spilling over from the General's bed.

Later, much later, Andropov awoke in a fetal position. He opened his eyes, but could not see. It was totally dark and cold. He was in a cave, underground. He sat up on the side of his hospital gurney, feet dangling over the side, and felt the chain around his ankle. He heard faint sounds and held his breath to get a bearing on the noise.

The echoes of scurrying feet, hundreds of little claws, then high-pitched screeches came to him. He felt a gentle, wet whip across the bottom of his foot and jerked his foot up, rattling the chains. Rats.

Andropov prayed out loud. "My God, my God, what have I ever done to deserve this?"

He felt the gentle, frantic rat claws scratching at the legs of his trolley. "Oh, my God, oh, my... God."

~

The Hilton Moscow Leningradskaya Hotel is one of the city's famous Stalin Towers, standing high above Moscow's skyline. Arkady arrived early to pick to up Gray from the lobby. Gray slipped into the back of the limo and greeted his Russian contact.

"Good to meet you."

The Zil took off into Moscow traffic. As it was only a short ride to the Kremlin, Arkady introduced himself fairly quickly. "I am a Colonel of the Special Red Guard assigned to the Kremlin. Also... How do you say it in the U.S.A. Ummmh...? A special assistant to the President... You know for those special assignments?"

Gray understood perfectly what that meant. Arkady was the go-to for the President; one day he might be opening a bottle of wine for the Russian leader, the next a hit man taking out a target.

Gray was a little impatient. "Viktor, we are running out of time. We have to question Andropov and get some answers."

Arkady nodded his head in understanding and responded, "David, I have two surprises for you. I think Andropov will be ready to answer all your questions."

Gray looked at him. "The other surprise?"

"Ahhh," the Russian answered, "for the second one you will have to wait and see!"

The official limo whisked the pair through Moscow into the center of the city, weaving in and out of traffic on the snowy roads past the Alexander Gardens into the courtyard of the Grand Kremlin Palace. As they drove into the Kremlin Complex, Gray looked over at Arkady, a concerned frown on his face.

Arkady recognized the look and said, "Don't worry, my friend. You are going to see what few outsiders have ever seen."

"That is EXACTLY what is worrying me."

Arkady chuckled at what he thought was Gray's humor. They pulled up in front of the two-story palace. Red Guards jumped out to open the doors on either side of the limo. Gray looked very uneasy. He gazed up at the building, a brownish-orange paint covering the front with recessed windows painted a clean white. Guards were stationed on either side of the open front door, holding the 12' wooden doors open for them. Arkady bid him enter.

Gray walked in, still suspicious, nervous even. "I believe many people have made one-way trips to this place."

Arkady replied, sensing his companion's uncertainty, "Don't worry, my new friend; you are safe with me. Not long now."

They walked across the foyer through a less opulent passageway and into the kitchen. On the other side of the kitchen was another keyed door, and Arkady opened it. He then turned around smiling and said, "This is the wine cellar."

Gray, obviously relieved, had never been so happy to see a wine cellar in his life, if it was, in fact, a wine cellar. Down rock steps they went, hundreds of wooden racks covering the walls. At the far end, Arkady stood in front of another very old wooden door. He waved Gray over and said encouragingly, "Come on."

Gray followed Arkady down more rock steps before he turned to say, "Hold onto the ropes."

THE EYES OF ATHENA

Gray could not hold back any longer; he blurted out, "Where are we going?"

"The Kremlin tunnels," Arkady said. "Many of these date back to the 1350s. Originally, they were built to be used in time of war as an escape route. If the Kremlin was ever besieged, they could bring water from the Moscow River and be able to survive the siege as long as necessary."

Arkady continued to lead the way down a cool, musty hall beneath the street to the entrance of a deeper tunnel blocked by another door. Old and rusted, he pulled hard to get it open. It screeched, and Gray felt more cold air coming up from below. At the bottom in the dim light, he could just see a subterranean chamber. He heard a faint voice from below moaning in terror, "Help me. Please, oh, God, help me."

Arkady stopped at a small alcove chiseled out of the rock wall and retrieved two oil lanterns. He lit them both and passed one to Gray. They continued down the steps, and Gray could hear a faint scratching sound below.

Andropov was whimpering audibly now. "Help me. Help me."

Further down, Gray's lantern shone on shadowy dark shapes running in and out of the light. Then he recognized them and shuddered. "Giant sewer rats. Yuck!"

Arkady and Gray reached the bottom of the stairway and walked toward Andropov. He was trying to sit up on the flat surface with his feet on the bed, straining to see who approached.

Gray saw Andropov's feet, covered in bites, raw and bloody. Andropov looked at him, frowning in concentration, suddenly lighting up in recognition.

Andropov was shocked and confused, "Weren't you traveling with the ..." Then he saw Arkady walking over to one side of the cavern.

"Andropov, look over here!"

He looked in the direction Arkady was shining his lantern. "Do you see what is over here?" Arkady asked.

Andropov had to squint to see in the corner where five or more skeletons were picked clean by rats, hair hanging down over meatless skulls.

"Oh, you monster," Andropov said. "What are my choices?"

Arkady shrugged his shoulders. "Andropov, you are going to die down here. The only question is when and how. If you cooperate with us, tell us what we want to know, I will give you a gun with one bullet and I will unshackle you. You can then make peace with yourself and die with dignity.

"On the other hand," Arkady continued, "if you do not tell us what we want to know, we will lower your hospital gurney by 10 centimeters a day. I think your little friends in here will persuade you to 'volunteer' the information." He laughed at his own sick humor.

Andropov, his voice betraying his fear by a thicker accent, said, "What do you want to know?"

Gray stepped in. "Two things – What is the 'The Arrows of Islam'? And why did you put the hit out on the Secretary of State?"

Andropov, still snickering defiantly, said, "You are too late; you can't stop our plan now. As to the Secretary of State, she has some powerful enemies."

"Are you going to play games with us, Andropov?" Arkady asked.

Seeing a defiant response, he moved over to Andropov, slapped him down on to the bed and secured his straps so he could not move his torso. Then he threatened, "Too bad; you must be getting very hungry. If you had cooperated, we were going to give the condemned man a last meal.

"As it is," he said, "we will have to feed your friends here. I hope they don't choke on you, Andropov."

Andropov asked Arkady to approach. "Come closer."

Then he whispered something, and realizing he was doomed, he struggled and tried to rebel, fearful. Thinking furiously, Andropov asked, "How long have I been here?"

Gray had prayed for this question and replied smoothly, "This is your fourth day. The dose we gave you was a little too strong."

"What time is it?"

"About 2 PM Moscow time," Gray said.

Andropov gleefully announced, "Then it is too late. Release me. In hours, I will be the President of the New World Order."

Arkady looked at him and said with emphasis, "You are crazy."

Andropov now sensed victory. "No, I am not. As we speak, dawn is rising over Sohae, North Korea, and missiles are launching. In less than an hour, Tel Aviv and Washington, D.C., will cease to exist."

Arkady was playing along, "You are quite mad."

He withdrew his pistol, steadied his arm and aimed at Andropov. "Yes. You are quite mad, indeed," he said. "By the way, you have been in here less than 12 hours."

Slowly comprehension spread across Andropov's face, then hatred. Arkady fired two shots then turned to Gray. "Isn't that the information you required?"

Moscow Airport
Thursday, January 21, 2010

Arkady's Zil went directly to the Moscow Airport, where the SecState1 was waiting. Gray and his Russian counterpart walked into the departure terminal.

Gray could not resist asking, "Viktor, what did Andropov whisper in your ear?"

Arkady responded evasively, "I'm afraid I can't tell you that; I have been asked to give that information to someone else."

As his vehicle pulled up to the plane, a lone figure descended the ramp and walked toward them. Gray immediately recognized her.

"What are you doing here, Jade? It's way too dangerous."

She smiled at him. Arkady moved toward McQueen to whisper in her ear what he had found out. She pulled back after hearing the report with a very satisfied smile. "Thank you, Viktor, and thank your boss for me, in fact give him this for me." She moved over to Arkady and gave him a kiss on the cheek, admonishing him, "Don't forget to give that to your boss."

Arkady actually blushed.

She turned back to the ramp and extended her arm out for Gray to take as they both ascended into her plane. He pretended to be a little mad at her. "What are you doing here? It is too dangerous for you."

"Ah, for a man who wants to look after me! David, come, we have a lot of catching up to do. And to answer your question, I couldn't ask you to risk your life over here and not come to surprise you in case you needed my help."

CHAPTER FORTY-NINE

Sohae Space Center, North Korea
Midnight, January 24, 2010 (Bethesda time)
The Prophet's Birthday

A C-17 flew 35,000 feet over Sohae Space Center in North Korea. The Jump Officer had his eyes glued to his watch. "Three minutes to green light, final gear check."

Ari and Gray tightened their oxygen masks and started taking deep breaths.

"High Altitude Airdrop Missions fail if you panic," the Jump Officer reiterated. Chutes will open at 3500 feet. Breathe regular deep breaths. Eyes closed if you want."

The pilot's voice came over the loud speaker, confirming the time. "Two minutes, gentlemen."

"We have not had jumpers before using latex masks and voice oscillators," the Jump Officer had to shout to be heard.

Ari and Gray straightened up, looked at each other, and neither recognized the face they saw. The latex mask changed their features to North Korean oriental faces.

"If your latex mask disintegrates due to pressure, abort, OK?"

They received two thumbs up from the Jump Officer and the jump light turned green. "Go! Go! Go!" he shouted.

Ari and Gray ran down the ramp and the air sucked them out into the dark, moonless night for a 35,000 foot free-fall. Ari's reaction was immediate, the wind slammed into him like a sledgehammer. He felt like the wind was going to rip his mask off. He couldn't keep his head and shoulders still, try as he might to control his body movements. The effort to bring his hand towards his face to protect his mask resulted in wild, uncontrolled movements of his body. He decided to close his eyes and wait for his altimeter to warn him when it was time to open his chute.

Once on the ground, they made quick time to the space center. Gray crouched, on full alert to any sounds. He stood erect and looked around the corner of the hangar. He leaned on the wall, wearing a dark cloak, only his eyes visible. They were the eyes of a hunter, on the lookout for any danger. The sounds of Koreans jabbering in the background were indecipherable.

He heard shouted orders, howls, and laughter. Somewhere in the background, an official-sounding voice came over the radio at full blast. He was tense. Suddenly, he moved, leaving the wall, he crossed to a large maintenance truck with side compartments.

A young Korean was at the steering wheel, a maintenance worker. Gray climbed into the cab. The truck was in motion, and the driver looked over at a Korean officer jumping into his moving cab with total surprise. He hesitated, not knowing whether to salute or scream in panic.

Gray lifted his arm and delivered a thunderous punch to the Korean's jaw. He slumped, unconscious. Gray grabbed the steering wheel and drove the truck toward the airplane terminal.

~

In the pre-dawn hours, there was a humming of motors. One truck after another passed with their headlights on along the runway. As they reached the launch site, they divided into two columns, as if to serenade the dignitaries arriving for the launch.

Hermann Gosslau rode on the giant mobile launch platform the last 100 yards, as the platform supporting the rockets was wheeled into position. He descended from the platform, and the launch crew took over.

Gosslau turned around to walk back to the hangar, but saw General Kim Lee marching toward him. Confused to see Lee in the launchpad area, he was absolutely dumbfounded when the little general held up his hand and bellowed in a mocking snarl, "Do you imperial fools think we are that stupid? Do you think we wouldn't check up on you? You mad western dog!"

Lee turned to his squad, screaming in an even higher pitch, "Arrest this capitalist fool! Shackle him and put him in the cell close to my office."

THE EYES OF ATHENA

The North Korean guards handcuffed Gosslau savagely and pushed him on his way. As they left, Kim Lee taunted, "Did you think we wouldn't check the target coordinates? You imperialist fool!"

Gosslau looked at Kim Lee in total shock, his jaw dropping to his chest. "What are you talking about? ... I don't understand!"

He was taken to a small cell in the same hangar where he had been working and was thrown to the floor as the cell door slammed shut and locked behind him. Less than five minutes later, Lee entered the cell and lashed out at Gosslau with a short whip. He walked menacingly around the cell, continually slashing his whip.

"Why have you changed the target coordinates?"

Gosslau shook his head vigorously, shouting, "I don't know what you are talking about! The target coordinates are the same as before! Here I can show you."

He reached into his pocket to pull out his cell phone. He was visibly shaken as he pushed his phone toward Lee. "I can show you. Look."

Beneath his latex mask, Ari looked at the program on Gosslau's phone, trying to memorize whatever he could as marching boots sounded outside. The door to the cell was thrown open again, and the real General Kim Lee exploded in in anger, jabbering in Korean. He looked at his impostor, seeing his own face standing in front of him and was totally confused. All he could resort to in a very loud voice, was, "Seize him! Seize him!"

"What are you doing here?" Gosslau stuttered, still unsure of himself. The confused guards seized not only the impostor, but Gosslau as well.

Lee shouted again, "WHO are you?" The Korean General walked around the impostor, examining him. General Lee was much shorter than Ari, so he had to stretch as he looked up to try to understand what he was seeing. He started poking at Ari's face with his index finger. When he felt the unusual substance, he started pinching his fingers together to pull at the latex of the mask, which started to give way, revealing the man beneath.

Lee, seemed tremendously relieved. "Ah ha!" Then, to his guards, "Cuff them both!"

A moment later, the questions began again. "Who are you? What are you doing here? What do you want?"

The general and his guards, unable to get any answers, left Ari and Gosslau, locking the door on their way out. The metal door banged noisily as it closed, and both felt relief to be alone, without the aggressive Korean guards.

Ari looked at Gosslau with contempt and asked, "Do you know what you have done?"

Gosslau just stared at him in response, giving no answer.

Ari tried again indignantly, "You want to plunge the earth into World War Three?"

Gosslau replied defensively, but proudly, "I am a scientist, not a madman, and... and what gives you the right to question me? I am the top scientific mind in my field. I have even managed to exceed the wildest dreams of my father."

"I'd be happy to debate you on whether you are a madman or a great scientist if we had more time," Ari said. "Right now, your invention is helping some lunatics plan to murder millions of innocent people. For all you know, your grandchildren might be among them."

Gosslau stopped ranting immediately, turned to Ari and asked, "What do you know of my grandchildren?"

"Obviously, I care about your prodigy more than you do." Then switching his line of questions, "Do you still think this is a test launch?"

"I did until last week," Gosslau said. "I learned then that I was not going to be a part of the missile warhead assembly team; they had brought in another North Korean scientist, who I later learned was an atomic weapons expert. It was fairly obvious that they intended to install atomic warheads."

"Nukes?" This was bad, Ari thought. There was no way even Athena could clean up this mess.

"Yes, but I made certain ... adjustments ... to the warheads last night that no one knows about." Gosslau said.

"You disarmed them?"

"Not completely. But I removed the nuclear component. I couldn't completely remove all explosive capability – they appear untouched to pass inspection this morning – but I did what I could in the time I had."

THE EYES OF ATHENA

There was hope ... maybe, Ari thought. "Do you know the scheduled launch time of the missiles?"

Gosslau was beginning to cooperate now. "Yes, 6 AM." Then he added, "Are you CIA?"

"Kinda," Ari responded. "He was already deep in thought. 6 AM was creeping up on them quickly."

Gosslau obviously took that as a yes. "What can you do for me IF I cooperate?"

"What do you want?"

"My freedom and a ticket back to Buenos Aires."

"What will you do for us?"

"Full cooperation," Gosslau said.

Ari shook his head. "You know the North Koreans are going to kill you."

From the expression on Gosslau's face, it was evident that he had not thought of that eventuality. They both turned their attention to the noise of guards outside their cell. The guards pulled back the peep slot, dark eyes peered through. Seconds later, the slot slammed shut.

Gosslau returned to their conversation. "My professional curiosity has led me astray."

Ari shook his head again, this time in amazement. "You raised a murderer and now, unknowingly or not, you are an accomplice to murder. I might be able to save your life, but not give you your freedom."

Gosslau nodded his head in understanding and furrowed his visibly aging his brow.

"Heinrich was ... a disappointment. I fear he was too much like my father," Gosslau said. "He was not my only son ... and there are grandchildren."

"Your ultimate sentence and level of 'accommodation' will depend on your cooperation," Ari told him.

Gosslau responded almost as if in a dream. "I understand."

Ari was beginning to think that all might not be lost. "Are you able to change the destination coordinates on the missiles?"

Gosslau looked at him and raised an eyebrow, questioningly. Clarifying his question Ari added, "Can you change them even after launch?"

"Yes." Gosslau responded proudly.

"I need to know all the specifications, such as range, speed, etc."

Gosslau assumed his professorial pose and started his dissertation. "The range of the missiles depends on the payload, but with an expected weight of 500 kilos, 9,200 kilometers is the maximum range," he said. "If we keep the targeted range within these limits, we can achieve an accuracy of within 10 meters."

Ari was absolutely stunned. He might have expected this type of weaponry from the U.S., but not in Tehran or Korea. Then Gosslau added proudly, "The propulsion system can achieve a cruising speed of up to Mach 12."

Ari must have been dreaming – a nightmare. He hesitated to ask his next question. "Is it a Stealth?"

"During launch no," Gosslau said, "after reaching cruising altitude, yes. After reaching cruising altitude, target acquisition is re-calculated, and the missile is able to alter course in stealth mode."

Ari stared at the scientist in amazement. Gosslau watched his reaction, trying to gauge if he understood the scientific accomplishment entailed.

"Can you change the target of one of the missiles remotely, for example to the assembly plant in Baku?"

Gosslau paused, clearly thinking through the implications of his next answer. "Yes. I can re-program those now, but internet connection is blocked here."

After a few moments, Lee sent for Ari to be brought to his office. Ari was collected from his cell with Gosslau and forced to climb up the stairs to the executive area. Progress was slow, as his hands were behind his back and he was shackled.

He made his ascent look as difficult as possible, dragging his feet on the floor. The guard gave a double knock and pushed him into the office. Ari stumbled forward, unsure of his footing, peering around the door to see Lee dressed in full military uniform standing at his desk. He was gloating, a look of total superiority and confidence.

"I thought you would like to watch superior Korean technology, our glorious launch." Sweeping his hand toward the view before him, he ordered, "Come to the window."

THE EYES OF ATHENA

As Ari approached General Lee, the guard prodded him again with his rifle butt. In the distance stood a launch pad, fully rigged, looking more like tall scaffolding.

Lee pointed out the window to the platform, gleefully enjoying his moment of glory. He encouraged Ari to approach closer. "Did you really think you could get away with impersonating me?"

The monitors on the wall flashed to life. On the screen was a distant rigging. Sticking out of the top were two cylinders, tapering to a round end, rather like a torpedo's nose.

General Lee turned his attention to the monitors, then back to Ari. "Get ready to say good bye to Tel Aviv and Washington, D.C."

Within a minute of launch, the rockets seemed to respond to some unknown flight program. They began to move from a nearly vertical flight path to a more level heading, each starting their final journey to self-destruction. As they leveled off their flight trajectory, debris fell away from the body. The rockets were lost to visual monitors.

Unseen by Lee, Ari picked up a paper clip and began working at his handcuffs. He finally opened them just as Lee turned to see his prisoner was free. General Lee went for his holster, but Ari pivoted, turning so that his arm, preloaded with a stiletto, thrust the knife at Lee. The blade entered Lee's shoulder, and Lee grimaced in pain. He slouched to favor the injured side, his arm and shoulder disabled.

The guard turned around, pulling his holstered revolver and swinging his arm around to target Ari, but Ari beat him to the punch and threw another stiletto. It flew true and lodged in the guard's throat. The guard had a look of complete surprise on his face as he frantically tried to pull the knife free. He slowly buckled, sinking toward the floor, dying.

Ari rushed over to General Lee, retrieved his gun and pushed him back into the chair and away from the desk. "Don't say a word or do anything, or it will be you that is dying today, understand?"

General Lee's face still had an expression of total surprise. He made a painful move with his uninjured arm toward the telephone. Ari noticed and just nudged the stiletto in his shoulder. Lee turned white and pulled his hand back, the discomfort overwhelming.

Ari put his hand back on the knife handle. "You are going to do exactly what I tell you, right?" He encouraged a nod, and Lee obliged. "Where is my phone?"

Lee looked toward his desk drawer. Ari opened it, retrieved his phone and turned it on. "You are going to call your assistant and tell him to get your plane ready to take you and us to Pyongyang, understand?

Lee nodded.

"In English. Tell him to bring Gosslau up here too." Ari reached for the desk phone and put it to Lee's ear.

General Lee's guard answered the phone. "Yes, Sir."

Lee, obviously in great discomfort, stammered out, "Have my plane ready to take off for Pyongyang immediately, and bring Mr. Gosslau up here too."

Lee's guard, detecting nothing out of order, said simply, "Yes, Sir."

Ari hung up the desk phone. He turned behind Lee and slugged him on the head. General Lee slumped over the desk, unconscious. Ari quickly bound him, covered his mouth and removed the knife. Ari cleaned his knife on Lee's uniform and cut the telephone line. He then sat down in the office to wait for the guard to bring Gosslau.

Ari heard the sound of the guard pushing and cajoling an uncooperative Gosslau up the stairs. But, instead of knocking and waiting to give Ari an edge, which was what he expected, the guard threw open the door and walked right in, pushing Gosslau ahead of him with his revolver.

Almost immediately, the North Korean saw Ari, then looked over at his unconscious commanding officer and swiveled to confront the intruder. Gosslau saw what was happening and pushed back to throw the guard off, but only caused the guard to pull the trigger.

Gosslau went down, shot in the upper back, but that delay gave Ari enough time to get close. He lunged, pushing his knife up through the guard's chest cavity, twisting, ending his life.

Concerned for Gosslau, Ari turned to him. "How badly are you hurt? Can you move?"

THE EYES OF ATHENA

Gosslau, gasping and grimacing in great pain, said, "No, I can't move, but we have a bigger problem. The rockets are on course for Tel-Aviv and the White House."

"Yes, I know."

"I watched the initial separation and course acquisition; both missiles are heading due west."

Ari got his satellite cell phone and started typing, texting Athena.

He hit the send button. Gosslau started coughing and spitting up blood, getting weaker by the moment. "We have to change target acquisition to our coordinates."

Ari was torn between his need to divert the missiles and loyalty to a man that had just saved his life. "How do we do that?" he asked.

"I programmed a private access to the missiles transponder from my smartphone," Gosslau whispered.

"How do I access that?" Ari asked.

"You will need Wi-Fi access and my smart phone." Gosslau struggled to pull his phone out of his jacket pocket. "Take it. Wi-Fi is blocked by security here. Get on the General's plane, get the access codes from the pilot, look for the icon named 'Arrows of Islam,' then just press transponder reset."

Ari was taken totally by surprise. "That's it? It's that easy?"

"That's it," Gosslau responded proudly, adding, "I designed it myself."

Ari put his hands under Gosslau's shoulders to help lift him, but the look of extreme pain made him stop. Still, he told Gosslau, "Let's go."

Gosslau groaned in great pain, obviously he was not going anywhere. He looked at his watch and said between painful gasps of air, "I can't move; leave me. You have an eight-minute window. After that, goodbye White House and Tel-Aviv."

Ari stood up to leave and wiped the blood from his hands.

"Give me the General's revolver," Gosslau said. "If he moves, I'll shoot him." Ari handed it over, nodded and left in a hurry. "Goodbye, Gosslau. I wish I could do something."

All business now and fully alert, Ari opened the door, peeked out to check for guards, and seeing none, he carefully moved to the stairs. At the bottom of the staircase, he heard one shot. Shortly thereafter, he heard one more muffled shot, as if at close range. He knew he must hurry now; that would have alerted any guards in the building.

Athena OPs Center, Bethesda

Burke was in the Athena OPs Situation Room with his team watching Sohae Space Center on a live feed from an overhead satellite. The pre-launch vapors coming from the launch pad were making everyone very nervous.

The situation was so tense that he had both the White House Chief of Staff and Ben Rosenberg in Tel Aviv on the line in case of any urgent developments. Everyone in the room was quiet, studying the live feed.

The sudden loud alarm from Burke's cell phone made everyone jump. His computer also started emitting a high-pitched emergency beep, indicating a high priority message was incoming. Burke turned around to his keyboard and entered a code, then read the text from Ari. "Missiles launched. Missiles are live. Evacuate D.C. and Tel Aviv."

His eyes bulged in fear and he bellowed, "Good sweet Lord in Heaven!" Then turning to his team, "Tell the Chief of Staff at the White House now, code red, and Ben Rosenberg in Tel Aviv."

Over the intercom, Burke heard an analyst's calm voice, "Chief, Mr. Rosenberg, two nuclear missiles are in bound; targets are the White House and Tel-Aviv. Evacuation is recommended."

Burke was busy on the computer and cell phone trying to raise Ari. He shouted out to the analyst talking to the White House, "We are trying to intercept. Keep these danged lines open!"

The White House

Chaos was rampant at the White House as Chopper 1 swooped in to land and POTUS was carried out unceremoniously, surrounded by Secret Service agents.

THE EYES OF ATHENA

The Knesset, Tel Aviv

In Tel Aviv, pandemonium ruled the Knesset as people came flying out of the building and nearly all cell phones were jammed with them trying to warn loved ones. Helicopters landed to rescue the elite.

Sohae Space Center, Pyongyang

Ari looked out the first-floor windows of the Space Center offices toward the launch platform. In the distance, toward the launch pad, Lee's guards were ambling back to the building talking animatedly.

Ari left the building and headed for a parked jeep. He jumped into the driver's seat and left the warehouse en route for the airplane hangar. As he approached the plane, the guards turned their attention to him. After a brief chat among themselves, two guards started his direction. He stopped the jeep at the ramp and waved, trying to exhibit a calm demeanor.

He muttered to himself, "I hope that fools them into thinking I am friendly." He started up the ramp to the plane, closing the door behind him. He looked around; he was alone in the passenger section. He turned to the flight deck, watching for any reaction from the front. The captain was sitting in the left seat, awaiting instructions. Ari walked down the aisle toward him.

"Take off now, the general will not be coming," he ordered.

The captain turned around as if to ask a question, but Ari pulled out a gun pointing it at the man.

"Hello, Ari," The captain smiled.

"David!" Ari exclaimed in total surprise. "I was arrested, lost my phone, couldn't check to see if you had made out OK.

He frowned then. "That mask is too good. Take it off."

Gray humored his friend. "Yes, Sir."

Ari continued up to the flight deck, sat down in the right hand seat, and said, "I need two things – the Wi-Fi access code and to change our destination."

Gray pulled out the flight check list and started reading, "The password is 'kimsung.' And where do you want to go?"

"Seoul," Ari said.

He turned to Gosslau's phone, looking for the "Arrows of Islam" icon. When he found the program, he opened it. Gosslau had prepared a message, "Ari, if you are reading this, I didn't make it. You asked me if I wanted to start World War III. No, I don't. Hit the enter button below. Password is my grandson's name, Martin."

Just as Ari entered the password, his phone rang. He answered, "Yes."

Burke asked urgently, "Can we do anything?"

"If I am not too late. I'm in a plane with David Gray, trying to get to Seoul. Can you clear us through the no-fly zone?"

"Done."

"Gosslau told me all I needed to do was to hit the reset button. He told me that he had already preset the new flight coordinates. I'm pressing reset now. Wow. He even has a 'Remove Stealth' option here so we can track them."

Burke was desperate, he shouted down the line, "Ari, do it now!"

Ari, knowing he had already changed the coordinates, said, "You'll owe me big time."

Burke shouted at the top of his voice, "Now!"

"Done," Ari replied calmly. "Well, I'll be, this phone even has a tracking function. I'm watching, and the missiles are turning. By the way are you tracking Mahmoud?"

Burke responded, getting a little calmer now that catastrophe was avoided, "Yes, remotely by phone tracer. He is monitoring the launch from the ball bearing factory in Baku. Why?"

"Could you text me the GPS coordinates?

"Done."

Baku, Azerbaijan
January 24, 2010

After a brief layover in London's Heathrow Airport, Konstantinos's Gulf Stream took off again for the flight to Baku. Five hours later, his jet was turning over the Caspian Sea to get into the landing sequence for Heydar Aliyev International Airport.

THE EYES OF ATHENA

After disembarking from his plane, Konstantinos made his way to the limousine at the private jet terminal provided by the ball bearing factory.

"How far to the Azerbaijani Ball Bearing plant?" he asked the driver.

The driver responded in his limited English, "Some 20 kilometers, Sir."

The short trip did nothing to improve Konstantinos's mood. In fact, he was in the back of the limo, fuming the whole time. *Russian arrogance,* he thought. *General Andropov had "ordered" him to come to Baku to watch the launch and attend a party to celebrate the successful completion of their mission, but didn't even show up to meet him at the airport.*

He thought it was probably a very good idea to be far away from Tel Aviv and Washington D.C. when those missiles landed. But even so, nobody was even here to greet him.

After a 45-minute trip through the early-morning rush hour, the Mercedes arrived at the ball bearing factory, was waived through security at the entrance and took him directly to a VIP waiting area at the plant.

Again, nobody to greet him, and he was shown into a rather plain reception area and asked to make himself comfortable by an attendant. Konstantinos looked around the room, bare except for a photo of Ilham Heydar Oglu Aliyev, the President of Azerbaijan. He felt drawn to the photo, felt as if the eyes were watching him. He got up to change seats, and the eyes seemed to follow him across the room. A coffee pot was simmering on a table at the far end of the room. He went to pour himself a cup, but when he looked up again, there were those eyes. It was very unsettling.

The waiting room door opened, and Mahmoud entered. They looked at each other, not sure whether they should acknowledge each other's presence. A few minutes later, Karim entered, and the release of tension in the room was palpable. He greeted Mahmoud with obvious warmth and gave a courteous nod to Konstantinos.

"Gentlemen, if you'll follow me. We have prepared an area in the mission control room for you to watch the launch."

Konstantinos was glad to be out of that room. As he left, he gave a faint shiver of relief. Karim led them through a second door into the plant. As soon as the door was opened, a barrage of shrill, high-pitched mechanical sounds overpowered their senses, ruining the relief they felt at having someone finally greet them.

Giant presses rhythmically exploded down on to sheets of steel fed into the machinery by a large conveyor belt. The resulting action released tiny particles of lubricating oil in a mist of steam that seemed to coat the suits of all three men as they passed.

After crossing this immense press room, Karim opened what appeared to be an air lock. He closed the first door after they all entered. The noise lessened considerably. Then he opened a second door and waited for the men to pass through before finally closing that door as well.

The relief from the stench and noise was miraculous. They entered a sterile-lab type conference room, and Karim led them into another room with a bank of computers in front of a large wall full of extremely large TV monitors, where he announced, "Mission Control Room, gentlemen. About thirty minutes to scheduled lift off."

Konstantinos was still miffed that Andropov was not here to personally greet him. Clearly agitated, he demanded, "Where is Andropov?"

Karim was far too proud of his accomplishment to even show the slightest reaction to the man's tone of voice. "From what we are told, there is an air traffic delay at Baku airport due to bad weather. A snow storm over the Caspian sea is backing up traffic."

The TV monitors in front of them flashed to life. On the screen was a distant rigging that looked like tall scaffolding. Sticking out of the top were two cylindrical missiles, tapering to a round end like a torpedo's nose.

Gradually, smoke started bellowing from underneath the scaffolding, building up higher and higher, as the smoke rose it fell away to the outside to be replaced by new smoke rising up from the center. As the smoke was about to envelop and cover the cones, the scaffolding seemed to shake, and the rockets began to rise. Soon they were free of the launch pad and gaining speed. In no time, they were above the horizon, surging up and up, each rocket on a different trajectory.

Konstantinos and Mahmoud were glued to the monitors, sitting forward in their seats. Suddenly they both jumped; Karim had popped a bottle of champagne. He was beaming in self-satisfaction. "It's time to celebrate, gentlemen," he announced happily.

Both Konstantinos and Mahmoud rose from their seats, still reluctant to pull their eyes from the television monitors, and walked over to Karim, who extended an arm to each of them.

"Champagne, gentlemen?" he absolutely glowed.

British Airways Flight BA0145

Most flights that come from the west fly toward Azerbaijan over Turkey then enter into Azerbaijani airspace. They typically enter into a holding pattern over the Caspian Sea. In this pattern, they circle before being scheduled for landing. BA Flight BA0145 was on final for Baku International, and the pilot had just received final clearance to land on runway 290 when he noticed a huge dust plume or mushroom cloud rising to the north of his heading.

Slightly concerned, the pilot decided to check in with traffic control.

"Baku, do you copy?"

The Baku Air Traffic Control Tower responded, "Go ahead BA 0145."

"We are seeing quite a disturbance; looks like an explosion of some type a few miles north of our flight path. Do we need to abort and go around?"

The tower responded, "BA0145, this is Baku. Maintain path, will advise."

After a minute delay, the tower came back on. "BA0145, this is Baku. Local services advise us that there was an industrial explosion in a suburb 20 miles north of your bearing for runway 290. Please continue flight plan for landing on 290."

"Roger, Baku," replied the British Airways pilot.

Baku International Airport prided itself on having the most state-of-the-art facility in the region. One of the nicer amenities was the private aircraft terminal where the crew room was so luxurious that some crew members did not even think it was necessary to book a hotel for overnight stays.

Konstantinos's pilot and attendants were relaxing in the crew room, idly listening to air traffic control and waiting on flight orders to file a flight plan. Neither the pilot nor the crew paid any attention to the conversation between the control tower and the British Airways pilot. In fact, it would be two more days until Konstantinos's body would be released by the Azerbaijani authorities.

As for Mahmoud, only one man would question his death.

CHAPTER FIFTY

Gray's Georgetown Apartment
January 26, 2010

Gray stood at the sink washing vegetables for dinner. Pasta was boiling on the stove and soft blues music played through the surround sound speakers in the house. He was in a pensive mood after all that happened, trying to consider the mission a success.

"You know I don't like yellow peppers."

Gray didn't need to turn to know Ari was sitting at his bar, drinking one of his beers, having let himself in despite him having his third state-of-the-art security system installed while they were gone over the weekend.

"I'm not cooking for you, you sneaky Arab."

Gray turned with his assortment of peppers, onions and tomatoes to begin chopping them on the center island butcher block.

"Haven't you seen enough of me for one week, Ari?"

"I'm hurt, friend. Truly." The smile on Ari's face belied the mock sentiment of his statement. "I needed to talk to you away from Athena and Burke and any other little ears."

Gray looked up from where he was chopping. "Oh?"

"I know having Mahmoud ... dispatched ... the way he was Sunday was inconvenient for you. You hoped to get him alone to find out more about Heinrich."

Gray just turned back to his vegetables and nodded. "Is what it is, brother. Safety of the free world and all that."

"When I was alone with Gosslau, he told me Heinrich was a disappointment to him. Used the word 'was' as if his son was no longer with us. The old man also told me had another son and a grandson named, Martin."

Gray was looking at Ari now, waiting to see where his old friend was going with this unraveling little mystery.

"I did some digging. Turns out Gosslau took to a lovely native woman in Buenos Aires soon after he sent Heinrich off to military school. Margarita had a son, Joseph, who spent his entire life in Buenos Aires, living simply as a shop keeper in the same neighborhood where he was born."

Gray moved to sit on a bar stool next to Ari.

"Eventually, he married and had his own son, Martin. The old man had only ever seen pictures of the boy, born after Mahmoud moved him to Baku.

"Joseph and Heinrich had very little to do with one another – not cut from the same cloth, shall we say. They moved in different circles while Heinrich was in Buenos Aires, but Joseph kept tabs on his brother for his father's sake.

"When his brother showed up in Buenos Aires after Fairbanks looking for a place to hide, Joseph took him in, and one day, he simply disappeared."

Gray looked at Ari with curiosity, now, but Ari had not looked up from where he was peeling the label off the beer in his hands.

"Seems our friend Mahmoud was as unhappy with Heinrich as the Secret Police, and he had connections."

"That's why he disappeared," Gray said with dawning understanding.

"I am told he is spread about the countryside of Buenos Aires in very small pieces, yes."

Gray went back to his chopping block. He was not entirely sure how he felt about this information. He had wanted to kill Heinrich to avenge Mike, and he had wanted Mahmoud dead for the massacre of his fellow paratroopers. But to have one kill the other...

"I know how you feel," Ari said. "It is an unsatisfying ending to the story."

There was a knock at the door.

"Company?" Ari asked.

Gray smiled. "It's my night off, and Secret Service is delivering my evening dinner guest."

Ari grinned then, as he made for the back door. "Maybe not such an unsatisfying ending after all."

CHAPTER FIFTY-ONE

Athena OPs Center
January 28, 2010

Burke's desk was a sea of paperwork, most of it related to Operation Boris. The consternation on his face was enough to make Ari think twice about knocking on his open door.

"Got a sec?"

Burke looked up and smiled, happy to be rescued from his paper jungle for even a brief respite. "For my star agent, always."

Ari laughed.

"Finishing up the paperwork, I see."

Burke looked at his desk as if it might bite him. "It never, ever ends." Looking back up at Ari, he knew the ex-Mossad agent had some questions.

"What can I do for you, Ari?"

"I think I've wrapped my head around most of it, Tom. The crazy Iranian wanted to take over the world for Iran using our Stealth technology and Russia's stolen military weaponry. He managed to wrangle together quite a menagerie of crazy generals and other assorted cohorts to get the job done."

"And one not-so-crazy little German scientist that helped save the day. Yes, I think that is a very basic summation of a very insane plot. So what's troubling you?"

"The Suits." Ari spread his hands before him in a questioning gesture. "We never fully connected them to anyone – Bratva or otherwise – and they just kind of fell off the radar. I mean, they seemed to be killing off pretty much everybody, and then they quit. Were they responsible for the attack on McQueen's plane? If so, that's some super-scary connections."

He was pacing now. "I mean I just have to wonder what they were looking to get out of all of this ... and if they got it."

"We haven't nailed that one down yet, Ari. And I hate to tell you, kid, but when you get to play in the middle of the Situation Room like you are now instead of out in need-to-know land, you learn that sometimes the reason we don't tell you out in the field isn't so much because you don't need to know as it is because we just don't know ourselves."

Burke walked around his desk to pat Ari on the shoulder. "It'll make you crazy if you let it. I prefer to think that is one part of the puzzle we haven't figured out ... yet."

He headed out into the hall. "Come on, Mossad. I feel a need for target practice. Any time I get too buried up in paperwork, I have a real desire to hunt and kill things. This being the quiet hamlet of Bethesda, the firing range is as good as it's going to get."

CHAPTER FIFTY-TWO

The White House
September 12, 2011

As the Athena member from Massachusetts entered the White House through the West Wing entrance, he couldn't help but think that it was almost like returning to a very familiar home, perhaps the home of a favorite uncle.

John Adams moved into the White House in 1800 and Thomas Jefferson, shortly thereafter – both early Presidents of the new found Republic and both responsible for creating the Eyes of Athena.

Ironic, he thought, *the very enemy that prompted the formation of Athena was also the culprit of the first "assault" on the White House in 1814, when the mansion was set ablaze by the British Army in the burning of Washington.*

A Marine Guard escorted the Massachusetts Eye through the West Wing to the White House Gym, where he was left to reminisce for a short time before President Klein entered, spotted him, and walked over.

From the look on his face, he was busy, but then, he was the President of the United States and one must assume that is to be expected.

"I'm told you needed to see me. I've had no recent alerts. Is there something new I need to be made aware of?"

Klein was obviously not used to being kept in the dark. The Athena Board Member from Massachusetts responded, "January 24th, 2010, Pyongyang, North Korea"

"Yes, that was quite a scare. I got a full report from my Secretary of State. Was there something we missed?"

"What you don't know, Mr. President, is that if your Secretary of State hadn't interceded, those missiles would have gone in a whole different direction."

Klein sighed then, warming up a little and remembering this was someone he could trust. "What do I call you?"

"Mr. President, most of my colleagues call me John."

"OK, John, you want to give me some particulars here?"

"It's a very complicated story, Mr. President. Suffice to say, Madam Secretary brought us the first tip and ran this OP as the key Eye from the beginning."

The President's eyebrows rose at that. McQueen had only told him enough Intel to avoid war with Russia without giving away her involvement with Athena.

"She oversaw a mission that ran the gamut of bad guys from Iran to Russia and back, with North Korea thrown in for good measure."

"Superb work, John, but I am baffled. Why are you telling me this? I had no idea she was even a member. Isn't it Athena's procedure to maintain complete secrecy regarding your operations unless absolutely necessary? You have taken care of all of the details. There is no advantage to telling me about this, is there?"

John was quiet, seemingly pensive for a moment. "Mr. President, our organization is made up of thirteen board members, one from each of our founding colonies – now states."

Klein was nodding his head now, he had learned this much in the Book.

"The Board Member from New York – your Secretary of State – is directly responsible for discovering this plot and leading the counter-measures effort," John said. "Her dedication was a big part of Athena's efforts to figure out the plan, save Washington, D.C., and, simply put, Sir, save your life".

"So, you've brought me this information so that I can honor her in some way? I suppose that is appropriate. I do need to think of some special way to thank her for her service."

John smiled then. "The point of my visit, Mr. President, is there is a rumor in Washington that you might be considering a new VP."

"I haven't made any of that public, John." Klein was starting to feel uncomfortable.

THE EYES OF ATHENA

"Be that as it may, Mr. President, we've heard there is a possibility that the Vice President may retire due to health issues. We think Jade McQueen would make an excellent replacement."

Klein paused in thought. After a few moments, he picked up his phone. The Eye from Massachusetts waited to see what was going to happen.

Klein spoke into the phone, "Morning, Chief, I want the Vice President in my office at 10:00 tomorrow morning."

Then he added, "And would you mind calling the Secretary of State after you confirm the VP's appointment and ask her if she has time to fit in a lunch with me at the White House tomorrow?"

The President turned to the Athena member from Massachusetts, smiled, and nodded his head. "Thank you, John."

The End

About the Author

Spencer Hawke was born in England and educated in the United Kingdom and set off as a young boy seeking adventure abroad. At the age of 21, he and a friend set off for Africa and crossed the continent North to South through the Sahara, sometimes on foot when their old Land Rover did not want to travel as far as they did.

Eight months later, having dodged many conflicts and machine-gun-toting patrols, the pair rolled into South Africa bound for Australia, determined to swim the coral of the Great Barrier Reef. But fate had a different plan for Spencer. In Johannesburg, he met a Brazilian girl who professed undying love for the young Brit. He changed his ticket and flew off to Rio de Janeiro in search of his love.

Once in Rio, she was nowhere to be found, and short on funds, he was forced to get a job. He went to work for General Motors in Sao Paulo. Eight years and two children later, he again had enough money to take off for what he thought would be his final destination.

Spencer landed in Oklahoma in the middle of the 1980s oil boom, and he and his children made a home for themselves in Oklahoma City.

Fate again intervened on a trip to Texas when he met the one true love of his life, wife Jenny. The poor misguided soul decided to take him on and has been his inspiration for the last 20 years. Together they are raising another gift from God, grandson Devon, who is already as avid adventurer as his grandfather.